MOURNING AFTER

HAUNTED EVERLY AFTER MYSTERIES
BOOK FOURTEEN

REGINA WELLING
ERIN LYNN

Willow Hill
BOOKS

CONTENTS

MOURNING AFTER

CHAPTER ONE

I know I said I'd never get married again, but I lied. And I'm not even sorry.

The noonday sun etched diamond-bright glitters across the lake as we crested the final hill, and the view of Oakville spread out in front of us. Colorful sails dotted blue water under an even bluer sky.

"Pretty as a picture, isn't it?" I said as Molly rested her chin on the back of my seat and let out a little huff of anticipation.

It's a common generality that chocolate labs love the water, and mine certainly fit the stereotype. Two weeks on the water—extended from one when his partner Riley insisted she had already rearranged her class schedule for our aborted honeymoon trip and that she didn't want to see Drew back at the gym for at least that long—would be Molly's dream vacation.

Two weeks spent in my new husband's arms without ghosts or drama would be mine, I decided as we followed the road down and around a curve that hid the lake from view.

In one thousand feet, turn right onto Lakeside Road— Drew's phone GPS warned.

"I don't see a sign. Are you sure this is it?" I leaned forward and peered at the phone in its holder attached to the dashboard as Drew flicked on the blinker and eased onto a narrow dirt road. "I thought the house was on the lake. We can't be that close to it yet, can we?"

Reaching over, he patted my knee. "Google Maps never lies."

"Except when it does. If you trust it to get you to Momma Wade's house, you'll end up in a field half a mile away." Leandra didn't seem bothered. She figured anyone who knew her well enough to visit would have asked for directions anyway.

"Don't worry," he said, his grin lighter than I'd seen it in days. "If we get lost, we'll backtrack and call Amethyst."

In a quarter mile, slight left to stay on Lakeside Road.

At the fork, a signpost for Bailey's Cove Getaway set my mind at rest, and I relaxed. With as many setbacks as we'd had between the wedding, Drew's arrest at the reception, and the clearing of his name, I didn't realize how fine of an edge my nerves had been dancing on. Extending our stay for the extra week had been the right call. We both needed to reset and relax.

Taking a deep breath, I let go of every last bit of tension and prepared to enjoy my drama-free honeymoon.

The gravel camp road wound through the woods for at least three more miles until we came to a T and followed the directions to turn right. Flashes of sparkling water finally began to show between the trees and a row of cabins lining the shore.

"This reminds me of the first time I met you at the Wade's camp," Drew said, his voice husky in a way that sent shivers across my skin. "I don't suppose there's any chance you have a pink bikini in your suitcase? I'd love to recreate a fantasy."

I laughed. "That was Jacy's swimsuit. You know pink isn't my color."

"Worked for me." He waggled his eyebrows and took a slight left at the next fork when GPS told him to.

In five hundred feet, your destination will be on the left.

"But I have one in blue that I think you'll appreciate."

"Count on it," he said.

Just as Drew's phone announced we had arrived, the lake house came into jaw-dropping view. The sleek, modern structure stood out like a shiny new penny among the rustic cabins and cottages we'd passed along the way.

"Holy mid-century modern, Batman," I breathed, taking in the floor-to-ceiling windows and clean lines. "Are you sure we're in the right place?"

Drew chuckled, reaching over to squeeze my hand. "Pretty sure, unless there's another place with a sign that says Bailey's Cove Getaway hiding around here somewhere."

We pulled up to the driveway, Molly whining and scratching at the window before Drew could put the car in park. As soon as I opened the door, she bolted for the water, brown fur a blur as she raced down the gentle slope to the lake.

"Well, I guess someone approves," I laughed, watching as our goofy flufferpup splashed into the crystal-clear water with abandon.

Drew came around to my side of the car, wrapping an arm around my waist. "What do you think, Mrs. Parker-Dupree? Will this do for our honeymoon getaway?"

I leaned into him, savoring the warmth of his body and the scent of his cologne. "I think it'll do just fine, Mr. Dupree-Parker." We needed to sort out our last names, but it was fun just considering the possibilities for now.

We stood there for a moment, watching Molly frolic along the shore, her joyful barks echoing across the water. I felt a lightness in my chest that I hadn't experienced in a long time. No ghosts, no mysteries, just Drew and me and our lovable dog.

"Should we go check out the inside?" Drew asked, pressing a kiss to my temple.

I nodded, eager to explore our home for the next two weeks. He called Molly out of the water and ordered her to wait for us on the deck. Open and airy, the place was as stunning inside as out. Windows lining the entire back wall gave the illusion it was made of glass, offering a breathtaking view of the lake.

"Wow," I whispered, dropping my bag, kicking off my flip-flops, and moving toward the windows. "This is... incredible."

Drew whistled low. "No kidding. Check out that kitchen."

I tore my gaze away from the view to take in the rest of the space. The kitchen was a chef's dream, all gleaming stainless steel and granite countertops. Plush throws draped over the leather sofa and colorful pillows added warmth, making the living area cozy despite the modern aesthetic.

As we explored, I kept running my hands over every surface. Everything felt luxurious and indulgent, from the smooth coolness of the marble fireplace to the soft texture of the area rug under my bare feet.

"I love our place, but I think I could get used to a space like this," I said, flopping down on the ridiculously comfortable sofa.

Drew joined me, pulling me close. "Me too. Though I have to say, the company is the best part."

I rolled my eyes but couldn't keep the smile off my face. "Smooth talker."

We cuddled for a moment before reluctantly getting up to unpack. As Drew moved our bags to the bedroom, which was just as impressive as the rest of the house, I wheeled the cooler into the kitchen, where I noticed a note, a key, and a small binder near the coffeemaker.

"Hey, we've got mail," I called to Drew. "It's from Bailey, the owner." The note welcomed us to the house and explained that the binder held information about the town, including phone numbers we might need, and that the key went to the boat docked outside.

Joining me, Drew looked over my shoulder as I read aloud. His eyes lit up when I got to the part about the boat key.

"A boat? Seriously?" He grinned like a kid on Christmas morning. "This just keeps getting better and better."

I laughed, shaking my head at his enthusiasm. "Let's at least finish unpacking before you go all Captain Ahab on me, okay?"

As we settled in, arranging our clothes in the spacious closet and stocking the fridge with the groceries we'd brought with us, I found myself humming contentedly. For once, no spectral voices were whispering in my ear, no unsolved mysteries hanging over my head. Just me, my new husband, and a time of pure relaxation stretching before us.

Of course, with Drew wanting a boat ride soon, that peace probably wouldn't last long. But for now, I was determined to enjoy every second of it.

The sun warmed my skin as we stepped onto the back deck. I inhaled deeply, savoring the crisp aroma of pine and the clean scent of the lake. Taking our presence as permission for another swim, Molly sailed off the end of the wharf while a pair of cushion-covered wooden chairs served as the perfect spot to sit and watch her cavort with the fishes. Drew pulled them close together so we could hold hands while we sat.

"This is nice," he said. "Just the three of us." Lazily, he turned his head to catch my gaze, and I nodded to confirm the lack of ghosts. "Maybe we could make it a yearly thing. A family tradition."

Visions of what that might look like played across my imagination in flashes. I don't claim to have ESP—seeing ghosts is about all the extrasensory input I can deal with —but the image of Drew standing waist-deep in the water, a boy with his smiling eyes, and a girl with my flaming hair shrieking with laughter as he played with them felt something like a premonition.

"I could go for that." All of it.

We fell into a companionable silence that threatened to turn into a nap until Drew said, "About that blue bikini..."

A dip in the lake led to a shower together, leading to other honeymoon activities, followed by dinner on the deck with Molly lying contentedly under the table. I couldn't have asked for more as we watched the sun turn a few puffy clouds to cotton candy pinks and blues.

"Walk with me?"

"Til death do us part," he replied, standing and pulling me up.

A strip of sandy beach arched in both directions from where the lake house sat at the center of a wide but shallow cove. With Molly splashing beside us, we veered left, following the curve of the water's edge.

"Hey, look at that," Drew said as we passed the property next to the one we'd rented.

I followed his gaze and saw a cluster of tiny house-style cabins nestled in a tree-lined clearing, arranged in a neat semicircle facing the lake, each one a different pastel shade that reminded me of saltwater taffy.

"Cute," I remarked. "I wonder if those are rentals, too. There's only one with open curtains and a car parked out back. The rest appear vacant."

Drew shrugged. "Probably. If so, renting five of them and bringing everyone down for a long weekend might be fun. Or all six if I can talk Riley into coming."

Knowing he meant Jacy, Brian, and their son in one cabin, Chris and Patrea in another, one for us, one for Neena, and one for David, I nudged him with my elbow. "We might only need five even if Riley does come. Neena and David are looking more and more like a thing."

I told him about the little glances and "accidental" touches they'd shared during the investigation that cleared his name. "I definitely caught date vibes between them at the bowling alley. I give it a month or less before they stop tap dancing around their feelings for each other."

"Um, hm." He seemed distracted.

"What?"

"I was just thinking about that one piece of property we looked at back home. The double camp lot. Something like this could work if we all chipped in and bought it as a group."

Thanks to my ex-husband's family, I could have written a check for the waterfront lot he was talking about, but since I didn't feel right about taking the money in the first place, spending it on land that was twice what we needed didn't sit well. But now that he mentioned it, a tiny house enclave with our closest friends sounded interesting.

Admiring the quaint structures with more interest, neither of us heard Molly come racing out of the water, so the cold shower that drenched our backs when she shook herself off was an unwelcome surprise.

"Ack!" I sputtered, laughing despite myself. "Molly! No!"

Drew chuckled, running a hand through his now-damp hair. "I guess that's one way to cool off."

Still giggling, I suggested, "We'd better take her for a walk. Give her a chance to dry off a bit on the way. I don't want her tracking wet sand into the house."

We followed the shoreline to a public boat launch with access to the gravel camp road and turned back toward the lake house with Molly trotting happily ahead of us. Listening to the wind in the trees, the occasional bird call, and the crunch of gravel under our feet, neither of us felt the need to talk.

After a minute or two, the rumble of approaching vehicles shattered the quiet twilight. Drew tugged me gently to the side of the road and called Molly as a small shuttle bus whizzed past us, kicking up a dirty cloud in its wake.

"Whoa," I coughed, waving away the dust. "Where's the fire?"

Drew squinted after the bus. "Looks like it's heading to those rental cabins we saw earlier."

I nodded, a tiny spark of curiosity igniting in my mind. "Group tour, maybe?"

"Probably," Drew said with a shrug. "Let's head back. I'm thinking of popcorn, a movie. You know, your honeymoon activities. Or ours, anyway."

Laughing, we continued on our way. I couldn't find a single thing wrong with any of his suggestions. There had been a short time during the past week when I wasn't sure we'd ever be together like this again, and now that we were, I meant to make the most of it.

CHAPTER TWO

Our new neighbors had other plans for us.

"Hey there!"

I turned to see a tall, rugged man with a grizzled beard waving enthusiastically our way while the rest of the group unpacked the shuttle. Waving back ended with his long strides eating up the ground between us. The smell of smoke and spices clung to him like a second skin.

"Name's Tommy O'Malley," he introduced himself with an outstretched hand. "You folks must be staying at the big house?"

I shuddered at the unintended second meaning of the term, but Drew only nodded, shaking Tommy's hand. "We're at the Getaway. I'm Drew, and this is my wife, Everly."

Wife. The word still sent a little thrill through me.

"Nice to meet you," I smiled, then gestured to our four-legged companion. "And this is Molly."

Tommy's eyes lit up when Molly flashed him her best doggy grin. "Well, ain't she a beauty!" He knelt to scratch behind her ears, then looked back at us. "Say, you two wouldn't happen to be foodies, would you?"

I exchanged a glance with Drew. "Not in the gourmet sense, but we like to eat," he said. "Why do you ask?"

Tommy's grin widened. "Well, you're in for a treat! What you've got right here," he jerked a thumb toward his fellow shuttle passengers, "are the best food truck vendors in the state. We're in town for the final round of a big regional competition starting tomorrow."

"That sounds fun," I said, genuinely intrigued. "What kind of food do you serve?"

Tommy puffed up with pride. "Best damned barbecue you ever tasted."

That explained the scents clinging to his clothes.

He gestured toward the contraption he'd been loading wood into near one of the cabins. "Cooked low and slow, and all night long. That's how I roll. Come on over and meet the rest of the crew."

"We're on our honeymoon," I said, hoping we might get out of having to be social, but that only delighted Tommy even more.

"That's even better. Come on over. I won't take no for an answer," he said, his voice carrying across the empty space. "Hey, guys! I want you to meet my new friends. They just got hitched. Let's help them celebrate!"

His voice set off a spate of barking inside one of the cabins. Sounded like a hound, to me. Molly quivered with excitement over the possibility of making a new friend.

Reluctantly, we followed him toward the others. This was shaping up to be anything but the quiet, secluded honeymoon we'd planned. Still, the idea of sampling dishes from food trucks piqued my interest. After all, what's a vacation without a little local flavor?

As we approached the group, I counted five other vendors. Three men and two women. I found myself cataloging each new face, a habit I'd picked up from years of dealing with both the living and, lately, the not-so-living.

"Ollie Henson." A jolly man with thinning hair introduced himself and shook our hands. A t-shirt with "In Pizza We Crust" written across it in fancy script stretched across his round belly. "Pizza Guy's the name of my truck. I toss a mean pie if I do say so myself."

He might have said more but was interrupted by the petite vendor standing to his right.

"Sophia Clark. Sorry, I'm a hugger." And she was. Even Molly got a hug. "Coffee and pastries are my thing. Well, besides Waffle Wednesdays when it's all about the toppings. Except I'm doing waffles every day for the competition, so I guess it's Waffle Whatever."

"I love waffles," I said, making a mental note that Sophia was a conversational rambler, and we should probably go into town for breakfast.

The next to introduce himself was, "Jake Ryder. Salads and sandwiches." Lean and athletic, he had a quiet intensity about him that suggested hidden depths and maybe a story lurking in his background.

The taller of the two women pulled one last suitcase out of the shuttle bus and put it with the rest of the matched set before coming over to offer her hand.

"I'm Cleo. Cleo Martin," she said as if her name should mean something.

"Nice to meet you," I said, and Drew repeated when she shook his hand.

Dark to light ombré curls rippled to her shoulders as if each one had been placed by a careful hand. I suppressed a twinge of envy over her curls being so neatly tamed while mine corkscrewed in every direction.

"My tacos are an elevated fusion of global flavors, carefully curated to tantalize your palate and offer an unparalleled culinary experience. Each ingredient is hand-selected for its freshness and vibrancy, sourced from sustainable farms to ensure ethical eating." She gestured animatedly, her perfectly manicured nails catching the last glimmers of sunlight. "I blend traditional techniques with avant-garde presentations, creating bold, Instagram-worthy creations that redefine what street food can be. What I serve isn't just a meal, it's a movement—a celebration of the senses and a journey through taste."

I caught Sophia's smirk out of the corner of my eye but managed to keep my face neutral. "That sounds like quite an experience."

It sounded like ad copy, but who was I to fault a woman for being on point with her branding?

"Trust me," she said. "It is."

Next to her, a scruffy-looking guy in well-worn jeans fidgeted with the hem of his faded t-shirt looking like he'd rather be anywhere else.

"That's Chase," Tommy said when no one else seemed

inclined to speak, pointing a thumb at the disheveled man. "He's not competing, just...visiting."

Chase shifted uncomfortably, his eyes darting to the stylish woman. "Uh, yeah. I'm not a vendor or anything. I'm here for Cleo."

I raised an eyebrow. Oh boy, I thought. There's definitely a story with this one.

Chase rubbed the back of his neck, his grin turning sheepish. "We're involved."

I raised an eyebrow, sensing the awkwardness hanging in the air. Cleo's previously animated expression had cooled considerably.

"We were," Cleo rolled her eyes so hard I was surprised they didn't fall out of her head.

Chase's casual posture as he slumped back against the side of the shuttle came off as a desperate attempt to appear nonchalant. "Come on, Cleo," he said, his voice a mix of hope and desperation. "We were good together and you know we could be—"

"Chase, honey, we've been over this," she said, her voice syrupy sweet but with an edge that could cut glass. "It's not happening."

I winced internally. Poor guy. But before I could feel too sorry for him, Cleo's demeanor altered abruptly. She flashed a dazzling smile at Drew and me as she pulled out her phone with a flourish.

"Did I hear Tommy say you were newlyweds?"

I nodded, slightly bemused. The woman changed focus so fast it made my head spin.

"This will be perfect content for my socials. My followers will just eat you up."

Before either of us could say we'd rather they didn't, she'd risen, adjusted the silk scarf around her neck—a pretty pattern of cobalt swirled with emerald—and positioned herself next to Drew, angling her phone to capture all three of us and Molly against the backdrop of the rippling lake.

"Hey Street Stars!" Cleo chirped into her phone. "Your girl Cleo here, coming at you live from my former hometown, beautiful Oakville, Maine! Check out this view, and this cutie pie doggo!"

On cue, Molly wagged her tail and posed. The ham.

As Cleo introduced us and continued her impromptu livestream, I smiled and wished I'd known what to expect when we left for our walk. I'd have put on mascara at least. And blown my hair out.

Somehow, over the next few minutes, Cleo turned the camera completely on us and managed to extract the story of our wedding, including Drew's arrest and my near-death experience.

"You're saints, the pair of you. I don't know how you managed to pull together the energy to go on a honeymoon. I'd be hiding under the bed covers by now. You're my new favorite couple. I'm obsessed."

I hoped not and thought we'd weathered the worst of it, but she snapped her fingers and said my name a couple of times.

"Wait a minute. Are you the same Everly Dupree who used to be married to Paul Hastings?"

Ugh. No.

"Yes."

"Did you really find him chained to a bed in a hotel room? Naked?"

It had been all over the news, so there was no reason to deny what happened or spare Paul's feelings, but I didn't need someone dredging up past scandals. "Paul and that unfortunate incident is in my past. I'm here in Oakville to celebrate my marriage to the love of my life, and begin my future."

Making eye contact with her, I channeled my mother's sternest look and let Cleo know I wouldn't be discussing the sordid details of my past. She took the hint. Spinning back around, she included herself in the frame.

"I can only imagine what you must have felt. Anyway...after everything you've been through, I think you deserve a reward. Your first meal at my truck is on me, and you'll receive a ten percent discount on every order for the rest of your honeymoon stay. How does that sound?"

Tommy and Ollie watched Cleo put on her show with similar expressions reflecting the same horror as passing an accident on the highway. Sophia quirked a brow but kept a smile on her face that didn't quite reach her eyes. Jake had taken his chance for escape once the camera turned on us, but Chase hovered at the edge of the group like a lost puppy. The contrast between his hopeful glances at Cleo and her complete indifference was painful to watch.

"Uh. Thanks," I said. "But you don't have to—"

"Don't you worry about a thing. You just come on down and find me. Street Chic Tacos parked at the corner of High Street and Main. I promise it'll be an experience you'll never forget."

I caught Drew's eye when she spun and angled her phone away from us again. He gave me a subtle wink, and I had to stifle a laugh. My husband knew me well enough to guess I was already piecing together the group dynamics. None of the other vendors looked happy at Cleo's obvious attempt to suck up to someone she now saw as a minor celebrity. Which I wasn't, really.

I leaned closer to Drew, whispering, "Well, this just got interesting. Think we stumbled into a reality show by mistake?"

Drew chuckled softly. "If we did, I hope we at least get royalties."

Cleo finally ended her livestream with a chirped, "Ta ta for now," and I saw my moment.

"Well, we should probably head back and let you all get settled," I said, resting my hand on Molly's head. "It was great meeting everyone."

"You can't leave yet." Tommy shook his head. "I've got some homemade peach wine. Stay for one drink. A honeymoon toast, if you will."

Before we could offer a polite refusal, he'd gone inside to grab the bottle and a sleeve of plastic cups. It would have been churlish to refuse, so we let him pour us a generous glass, then watched while Chase, at Tommy's instruction, lit the campfire already laid out in the center of a circle of stone benches.

"Jake!" Cleo called out toward the open window of the cabin he'd entered earlier. "You're missing all the fun."

"I'm good, thanks," he called back.

"The man is as fine as this wine, but he's not much of a joiner."

"You mind if I let Prescott out?" Chase said as the howling intensified. "He's good with other dogs. People, too."

"Molly would love to make a new friend. She's good with other dogs as well."

My guess of the dog being a hound hadn't been too far off the mark. Prescott turned out to be a beagle mix. When Chase opened the door, he shot out like his butt was on fire and made a beeline for Molly. The two dogs wiggled and sniffed each other, then ran for the water to splash around together.

One glass turned to two and a round of pleasant conversation where we learned the vendors had competed in a series of regional competitions all over the state to qualify for the finals being held here in Oakville. Tommy left long enough to fire up his smoker, then returned to rejoin the conversation.

"There was twenty of us when we started. We're down to five now. May the best truck win," Ollie said, draining his plastic cup. "And on that note, I'm off to unpack and get ready for bed."

Thinking more time had slipped by than I expected, I checked my watch and saw it was only eight pm. It wasn't even fully dark yet.

"I'll head in as well," Sophia also rose. "I need to make up a batch of brioche dough so it can chill overnight, and call my mother. We talk every night. It was good to meet you, Everly, and Drew."

"We should be heading back as well." We said our goodbyes, with promises to visit their trucks soon, and escaped toward the lake house, hand in hand, the gravel crunching beneath our feet.

The moment we stepped inside, the rest of the world fell away. Drew pulled me close, his blue eyes twinkling and strong arms encircling my waist. "Now, Mrs. Parker," he murmured, his breath warm against my ear, "where were we before we were so rudely interrupted by civilization?"

I grinned, wrapping my arms around his neck. "I believe we were about to start our honeymoon properly, Mr. Parker."

As Drew's lips met mine, I pushed thoughts of food truck rivalries and unrequited love to the back of my mind. For now, at least, the only mystery I wanted to solve was how I'd been lucky enough to marry this remarkable man.

CHAPTER THREE

The aroma of freshly brewed coffee and maple syrup lingered in the air as I scraped the last bite of blueberry pancake from my plate. Sunlight streamed through the floor-to-ceiling windows of Bailey's Lakeside Getaway, casting a golden glow across the modern kitchen.

"That was delicious," Drew said, leaning back in his chair with a contented sigh, "Looks like Molly wants a quick run. Want to join us?"

I glanced at Molly, our eager chocolate lab, her tail thumping against the hardwood floor, her chin resting on Drew's leg as she gave him her best pathetic look. "As tempting as it is to watch your backside while you two out-pace me, I think I'll pass. Someone's got to clean up this mess, and I have a date with the last chapter of this mystery novel I've been trying to finish since before the wedding. I think I know who the killer is, but I really want to find out."

Drew stood, his blue eyes twinkling. "Suit yourself, but you're missing out on all this," he said, gesturing to his muscular frame with a playful grin.

I rolled my eyes, fighting back a smile. "Oh, the tragedy. However will I cope?"

As Drew bent to clip on Molly's leash, I was drawn to how his faded blue t-shirt stretched across his broad shoulders. Not a bad view at all, I mused.

"Have fun, you two," I called as they headed for the door. "When you come back, I'll take advantage of all of that." I mimicked his earlier gesture.

Drew's laughter echoed as the door closed behind them. I sighed contentedly, savoring the peaceful quiet of our honeymoon hideaway. The lake sparkled beyond the windows, a perfect backdrop for a cozy morning of reading.

I had just loaded the last plate into the dishwasher when my phone buzzed. A text from Jacy lit up the screen:

Two things. First, OMG, Ev! Have you seen what's happening online? #HappilyEverlyAfter is trending.

My brow furrowed as I typed back: *What are you talking about?*

Jacy's response was instantaneous: *Cleo's video post about you and Drew has gone viral. You're all over social media with #EverlyAndDrew and #MysteryLoveAndTacos, too.*

I groaned, my peaceful morning evaporating like mist on the lake. So much for escaping into the drama of my mystery novel. It seemed I'd be dealing with real-life drama instead.

"Great," I muttered, sinking onto the plush sofa. "Just

what every newlywed wants—their love life turned into viral hashtags."

What's the second thing?

Mooselick River has its very own escape room. That's what went into our old place. We're going to the soft opening tonight unless you want us to wait until you come home.

It was nice of her to ask.

No, I texted back. *You guys go and have fun. Let me know how it goes!*

As my phone continued to buzz with notifications, I couldn't help but wonder how many followers Cleo had and why a post about an unknown couple was causing such a stir. More importantly, how was this going to affect our honeymoon?

I glanced longingly at my abandoned book. The last chapter would have to wait. It looked like I had a different kind of mystery to research now. The sound of the front door opening jolted me from my social media spiral. Drew came in, his blond hair damp with sweat and blue eyes sparkling with excitement.

"Have I got a story for you," he said, plopping down beside me on the sofa. He wasn't the only one with a story, but mine could wait.

I raised an eyebrow, intrigued. "Oh? Do tell, Mr. Parker. What juicy gossip have you brought me from your morning run?"

Drew leaned in for a kiss, then settled back and propped his feet on the ottoman. "So, I was jogging past the rental cabins, right? And Tommy's out back, pulling things out of the smoker. We'll need to hit his truck, by the way. The food should be excellent if the smell is anything to go by."

"Okay," I circled a hand to indicate he should get on with the story part of things.

"Anyway, I stopped to let Molly pee and ended up hearing a heated argument between Ollie and Tommy."

"That would be the pizza guy and the BBQ master?" I asked, already sensing drama.

"The very same," Drew nodded, his hands animatedly painting the scene. "Tommy had his earbuds in, so he didn't hear Ollie coming. Or Molly and me, for that matter. He'd just pulled a whole chicken out of the smoker when Ollie grabbed his arm. The chicken fell into the coals, Tommy yanked out his earbuds, and then, it was on."

Both men had seemed so affable when we met them the day before. "You have my attention," I said.

"Ollie said he'd just got off a call with someone in town and said it wasn't a mistake that they'd had him park his truck on the side street instead of the spot he'd paid for. His face got all red, and he kept jabbing his finger at Tommy, accusing him of bribing town officials to snag the prime vending spot."

The drama of it all. "Bribing with what? Burnt ends?"

Drew grinned, appreciating my quip. "More like greasing palms with secret sauce, I'd wager. Tommy denied having anything to do with the parking arrangements and offered to switch spots with Ollie if he wanted to. He said it didn't matter to him. He'd get plenty of business no matter where his truck was parked. And what difference did it make anyway? The competition was all about the food, not the number of customers."

"Sounds logical to me. Did that calm Ollie down?"

"Some. I figured that would be the end of it and once Tommy put his earbuds back in, I could slip away, but they both started griping about Cleo."

"Cleo?" I echoed my earlier unease about her social media post resurfacing. "What's she got to do with anything?"

"Tommy said," Drew continued, his eyes widening for dramatic effect, "if anyone from the competition was behind Ollie getting shunted to the side street, it would be her. This wasn't the first time he'd come up against her, and she was a 'cutthroat competitor' who'd do anything to win."

I leaned back, processing this information. "Well, that's quite the food fight brewing. Who knew the culinary world could be so... spicy?"

Drew chuckled, wrapping an arm around my shoulders. "I know, right? It's like we've stumbled into the 'Great British Bake Off' meets 'The Godfather'."

I snorted at the mental image. "Oh, I can see it now. 'I'm gonna make him a cannoli he can't refuse.'"

We both dissolved into laughter, the tension from my earlier social media discovery momentarily forgotten. As the hilarity subsided, I marveled at how easily Drew could find humor in any situation.

"You know," I said, nestling closer to him, "I think I prefer our version of honeymoon drama to the one happening online right now."

Drew's brow furrowed. "Online? What do you mean?"

I sighed, reaching for my still-buzzing phone. "Buckle up, honey. We've got more than just food truck wars to contend with. Cleo's little livestream yesterday has taken on a life of its own. We're on our way to becoming social media stars."

"Really?"

He reached for my phone, but I shook my head and pushed it away. "You know what? Let's deal with that later. We're on our honeymoon, and I refuse to let anything disrupt our day."

Drew's face lit up with that boyish grin I adored. "Now that's the Everly I married. What do you say we make the most of this gorgeous weather and take a dip in the lake?"

Snorting, I teased, "You just want me to put on that blue bikini so you can ogle me in it."

"Busted," Drew agreed, already heading for the door. "I'll grab the towels."

When Drew stepped onto the dock, Molly bounded ahead, her tail wagging furiously. The water lapped gently against the shore, inviting us in. I padded across the brown sand to let the water swirl around my feet, pleasantly surprised by its warmth.

"This is how you do it," Drew called, cannonballing off

the dock with a splash that sent Molly into a frenzy of excited barks as she leaped in behind him.

I laughed, heading back to the dock and following suit with a less-than-graceful plunge. The cool water enveloped me, washing away my lingering worries. We spent the whole morning splashing around, playing fetch with Molly, and enjoying the simple pleasure of being together.

Later, as we toweled off on the deck, Drew glanced at the boat and then at the house. "Boat ride now? Or after lunch?"

"After. Definitely after. I'm starving, and I think we'll need some private time afterward. You know, to digest properly."

"Oh, absolutely. Proper digestion is crucial. Let's eat outside."

We went with sandwiches because hey, fast and easy. Drew carried the plates outside while I brought glasses, then returned for the pitcher of iced tea I'd brewed and stashed in the fridge.

When I got back outside, Drew was no longer alone. I found him standing next to a six-wheeled ATV, talking to a couple I judged to be in their mid-seventies.

"Hey, Ev!" Drew waved me over. "These are our neighbors on the other side. We were just getting to the introductions."

"Well, hello there, young lady." Everything about how she dressed and something about her smile reminded me of Grammie Dupree, which made me like her almost immediately. "We brought you a little welcome gift." She produced a plastic container that smelled suspiciously like freshly baked cookies.

Drew's eyes lit up. "You shouldn't have! But I'm certainly glad you did."

The woman beamed. "I'm Effie Paulson, and this old coot here is my husband, Carlton. We're celebrating our golden anniversary this year!"

Carlton wrapped an arm around his wife, his round face split by a beaming smile. "Fifty years of her putting up with me. It's a miracle, I tell ya."

"Oh, hush," Effie swatted at him playfully.

"I'm Everly, and this is my husband, Drew."

"Pleased to meet you." Effie looked down at the tea pitcher and then up at me. "If you've got extra glasses, we'd love some of that tea and a chance to get to know our neighbors!"

I glanced at Drew, who shrugged and waited for me to decide. "Well," I said, "we were just sitting down to a late lunch. We weren't expecting guests."

Effie waved that away with an age-spotted hand. "Don't you worry your pretty head about us. Carlton likes to keep to a tight schedule, so we ate at noon like we always do. But you go right ahead and have yours. Good conversation makes a meal better, I always say."

Not wanting to be rude, I went back inside and returned with two more glasses and some extra napkins.

"Now, don't you two look like something out of a

romance novel," Effie cooed, accepting her drink. "How long have you been married?"

"Just a week," Drew replied, his hand finding mine. I felt a warmth that had nothing to do with the summer sun.

Carlton leaned back in his chair, a mischievous glint in his eye. "Well, let me tell you about our honeymoon. It'll give you youngsters a laugh."

"In retrospect, it was a honeymoon marked for disaster. Two city slickers thinking we could rough it in the great outdoors? I'd never even seen a tent before, let alone set one up!"

As Carlton launched into his tale, I was drawn in by his animated storytelling. His weathered hands gesticulated wildly as he described the ill-fated camping trip they'd both expected to be a romantic start to their marriage.

Effie interjected, "Oh, honey, remember the raccoons?"

Carlton guffawed. "How could I forget? Those little bandits made off with our entire food supply. We lived off berries and the trout I pulled out of the creek for three days."

As he'd wanted, Carlton's picture of himself and Effie stumbling through the wilderness made us smile and laugh along with them.

"But you know what?" Carlton's voice softened. "Those three days taught us more about marriage than any self-help book ever could. We learned to laugh at ourselves, to work as a team, and most importantly, to always pack extra snacks."

"And socks," Effie added.

"You can never have too many pairs of clean socks," Drew agreed with her.

"He should know," I said, not ashamed of ratting him out. "Even knowing we had access to laundry facilities, he packed ten pairs."

Filled with more stories and laughter, another hour passed. One that left me feeling relaxed and happy, starkly contrasting the tension of the morning's events.

"You really want to have some fun, go on into town and rent yourselves one of these side-by-sides." Effie pointed a thumb toward the ATV. "They're easy to drive, and you'll find plenty of trails around the lake. The way Carlton opens her up on the trails makes me feel young again. Brings me right back to when we used to put on our leathers and take the Harley out for a spin."

Effie Carlson, younger and leather-clad on the back of a motorcycle, evoked an unexpected mental image.

"You know how to handle a firearm, young fella?" Carlton assessed Drew shrewdly. "Black bears roam these parts. If you decide to take to the trails, you'd best have some protection."

"Yes, sir. I do." Drew said without bringing up his military history. "I'll take that under advisement if we rent a rig."

By the time Carlton declared it was time to get Effie

home for her afternoon nap, we'd exchanged addresses and phone numbers and promised to keep in touch.

"What nice people," I said as they disappeared around the corner, Carlton's hand on Effie's elbow as if guiding her safely on the walk home. "They remind me of my grandparents."

"Mine, too," Drew admitted with fondness in his tone and helped me carry the remains of our meal inside. Later, I noticed Drew's gaze straying toward the dock. "You ready for a boat ride?"

At the word ride, Molly raced toward the door. "I guess she's ready."

Outside, I grabbed the life vests while Drew checked the boat over to make sure it was ready to go.

"Come here, Molls. Let's get you suited up."

Molly, however, had other ideas. She eyed the gently rocking boat with suspicion, backing away as I approached with her life jacket.

"It's okay, sweetie," I coaxed, trying to lure her closer with a reassuring tone. "You've worn this before, remember?"

Molly whined, her tail tucked between her legs. "You'd think we were asking her to walk the plank. Should we just leave her here? It's not like her to be so dramatic."

Drew joined in the effort, patting the boat's seat. "It's just new. I think she'll be fine once we get her on board. She loves canoeing with us, and this isn't that different. Come on, Molly! Want to go for a ride?"

At the word "ride," Molly's ears perked up. She inched forward, still hesitant.

"That's it, good girl," I encouraged, finally managing to slip the life jacket over her head.

With a bit more coaxing and saying the word *ride* several more times, we finally got Molly into the boat. She immediately plastered herself to Drew's leg, looking at him with pleading eyes.

"A sea dog, you are not," I teased her, settling into my seat. Once we got up to speed and the nose of the boat leveled off, Molly realized this wasn't so different from riding in the car and calmed down, her nose pointed into the wind and her tongue lolling out in a doggy smile.

Despite the change in venue and the touch of neighbor drama, this was shaping up to be a decent honeymoon. My heart felt as light as the froth churned up by our wake.

Twice as long as it was wide, the lake was half again the size of the one back home. We spent a couple of hours just tooling around the perimeter, taking in the sights, and making way for other boaters. The waters were busy with fishers and pleasure riders even on a weekday.

"This is my happy place." The wind tried to whip Drew's words away as soon as they left his mouth. "I love being on the water. Want to take the wheel?"

"Thought you'd never ask!" I grinned, switching places with him.

A rush of exhilaration coursed through me as I gripped

the steering wheel. The boat responded to my touch, cutting through the water with ease.

"You've done this before," Drew shouted, his arm around Molly.

I winked at him. "What can I say? I'm full of surprises. Jacy taught me."

"I'm not sure I find that comforting."

"Jacy's need for speed is legendary, but she's an excellent driver and a great teacher." I whipped the wheel and took the boat through a series of tight curves that let us bump over our own wake. "We clocked a lot of hours on the lake."

Until I left for college and got married, anyway.

After pulling into an out-of-the-way cove for a leisurely swim off the back of the boat, Drew pointed its nose toward the southern end of the lake and put on some speed to let the open air dry us off. When the public docks came into view, I was as relaxed and stress-free as ever. A hot husband, a place on the water, and most importantly, no ghosts lingering to screw up the mood...absolute paradise.

"I think the water's my happy place, too. And we need to buy a boat." I hooked a finger in the tendril of hair that wanted to blow into my eyes and tucked it behind my ear.

"No argument here. We should probably fill up before we head back." He pointed toward the gas pump set up at the end of the longest wharf.

I cocked an eyebrow and patted my stomach. "I don't know about you, but I could use a fill-up, too."

"You want to check out the food trucks?" With Molly in tow, that seemed like the best idea.

"Might as well get our free tacos. I hear they're an experience." I grinned.

CHAPTER FOUR

*D*rew expertly guided the boat to the fueling station. Once he'd filled the tank and pulled into an empty spot out of the way of the pumps, I stowed our life jackets and clipped on Molly's leash.

"So, which truck should we hit first?" I asked, scanning the line-up of colorful vehicles.

Drew grinned. "Well, after this morning's drama, I'm kind of curious about Ollie's pizza."

I raised an eyebrow. "Feeling sympathetic to the underdog?"

"Maybe," he shrugged. "But also, who doesn't love pizza?"

We strolled hand-in-hand toward the food trucks parked on the grassy verge between the docks and the business district. Four trucks were lined up two by two, facing each other, with picnic tables and trash cans filling some of the space between. Ollie's truck sat alone at the end of a side street, still visible but some distance away.

"Looks like Ollie was worried for nothing." A line of waiting customers snaked around the corner.

Drew shrugged. "Good for him, but do we want to wait in line?"

I chewed my lip. "You're the one who suggested pizza. I'm easy."

"Barbecue sounds good, too," Drew mused. "Maybe we should try something from each truck. I'm not above a little taste testing."

The mix of aromas wafting through the air made deciding where to begin our culinary adventure difficult. I headed for Tommy's truck, then stopped and read the menu board at Jake's. Drew chuckled, squeezing my hand.

"Too many choices?" he asked, eyes twinkling.

"Let's start with Cleo's tacos. I'm dying to see if they live up to the hype. We'd better split one, though. Or else I'll have to swim back to the lake house to burn off all the calories."

"But which one is hers?" Drew asked, his tongue firmly planted in his cheek.

The one with her face splashed across the side, naturally. Below graffiti-style letters in hot pink with green outlines spelling out the name of her truck, Chic Street Tacos, Cleo stared at us with an Instagram-worthy smile. It was a bit much. And yet, it was totally her.

As we reached the order window, her megawatt smile greeted us. "Well, if it isn't the newlyweds! What can I get for you lovebirds?"

"We'd love to try your famous fish tacos," Drew replied. "Just the one order. We're doing the rounds and sharing plates."

"Oh, I don't think so! I promised you a free meal, and that's what you'll have. Trust me, you won't want to share once you get a taste!" Cleo winked, turning with a flourish to drop portions of fish into batter, then slip them into the fryer.

While we watched her work, I made small talk. "How's the competition going so far?"

She paused, a flash of strong emotion crossing her face before her smile returned. "Oh, you know, same old, same old. To get here, I had to place in three qualifying events, and I won all three."

"Really?" I said, surprised. "I didn't know there were so many of these competitions. This is the first one I've ever heard of."

"Oh, sure. We were all in Port Harbor last week, along with ten other vendors who didn't make the cut, and I'll be heading up north to compete in another regional after I win this one. I can't lose. I'm the hometown favorite."

That surprised me. "You're from Oakville?"

"Born and raised. Until I left for culinary school, anyway. Now, I'm here to prove myself."

Underneath Cleo's social butterfly exterior beat the heart of a serious competitor.

"Hold on," she cut our conversation short to slip each taco into a holder, then made a big deal of garnishing them with sliced scallions and a flurry of herbs. Satisfied, she pulled out her phone before sliding the tacos through the window. "I want to get a shot of you for my socials."

"But we..." I began, then trailed off when she ignored my protest and exited the truck to point her phone camera in our direction. Between swimming and boating, my hair probably looked like a bird's nest caught in a hurricane, and the cover-up I'd dragged over my swimsuit dated back to my high school years. Drew looked as carelessly handsome as he always did—his hair artfully tousled by the wind, his swim trunks and tank top showing off sculpted muscles.

"We're not camera-ready."

Cleo waved my protest away. "You're fine. You've got that honeymoon glow. Now, don't let your food get cold!"

"Okay. I guess we're doing this." We were, but not until Cleo had me unlock my phone and exchange numbers so she could send me copies of the photos.

Trying to ignore Cleo and her phone, I picked up my first taco. The first bite was a revelation—crispy, beer-battered cod nestled in a warm corn tortilla, topped with tangy slaw and a creamy cilantro-lime sauce.

"Cleo," I mumbled through a mouthful, "this is amazing." Drew nodded in agreement. His eyes closed in bliss while she stuck her phone in her pocket and knelt to give Molly some attention.

"Who's a good girl?" She crooned while Molly lapped up the attention. "Can she have something, too? Or is she a fussy eater?"

I laughed. "No, she's definitely not one of those. She's the queen of snapping up anything that gets dropped on the floor, which is plenty when my friend brings her toddler around for a visit."

"You don't let her have anything bad for dogs, though?" Cleo looked at us like we'd admitted to being abusers of innocent animals. "Chocolate can make them sick. Grapes and onions as well."

"No. We're careful," Drew assured her, but Cleo had already turned her attention back to Molly.

"I'll make you some of the fish and top it with shredded carrots," she baby-talked to our dog. "We wouldn't want to give you an upset tummy, now, would we?"

Molly wolfed down the proffered meal and finished it off with a drink from the water bowl Cleo kept near her truck for passing pets.

"Come see me again, won't you?" Cleo said though I was pretty sure she meant the dog, not us.

For our second stop, the aroma of smoked meat drew us to Tommy's truck like a siren's call.

He greeted us with a gruff nod that said he'd watched Cleo make a spectacle of herself and us. "What'll it be? I've got a special going on pulled pork sandwiches today."

"Sounds great," Drew said after cocking an eyebrow at me and getting my nod of approval. "We'll take one of those. No sides, and can you cut it in half? We're in a sharing mood tonight."

And we'd just eaten three tacos each, but we weren't about to say that to Tommy.

"Sure thing," he agreed, pulling a roll from a bag, dipping each half in butter, and dropping them on the grill.

"Quite a turnout today," Drew casually mentioned. "Seems like everyone's doing well."

"Sure does." He flicked a look at Ollie's truck. "Come for the pizza. Get distracted by the barbecue. We wouldn't be here if we weren't the best of the best. Or most of us, anyway."

This time, his gaze slid toward Cleo's truck, where a line had formed since we'd left. Her voice lifted above the hum of the crowd, tightening Tommy's smile. I filed that tidbit away as we accepted our sandwich. The tender pork practically melted in my mouth, perfectly balanced by a sweet and smoky barbecue sauce and a topping of freshly fried onion rings.

"If he serves this to the judges, he'll be a contender," Drew said, licking sauce from his fingers. "Best I've ever had."

We continued our culinary tour, cleansing our palates by sharing a crisp, refreshing salad served with a smile but without any additional conversation from Jake.

By the time we got to Ollie's pizza truck, the line had dwindled so that only three people waited ahead of us. The aromas of browning crust and spiced meats blending with the sharp tang of tomato sauce made the wait seem longer than it was. If his pie were half as good as it smelled, it would give Bertino's, my hometown favorite, a run for its money. Seeing us, Ollie's face lit up.

"Welcome, folks! What can I get for you today?" he asked, his enthusiasm showing in the smile lines around his eyes. "Anything you see on the menu, I can make up as a six-inch single or a ten-inch double if you want to share."

I felt my waistband tighten as Drew replied warmly, "We'll take a double. Any toppings are fine. Surprise us."

Beaming, Ollie busied himself with our order. "It's been busier than I expected. Small towns like this, you never know how things will shake out."

"You'd be surprised what a little judicious advertising can do," I said, having had some experience running events. "People like the cozy feel of a festival."

"I guess so! And now, it looks like I need to mix up another batch of dough."

I watched with fascination as he tossed yeast and water into an industrial mixing bowl on a low stand. While it bloomed, he rotated our pizza, slit open a fifty-pound bag of flour, and glanced around as if searching for something. A flour scoop, I assumed. Finding none, he shrugged and bent to lift the bag.

It came off the floor less than an inch before he let it drop back down and uttered a low oath.

"Everything okay?" Drew asked.

"Got a bum shoulder." Ollie gave up on trying to lift the flour and clapped his right hand to his left shoulder. "Plays me up more than it used to. After the season's over, I'll have to give in and have that rotator cuff surgery, I guess."

"Let me give you a hand." Always willing to help others, Drew rounded the truck and stepped in to lift the bag for Ollie.

"Thanks, young fella. Getting older isn't as much fun as I thought it would be."

While we waited for our pizza, I leaned in close to Drew. "First it was Ollie thinking someone was out to get him, then it was Tommy throwing shade. Food Truck Wars might be my new favorite reality show."

Drew winked. "All the drama but no popcorn."

A few minutes later, Ollie presented us with a steaming pizza topped with prosciutto, figs, and a drizzle of honey. The first bite sang on my tongue—the crust was perfectly crisp, and the flavors a delightful balance of sweet and savory. It was so good I closed my eyes to savor the moment.

"Now I see why people are lining up," I said and took a second bite. "This is incredible. I wouldn't want to be a judge."

Drew washed down his pizza with a drink from the water bottle he'd brought with us from the boat. "I would if it meant getting a chance to sample my way through Ollie's menu."

Our final stop was Sophia's dessert truck. As we approached, I noticed her fingers drumming nervously on the counter.

"Everything okay, Sophia?" I asked gently.

She startled slightly. "Oh! Yes, of course. Just...thinking about tomorrow's menu. What can I get for you? Mocha lattes are on special today."

Not wanting a hit of caffeine, I selected a London fog latte and a delicate lavender macaron. "Sharing time is over," I told Drew with a wink and a smile.

Grinning, he said, "You can keep your frou-frou little

lady cookie. I'm going for the triple chocolate brownie. It's manly."

"Lady cookie," Sophia burst out in giggles.

"Sounds dirty somehow," I said, giving Drew a joking nudge with my elbow.

"You're funny together. I like it," Sophia said, bagging up our order. "Come back tomorrow. I'll make sure to have an array of lady cookies and manly desserts on hand."

The subtle floral notes danced on my tongue as I bit into the macaron.

"These are divine," I told her sincerely. "All joking aside, I've never had better. Not even in Paris."

A genuine smile lit up Sophia's face. "Thank you. That means a lot."

Hand in hand, with Molly gamboling beside us, we strolled along the sand lining the curved edge of the lake where the docks gave way to a public beach. "Look at that view," I breathed, pointing ahead to a secluded outcropping of rocks overlooking the water. "It's like something out of a postcard."

Drew grinned. "Race you there?"

I laughed, already breaking into a jog. "You're on, Mr. Parker!"

We scrambled up the bank, giggling like kids, until we reached the top. Slightly out of breath, I settled onto a smooth, sun-warmed surface, Drew's arm wrapping around my shoulders, Molly happily settling at our feet.

"You know," I mused, leaning into him, "for all the craziness that usually follows us, this is pretty perfect."

Drew pressed a kiss to my temple. "Couldn't agree more, Mrs. Parker."

We sat in comfortable silence, watching the sun dip lower on the horizon. The gentle lapping of waves against the shore provided a soothing backdrop to our quiet contentment.

"I could get used to this," I murmured, my eyes drinking in the tranquil scene before us.

Drew chuckled. "No ghosts clamoring for your attention? No mysteries to solve?"

I elbowed him playfully. "Don't jinx it, mister. I'm thoroughly enjoying this ghost-free honeymoon, thank you very much."

Just beginning to sink toward the horizon, the setting sun cast warm light over fluffy clouds, turning their edges molten as we reluctantly made our way back to our lakeside getaway. Once the wake of our passing smoothed away, the still cove water mirrored the sky. I pulled out my phone to take a photo that didn't quite manage to catch the magical moment but came close.

"What a perfect end to a perfect day," I mused, linking my arm through Drew's as we made our way up the gravel path to the house.

Drew chuckled, patting his stomach. "If by perfect, you mean I'm perfectly stuffed, then yes."

We settled onto the plush outdoor sofa on the deck, snuggling close to wait until the last rays of sunlight danced across the lake's surface. I nestled my head against Drew's shoulder, inhaling the comforting scent of his skin mixed with the warm evening air.

"You know," I began, "We could—"

My words were cut short by the buzzing of the first mosquito that hovered nearly at the end of my nose before zipping over to land on my arm and get a bite of me before I slapped it dead.

"Go inside?" Drew slapped the second mosquito. "Before the rest of the...is it a swarm?...shows up."

"I think a group of mosquitoes is called a scourge," I said, slapping at a second bite, "for good reason."

Inside, a sudden cacophony of pings and buzzes emanating from my phone. Frowning, I fished it out of my pocket.

"What's up?" Drew looked over my shoulder.

My eyes widened as I scrolled through the flood of notifications. "Oh boy," I muttered. "Remember Cleo's post from this morning?"

"The one with the hashtags? How could I forget #HappilyEverlyAfter?"

I nodded, my brow furrowing. "Well, now that it's gone viral, her fans are reaching out to me directly."

Drew's eyebrows shot up. "Seriously? Let me see."

I tilted the screen toward him, showcasing the barrage of messages. "Look at this one: 'OMG! You're that chick with the chained-up ex! Was he really naked?' And this: 'Everly! No presh, but hear me out. You should collab with

Cleo on a line of pink taco shells! #GirlPowerTacos #PaybackTacos!' "

"Payback tacos?" Drew snorted. "Now that's a food truck that sounds like an insurance nightmare."

"Pink taco shells? Could you just imagine?" I could. Once the mental image popped into my head, I wished I hadn't, and the messages just kept coming. "This is...a lot. I mean, I've been a hot topic before, but not like this."

Drew wrapped an arm around me, pulling me close. "Hey, we'll figure it out. Maybe this is a good thing? Ten bucks says Martha finds a way to turn it into free publicity for the next Mooselick River event?"

I sighed, leaning into his embrace. "I wouldn't put it past her. This is just so invasive."

As if on cue, my phone pinged again. This time, it was a message from Cleo herself: "You're blowing up. Isn't it amazing? We need to talk ASAP. I have a proposition for you."

Dread swirled up and then settled in my gut. "If this is about payback tacos," I said, my voice tinged with resigned amusement, "she's doomed to disappointment."

"Are you planning to call her back?" Drew's fingers played along my cheek, his lips moving close enough to mine that I could feel his warm breath. "Or can I find a way to distract you?"

"Oh, I think you can." And he did.

CHAPTER FIVE

*a*T HAYWARD HOUSE
"A little to the left," Julie Kingsley directed her best friend Gustavia, who was standing on a step ladder nearby. "No. Your other left."

"Sorry." Gustavia tilted the reflector the other way so the soft morning light streaming through the window bounced off its silver lining to highlight the pretty teapot glazed in turquoise and white. "How's that? Better?"

"Perfect. Kat, could you tilt your hand just a little more toward me?" Julie peered through her camera's viewfinder to line up the shot. "Right there. That's good."

"What about me?" Amethyst held the position she'd been in for the past five minutes but felt a case of the shakes coming on. "Are you about done yet?"

"You're fine. Don't move." Julie clicked the shutter twice. "Almost done, now. Move into the second position. And hold." The shutter clicked twice more. "And done."

"Phew," Kat said, shaking her wrist to get the feeling back in her hand. "You wouldn't think a teacup was so heavy until you've held one in the same position for half an hour. I hope we got the shots you needed."

Her grin wide, Julie flipped her laptop around to show

off a series of gorgeous photos featuring the teapot and matching cups cradled in her friend's hands. "They're perfect. Amaya's gonna sell a lot of teapots thanks to your pretty hands and Gustavia's head for heights."

"I'll take the flattery," Amethyst rose and stretched to ease the kinks from sitting still for so long. "And the standard model fee since we decided to go with the premium windows Finn's been harping on about. I'll be glad when the building phase is complete."

Having climbed down the stepladder, Gustavia spun and clapped her hands. Yards of paisley in a sunny yellow swirled around bracelet-adorned ankles. "I stopped by on my way here to check on the progress. The addition is coming right along. I can't wait until you start buying fixtures. The best part of any remodel is putting in those personal touches."

Helping Julie gather the cups to take to the kitchen so they could be washed and repacked for shipping, Kat teased, "Three guesses what the color scheme will be."

Since purple had been Amethyst's signature color for a few years, it wasn't much of a leap to assume its varied shades would figure highly into her decorating.

"You might be surprised to learn I've decided to go with neutrals for the walls." Amethyst's chin tilted up in mock defense. "It was Reid's idea, but I've been considering a change anyway."

Three sets of eyes widened at the declaration.

"No kidding?" Julie tilted her head and let her eyes go slightly unfocused while imagining Amethyst in various shades. "I could see you as a Ruby or maybe Sapphire. With your skin tone, you should stay away from yellows. I can't see you becoming a Citrine or Sandstone. Jewel tones look better on you."

"Citrine would be better than plain Jane." Even though plain had never been a word to describe her, Amethyst's dislike of her given name had driven her to change it legally. "But I think I'll keep the name and just try some different colors on for size."

"Twenty bucks says you're back in purple by the end of the summer," Kat fished inside her pocket and pulled out the folded twenty she kept on hand for just this reason. She and Amethyst would put their money on the table for almost any reason.

"You're on." A second twenty joined the first. "Sucker bet." Still, they shook on it.

Since many hands make light work, twenty minutes saw the teacups washed and packed and a fresh pot of tea brewed to share.

"Did Everly and Drew get checked in okay?" Gustavia asked Amethyst while she added a dollop of cream to her tea, followed it up with a spoonful of honey, and selected an oatmeal raisin cookie from the plate Julie placed in the center of the table.

"As far as I know. She messaged me when they arrived but not since, so I figure they're settling in and doing the honeymoon thing. Didn't want to disturb."

Waiting for her tea to cool, Kat began to shuffle the Tarot deck she'd pulled from her purse, "I could read for her. Or just pull a card for one of you." She scanned her friend's faces.

"I'm good," Julie said, as usual.

"Same." Gustavia chose a second cookie, broke off a chunk, and popped it into her mouth. "Ammie?"

"Read for Everly. I've got no burning life questions at the moment—unless the cards can help me decide between Steely Gray and Morning Fog for my bedroom walls." Rising, she retrieved her purse and pulled out two paint sample chips.

"Morning Fog," Kat glanced at the samples and cut the deck. "It's softer. More bedroomy."

"Is that the technical term?" Julie teased.

"It is," Kat said, nodding her head with enthusiasm as she shuffled again and chose a five-card spread. She laid the cards face down on the table, all in a row, pausing theatrically before turning over the first. Her brows shot up with the revelation. "The High Priestess. Now that's interesting."

"I've had that one before," Amethyst said, leaning forward to get a better look. She reached across and tapped the card. "She stands for intuition and secrets, right? Do you think something's up with Drew? Maybe he's hiding something from her. Not the best way to start a marriage."

"Could be Everly with the secrets," Kat mused, tapping her lip with the tip of her finger. "She's been known to keep a thing or two to herself."

Julie cradled her teacup and blew gently on the

surface to cool it. "Probably wise in her case since few people would believe her if she told the truth."

Shrugging, Kat turned over the rest of the cards, showing the Page of Swords, the Tower, the Five of Cups, and Judgment. She frowned at the combination. "Hmm. Definitely interesting and more than a little concerning." She glanced up at her friends, gauging their reactions before diving deeper into the interpretation.

"Why?" Julie asked, curious and without the others' depth of insight into what the cards meant.

Kat pointed to the Page of Swords. "Well, this little guy suggests curiosity and a search for the truth, maybe even some cleverness or manipulation involved. It could mean someone's hiding something, and Everly's on the hunt to figure out what it is. Then there's the Tower, which represents unexpected events or an upheaval that leads to a breaking down of existing forms. Probably means she'll get more than she bargained for. Shocking secrets, maybe?" Her eyes sparkled a bit at the dramatic turn of events the cards predicted but softened as she considered Everly's penchant for landing in hot water.

Julie's brows drew together in concern. "Like, something's going to happen to shake things up?"

"Exactly. Most likely when she's not expecting it. And it doesn't look like it will be a small thing. Very disruptive." Kat sighed and tapped the Five of Cups, her finger lingering on the dark card.

Gustavia frowned down at it.

"This doesn't bode well." Kat turned to Amethyst.

"See all these spilled cups? Maybe Drew has something in his past. Something Everly won't be happy to find out about. This card is all about disappointment and emotional loss."

"I'm not buying it," Amethyst declared. "There's nothing in Drew's aura to suggest a sordid past. Couple of dark spots, but nothing different than I've seen with other veterans."

"The cards don't lie," Kat said, her tone mild. "But they could be open to other interpretations depending on the circumstances. It's hard to tell, but this is not the reading I'd want to get on my honeymoon, and three major cards out of five lend more weight."

"And just when will that be, anyway?" Gustavia quirked a brow at Kat. "You and Zack have been married for almost a year. Seems like the honeymoon phase is over, and you missed it."

Grinning, Kat scooped up the cards and returned them to the deck. "We haven't figured out a destination, and Zack couldn't get time off right away. And you know he has to think every decision to death."

"Pfft." Gustavia waved that away. "I love my brother, but he's an idiot."

"He's not." Kat defended her man. "And I'm not in any rush. I like the scenery here."

"What about Everly?" Julie offered a gentle reminder. "Should we drop by and see how things are going? I don't want to be a honeymoon crasher, but if something's up..."

"Something's definitely up," Kat agreed, nodding.

"Then we should go." Gustavia began to rise.

"I think we have time to finish our tea first," Amethyst said, picking up a cookie. "Then we'll go."

"Should we call first?" Julie wondered.

"Not if we want to get a solid impression of things. Better to show up without warning, I think."

"You're probably right."

CHAPTER SIX

*E*ager to see if Sophia's waffles were everything she promised, Drew and I took a leisurely morning boat ride back to the public dock at the lake's southern end. I let Drew pull me onto the dock while the scent of bacon waged an aromatic war against my resolve.

"Hope Sophia has blueberries as one of her topping choices," I mused aloud, visions of fluffy yumminess already dancing in my head. "Then, I can fool myself into thinking I'm getting a serving of something healthy."

"I can think of at least one way to burn off any excess calories," Drew said, waggling his eyebrows and scanning the scene as if his stomach wasn't the only thing on his mind.

As we navigated our way toward Sophia's truck, I decided Oakville's early birds were a ravenous bunch, flocking to their chosen vendors like seagulls to a forgotten hot dog on the beach. The eclectic mix of aromas—robust coffee blends battling it out with the earthy notes of artisanal sausage—created a sensory blend that had drawn quite a crowd.

Noticing us, Ollie offered a flour-dusted wave.

"Hey, neighbors! Fancy a breakfast pizza? Got one with eggs and bacon that'll knock your socks off!"

"Next time," I replied, giving him a thumbs-up.

Seeing Jake's truck across the way, I noticed he'd also jumped on the breakfast bandwagon, featuring a fruit-filled salad that looked tempting but not tempting enough to forgo the decadence we'd come here to enjoy. As we sidestepped a puddle of spilled coffee, which I'm sure had its own tragic backstory, we passed by Tommy's barbecue truck.

He, it seemed, had not figured out how to turn barbecue into breakfast fare. Or hadn't bothered to try. Still, cabinet doors banged, and utensils rattled as he set things up for the day.

"No," Tommy barked into his phone, the words sharp as the edge of a cleaver. After a short pause, "I told you already, the competition doesn't end until next Friday. I can't do anything until then."

"He sounds annoyed," I said, veering away from the cloud of tension hovering around Tommy's truck before it spoiled my appetite.

At Cleo's truck, the chalkboard offered a new addition to the menu: waffle tacos—whatever those might be. I wasn't sure I wanted to know, but the fact that we couldn't get to Sophia's truck without passing Cleo's meant I was likely to find out.

"Everly!" Cleo called out, proving me right and handing me a free sample from a plate of them when I stepped up to her window. "You have to try my latest brainstorm. It's a deconstructed waffle in a cinnamon-coated, fried tortilla topped with pastry cream and syrup. Think cake pop meets breakfast."

What was a deconstructed waffle? I took a bite and decided delicious was what it was. Not wanting to spoil my appetite, I turned and popped the rest in Drew's mouth.

"Everly! It's so good to meet you." The woman who practically shouted my ear off also grabbed me and gave me an unsolicited hug. Once she let me go and I got a good look at her, I quickly pegged her as a Cleo fan.

"This is Tawny Ray," Cleo made the introduction, her expression betraying nothing of her thoughts about being emulated so closely. Tawny's hair might be a couple of shades off, but it sported a similar fade effect and the same rippling curls. Maybe they weren't as precisely placed as Cleo's, but the intent to copy was evident. "We went to school together, and she's a fan."

"Your biggest fan," Tawny corrected, hovering near Cleo's food truck with the intensity of a hawk studying its prey, clutching her phone like it was the last lifeline on "Who Wants to Be a Millionaire."

"Nice to meet you." I just stood there awkwardly while Tawny launched herself toward Drew next. Anticipating unwanted contact, he dragged his hand out of his pocket and put his arm around me, neatly avoiding being hugged. The man was smooth. You had to give him that.

"You look fabulous this morning." Cleo exited the truck and stepped close to take a selfie of us. Noting how

Drew maneuvered his way out of the shot, I slanted him a narrow-eyed look, which he returned with a quirked brow over twinkling eyes. He might not have wanted to end up on Cleo's socials again, but Tawny had no such reticence. But while she angled to get herself included, Cleo was a step ahead of her and pivoted us away while snapping the shot.

I felt like I'd walked into the middle of something weird between them. Or just something weird altogether.

Not to be outdone, Tawny spun and grabbed the last taco sample from the plate. Putting it to her lips, she tilted her head and offered her phone an exaggerated pose before thumbing the record button.

"Lucky me," she chirped, her tone and inflection a carbon copy of Cleo's, minus all of the polish and most of the sass. "Your girl just got herself a personalized sample of Cleo's newest taste sensation. You've never had a waffle taco like this before. I think I'll call this one #BrunchGoals."

"Ah," I said, feigning enlightenment, "the sacred rite of social media communion."

"Totally! I've seen you in her Insta stories. They're epic," Tawny gushed, eyes glazed with a fervor that bordered on zealotry. "You have to friend me on all your socials."

"Will do," I lied as seamlessly as someone who'd spent years pretending not to chat with the dearly departed.

Tawny must have sensed the untruth because she held her hand out and snapped her fingers. "Give me your phone. We'll take a selfie and tag each other. Any friend of Cleo's is a friend of mine."

"Everly loves making new friends," Drew added, winking at me. Tawny nodded vigorously, unaware of the minor sarcasm he'd injected into the statement.

"Oh, good!" she exclaimed before returning her gaze to my phone, thumbs moving at the speed of light as she added herself to every one of my social media accounts, keyed her phone number into my address book, and sent herself a text so she'd have mine.

I ignored Drew's smirk when Tawny returned my phone, pulled hers out, slung an arm around my shoulders, and snapped a shot of us. She didn't seem bothered that I looked like a deer in headlights as she posted the photo to her account.

"Can I get one with you now, Cleo?"

"Sorry, Tawny. I've got to whip up a new batch of samples." *Because you took the last one* was implied. Cleo turned her attention to me again. "What can I get you?"

"Oh, sorry. We're here for..."

"Do not tell me you're one of those salads for breakfast, people. I mean, Jake's are almost as yummy as he is, but you're on your honeymoon. You should indulge a little."

At the mention of Jake's yumminess, Tawny's focus arrowed his way. She tilted her head and surveyed him with great interest, which Cleo noted, and based on the narrowing of her eyes, without approval.

"We'll let you get to it then, Cleo. Shall we?" Drew

gently tugged me away from Cleo's Haven of Drama and toward Sophia's dessert truck, where the promise of waffles hung in the air like a sweet melody.

"Lead the way, my knight in tarnished armor," I replied, falling into step beside him. Once we were out of earshot, I added, "You could have saved me from that Cleo wannabe."

"You think so?" He grinned. "How?"

"I don't know," I admitted and gave him a nudge with my elbow.

Sophia's smile greeted us before we even reached her window, her cheerfulness as genuine as a puppy's enthusiasm—if puppies ran on caffeine and sheer willpower. Yet her fingers drummed an anxious tap dance on the polished countertop, betraying some strong emotion she kept tucked behind the sunny facade.

"Morning, you two lovebirds," she sang out, eyes crinkling with good-natured warmth. "Ready for some waffle wizardry?"

"Absolutely," Drew confirmed. "The smell alone is pure sorcery. I'll have the caramelized bananas and granola on mine."

"Got it," Sophia keyed his order into her cash app, then looked at me expectantly.

Until I got a look at the menu, I'd planned on having the blueberry waffles, but when I saw the black forest option, the idea of chocolate for breakfast won me over.

"I'm on vacation, so I might as well indulge."

"I'll have those ready for you in a jiffy!" She turned to a

pair of waffle irons, scooping chocolate batter with her left hand, regular with her right, and depositing both with a flourish that would make a maestro jealous.

"Looks busy this morning," Drew commented.

"It has been," Sophia's laugh lacked its usual bell-like clarity. "But busy is good, right? Keeps me from worrying about today's judging."

Soon enough, Sophia pushed two plates piled high with waffles that might have been crafted by breakfast fairies through the window. "Enjoy!" she said, with a bit more cheer than before.

"If you're serving these waffles to the judges, you shouldn't have anything to worry about," I said as we settled at the picnic table in front of her truck to eat. "If they taste as good as they look and smell, you'd get my vote."

Spoiler alert: they did. Light and airy but filled with chocolate goodness, the waffles made a perfect delivery system for tart cherries in a delicate sauce. I traded bites with Drew. His waffles were just as yummy as mine.

"Wow, Sophia. These are so good, I might just forget how many laps I have to swim to work them off."

Drew took a bite. "Everly's right. They're like eating clouds if clouds were made from delicious, crispy dough."

"Cloud-eating would certainly cut down on the food truck drama," I quipped, gesturing discreetly toward Cleo's truck. "Imagine the peace and quiet."

"Ah, but then what would we gossip about over breakfast?" Drew winked, taking another blissful bite.

"Fair point. I suppose one must endure the occasional tempest in a teapot—or, in this case, a tornado in a tortilla —for the sake of vicarious entertainment."

Taking another bite, I sighed and chewed slowly to savor the moment. A flurry of motion at the corner of my eye drew my attention.

"Look at Tommy go," I murmured, nodding subtly toward the marina's sales and service building. The way he'd crossed the distance and hustled inside, you'd think his smoker had grown legs and decided to take a dip in the lake. And here I thought brisket preferred dry rubs over swims.

"Something's got him more spooked than Molly at a vacuum cleaner convention," Drew mused. "And that's saying something, but I hope nothing's wrong with Tommy's truck."

Molly's deep and abiding fear of the vacuum cleaner sent her skittering for the door every time I turned it on. Poor thing.

Spearing my fork into the last piece of waffle on my plate, I waved it toward Drew and teased, "Because you're so addicted to his pulled pork, you're likely to turn into a Cleo-esque groupie over it."

"Could be," he said without shame. "I wouldn't be upset if all of these vendors showed up at the next Mooselick River shindig. Just saying."

"Way ahead of you, sweetie. I'm planning to get phone numbers from everyone before we leave. Ten bucks says Martha jumps on the competition bandwagon as soon as she hears about this."

Drew shook his head. "Not taking that bet."

"You're as smart as you are cute." Rising to clear our trash from the table, I gave him a peck on the cheek.

"Ready to hit the lake?" Drew asked, standing up and patting his pockets. A frown creased his brow as he patted again, more insistently this time.

"What's the matter?" I asked when he turned the air blue.

"Boat key's gone," he said, irritation threading through his usual calm demeanor.

"Okay, no need to panic," I replied, sliding into problem-solving mode. "We'll just retrace our steps. It has to be around here somewhere."

It wasn't anywhere near the picnic table or Sophia's truck.

Drew and I wove through the food truck crowd, the morning sun casting a warm glow that belied our growing concern. Losing the boat key wasn't on my list of fun things to explain to our temporary landlord.

"Let's split up, cover more ground. You check near Ollie's truck, and I'll search near Cleo's," I suggested.

Tawny had gone, and the line for Cleo's new taste sensation stretched halfway back to Tommy's truck. Still, she took a moment to shake her head when I approached the window from the side and asked if anyone had turned in a set of keys.

"There's a lost and found box over by the judging

tent," one of her customers informed me once he realized I wasn't trying to cut the line.

Completing my circuit, I met Drew in front of Tommy's truck. The tense set of his shoulders told me he hadn't had any more luck than I had.

"Hey, you lovebirds looking for these?" Tommy's voice cut through my reverie as he dangled a set of keys out his ordering window. A glance proved they were Drew's.

"Tommy, you're a lifesaver!" Drew exclaimed, his relief palpable as he reached for the keys with eager hands.

"Found 'em by the trash cans. Odd place to drop your ticket to paradise," Tommy remarked, the corner of his mouth ticking up in amusement. "I spent fifteen minutes looking for you before I realized you'd probably pass by here eventually."

How hard had he looked? We'd been eating waffles within a stone's throw of his truck for the past half hour, and he'd walked right past us on his way to the marina. But it seemed churlish to bring that up.

"Thanks, Tommy. We owe you one."

"Anytime." He went back to slathering fresh sauce on a rack of ribs, but not before shooting us a look that lingered a second too long. "You sticking around for lunch? I'll be opening up in another hour."

Drew shook his head, but his gaze strayed to the ovens. "But if you wanted to sell us a container of pulled pork right now, I'd take it home with me and sing your praises."

"Not literally." I winked at Tommy. "He never even sings along when we're listening to music in the car."

Already pulling out a container, Tommy laughed out loud. "I guess it's a good thing I don't sell my wares for a song, then." He took our money and bagged up our purchase.

"Let's head back before Molly thinks we've deserted her," I said, steering Drew away from the scent of smoked meat and tangy sauce.

Halfway back to the boat, my phone dinged with one new notification after another. It seemed Tawny had followed through on her promise to tag me in her socials. After two more dings, I muted my phone and left it muted all the way back to the lake house.

While Drew cut the engine and let the boat drift gently up to the dock at our rented home, I couldn't shake the uneasy feeling that had settled over me in town. But the sight that greeted us as we stepped out of the car quickly pushed thoughts of Cleo aside.

"Surprise!" A chorus of familiar voices rang out, and I found myself enveloped in a whirlwind of hugs from Julie, Gustavia, Kat, and Amethyst.

"What are you guys doing here?" I laughed, my heart swelling with joy at seeing my friends.

Julie, her blond hair glinting in the sunlight, grinned an apology. "We know you're on your honeymoon and might not want to socialize, but we figured we'd come out and bug you anyway."

"There's nothing to say you can't be a little bit social

on your honeymoon." From the top of her head—a corona of brightly dyed braids—to the tip of her toes, painted in similar hues, Gustavia resembled a rainbow sprite. Her eyes, however, appraised us with some speculation.

Drew chuckled beside me, his arm wrapping around my waist. "I should've known our peace and quiet wouldn't last long."

Amethyst, her purple hair almost perfectly matched her cropped pants, reached up and playfully punched Drew's arm. "Peace and quiet are overrated."

"You should have let us know you were coming," Drew said, smiling at the diminutive woman.

"Is it a problem?" Kat frowned. "Should we have called first?"

"Not at all. But we could have brought back a selection of food truck waffles for you." Drew patted his stomach. "Best I've ever tasted."

"Seriously," I said, wondering what was up when Gustavia and Amethyst exchanged a look I couldn't quite interpret. "Sophia's waffles are works of art. And Cleo's waffle tacos are worth the trip, as well."

When Molly let out a short bark, Drew said, "We'd better let her out. Why don't you come inside? I can make coffee."

"I could go for a cup," Kat tilted her head back, appraised us with a look, then decided. "Besides, I haven't seen the place since Bailey repainted."

Molly squeezed out as soon as Drew unlocked the door. Torn between greeting the newcomers and doing her business, she hesitated, then shot off to water a patch of grass as we went inside.

Whatever tension I'd sensed dissipated as Drew headed for the kitchen and fired up the fancy coffeemaker.

"I love the saturated blue she used in the kitchen. What do you think, Ammie? I know you said you were going for neutrals, but this color really pops."

Considering, Amethyst tilted her head. "Maybe."

"Amethyst is building onto her house," Julie explained.

"Sort of," Gustavia qualified. "It's more of an annex or something since she's currently living in a burrow. But Reid needs a bit more headroom."

"He's only had one near-concussion from whacking his head on the laundry room door frame," Amethyst said, "but there's cozy, and then there's cramped. We're way into cramped territory, so it's time for things to change."

"You won't be losing your cave," Julie pointed out.

Amethyst nodded when Drew offered her a cup of coffee. "It'll work as a dedicated client space and keep Reid from embarrassing himself so often."

"That sounds like a story," I encouraged her to provide more details as I added cream and sugar to my cup.

"Not much of one," she admitted. "He only flashed his boxers at Mrs. Martindale twice. He forgets she likes her early Saturday readings."

"And," Gustavia leaned forward, her eyes twinkling with humor. "He favors the fancy pants."

When Drew nearly choked on his coffee, Amethyst

winked at me. "I think it was when she saw the Grinch splashed across his butt that really did the trick."

"I think I'll go see how Molly's doing." Drew excused himself as a hint of red crept up his neck.

"Red hearts for Valentine's Day," I said, pointing my thumb toward him as he headed for the door.

"I heard that. Can't a man have any secrets?" It was a rhetorical question that elicited a round of female laughter.

"Poor guy," Kat rose and rinsed out her cup. "I think we scarred him. Probably for life."

"He'll hold up. He's the best."

Gustavia tilted her head and gave me an assessing look. "So everything's good with you two? You got off to a rocky start."

"Everything's perfect."

"Perfect is a difficult word to live up to," Kat observed quietly, making me wonder if the comment had a deeper meaning.

"We could be in Milos with our toes dug into white sand while we consider taking a dip in blue-green water, but being here doesn't suck. All that matters is that we're starting our lives together, and what happened at the wedding simply proved we can weather any storm as long as we're together. Drew's my rock, and I hope I can be his."

"He seems great," Julie said. "How did you meet?"

I gave them the Cliff Notes version, including a rundown of our ghostly exploits since we'd become a couple. "We've been through a lot in a relatively short time, but being tested has given each of us a better sense of the other. I've dragged him into several situations that would have sent a lesser man packing. He just...sticks."

Amethyst rose and stepped over to the expanse of glass that overlooked the dock, where she could watch Drew throw Molly's toy into the water. "There's a hint of something in his aura," she said without turning around.

"I'd be surprised if there wasn't. He's carrying a few scars from his time in service. Therapy leveled him back out, and so does helping other people."

She watched him a moment longer, then turned and said, "He's a good man."

For some reason, it felt like she directed the comment more toward her friends than toward me.

"We'll get out of your hair and let you get on with your honeymoon," Kat said. "But we wanted to invite you guys to a cookout at Julie's place tomorrow night. What do you think?"

"The men," Gustavia pitched her voice low, "will make fire. Cook meat."

"And leave everything else to the women," Julie said, her grin taking away any condemnation that might have accompanied the statement. "It'll be fun. You can bring..." She gestured toward where having checked that the underwear discussion was over, Drew was toweling off a post-swim Molly.

"Her name's Molly."

"Bring Molly. She gets along with other dogs?"

"Molly gets along with everyone."

"Great. She can hang out with Lola and Fritzie." Gustavia crossed to pet Molly on her damp head. "They love making new friends."

I glanced at Drew to check his opinion, which he registered with a nod and grin. "Count us in!"

"Great," Julie said. "I'll text you the address. We're easy to find and, trust me, you can't miss the place. Show up around five, and I'll give you the tour before we eat. Hayward House has quite a story, but we'll get out of your hair for now."

"Thanks for the invite." We followed them as far as the deck, waving as they backed down the short drive. Turning back to Drew, I found his gaze fixed on me, a familiar warmth in his blue eyes that always made my heart skip.

"Sounds like fun," he began, a teasing note in his voice, "but you do realize we have the rest of the day free, right?"

"Indeed, Mr. Parker." I arched an eyebrow, leaning into him. "And how, pray tell, should we fill this vast expanse of unscheduled time?"

His arms drew me closer, the touch of his skin against mine electric even in the comfort of familiarity. "I was thinking," he said, his breath tickling my ear, causing involuntary shivers, "we might have a private honeymoon moment."

"Private, you say?" I feigned ignorance, relishing the playful banter that danced between us. "Is that anything like a public honeymoon moment, but with less chance of an audience?"

"Much less chance," he assured me, his hands tracing the curve of my back. The sunlight danced through the leaves overhead, casting a dappled pattern over our faces.

"Sounds promising," I whispered, standing on tiptoe to close the distance between us. Our lips met in a kiss that held the sweet promise of more—a promise that spoke of shared lives and intimate discoveries, of laughter and tender moments.

The world hushed around us. The only sounds were our mingled breaths and the soft water lapping against the shore. It was in his kiss, the depth of connection, the thrill of being with someone who knew all of me—even the parts that conversed with ghosts—and loved me still.

When we finally parted, a slow smile spread across Drew's face. "I think," he said softly, his eyes alight with mischief and desire, "this is going to be one unforgettable afternoon."

"Unforgettable and entirely ours," I agreed, my smile mirroring his. With a whole summer day stretching out before us, there were plenty of moments left to savor, and I intended to make the most of every single one.

It wasn't until much later, when the commotion drifted through our bedroom window, that I dislodged myself from the crook of Drew's arm and put down my book to peek out.

"Last chance, Sophia," Cleo's voice trilled across the

night air as she stood in the driveway of the rental cabins, her body lit up by the beam of a pair of headlights.

"I'm good." Her closed door muffled Sophia's response as Cleo hopped into the cab of a pickup truck. I couldn't tell what make or color it was, but from its shape, it was an older model. Vintage, even.

"Don't you want to have a little fun?"

If Sophia had an answer, she didn't offer it, but Ollie's voice rang out. "Pipe down out there. I'm trying to sleep."

"Your loss." Cleo slammed the door behind her, and the truck spewed gravel as it left.

"Nosy," Drew accused.

"Guilty," I replied, thinking it might just be my luck to spend my entire honeymoon trying to finish this book.

CHAPTER SEVEN

*T*aking in the sights and sounds of the food truck competition shaking up their little town, Julie and Gustavia strolled through Oakville's quaint downtown, each clutching a folded slice of breakfast pizza from Ollie's. The golden crust, crisp on the outside and pillowy within, cradled layers of melted cheese, scrambled eggs, and crumbles of bacon. Julie took a bite, letting the flavors bloom on her tongue, and the hint of black pepper and smoky cheddar added just the right kick.

"You have to admit, this is the best breakfast food ever invented," Gustavia declared between bites. "I do love a good waffle, but they're a sit-down meal. This is portable."

"I'll give you that," Julie conceded, swiping a napkin across her lips. "But keep your voice down, or Becky will hear us, and we'll lose our favorite table at the diner."

Gustavia grinned. "She does take her food seriously." She tilted her head, causing the charms woven into her braids to catch the light. "Speaking of taking things seriously, we need to decide on Amethyst's housewarming gift. Something spectacular."

Julie exhaled through her nose in amusement. "We're

talking about a woman who once debated the metaphysical properties of different shades of purple before painting her kitchen the color of an eggplant."

"Exactly. That's why we can't just show up with a scented candle and call it a day." Gustavia stopped abruptly, nearly causing Julie to bump into her. "Wait—what if we had a crystal grid designed specifically for her house?"

Julie sighed, adjusting the strap of her crossbody bag. "And where, exactly, do we get one of those?"

Gustavia's eyes twinkled with excitement. "Leave it to me. I know a guy."

Julie groaned. "Of course you do."

They weaved past families and couples, all drawn in by the magnetic energy of the food truck competition. It was like walking into a kaleidoscope of culinary delight. Each of the trucks boasted its own vibrant personality. With its large canopy, Ollie's emitted the cozy warmth of an Italian trattoria, his robust laughter mingling with the aroma of baking dough and fresh basil.

Nearby, Tommy's truck gleamed under the morning sun, promising stick-to-your-ribs barbecue options. Sophia's pink and brown confection, draped in patio and fairy lights, was a clear advertisement for her pastries and coffee. Jake's sleek black truck, minimalist in design, offered a sharp contrast to the riot of colorful vegetables and fruits ready to be chopped and sliced into salads.

And then there was Cleo's truck with her face plastered across the side, its bright colors and bold font drawing the eye.

"Tacos and pizza can both work for breakfast, right?" Julie said, walking past a woman eating a breakfast taco with evident pleasure.

"Maybe if you're having weird cravings. Are you?" Stopping, Gustavia grabbed Julie's arm, her face alight with hope.

"I'm not pregnant if that's what you're asking." Julie rolled her eyes. "We've only been trying for a little over a month. You need to give me a minute."

"I want to be an Auntie, so you'd better get with the program." Gustavia eyed Cleo's smiling face and the happy customers wolfing down her food. "But now that you've piqued my interest, I need one of those waffle tacos. We'll call it dessert."

"Since you brought the subject up, I'd like to be an Auntie, too. Anything going on with you in the baby-making department?"

"Not so far." Gustavia shook her head. "We even had sex in my copper pyramid, thinking it would move things along."

Julie's feet failed her. "You got Finn to do it in a pyramid?"

"Sure. I befuddled him with my charms." Grinning, Gustavia glanced down at her chest. "They're pretty good charms. Did the job, anyway."

Holding out a hand in the stop motion, Julie laughed.

"They are, but I don't need the details. At least not in public. Are you worried that you're not?"

"No, are you? It's fun trying, but if it doesn't happen right away, I'm good with it."

"Exactly, but I still want that taco. And we still have to decide on Ammie's housewarming present." Julie took her place in line for the taco truck.

"I saw a crystal ball the size of my head at my favorite antiques place in Wiscasset. The clarity was amazing, and the stand was a work of art. It's pricey, but she'd love it. We could go in on it together if you're not down with the personalized grid. You, me, and Kat."

"That pricey?"

"Enough she'd kick up a fuss if only one of us spent that much on her. You know how she gets sometimes."

"Okay. Check with Kat. If she's on board, I'm in too. Unless you want to go with something more traditional."

Gustavia snorted. "Have you ever known me to go that route?"

"No, I honestly have not."

The line had filled in behind them while Julie and Gustavia decided on a gift, the tantalizing scent of waffle tacos drifting through the air. But just as they inched forward, an excitable squeal pulled their focus.

"Oh. My. God. Shut up and hold my salsa! I can't believe it's you!"

Julie turned just in time to see Cleo herself—live and in Technicolor—bolting out from behind the order window of her truck, oversized hoop earrings swinging like pendulums, her vibrant pink apron embroidered with her business name in glittery gold thread. She winged a squeeze bottle of sauce back into the truck without missing a beat.

Gustavia blinked, mid-bite into her breakfast pizza. "Is she talking to me?"

"She's definitely talking to you," Julie confirmed, watching Cleo beeline toward them, her phone already raised in selfie mode.

"You're Gustavia. The. Freaking. Gustavia." Cleo stopped just short of colliding with her, her neon-painted nails fluttering excitedly around her phone screen. "My niece loves your books. This is fate. No, this is a manifestation. The universe put you in my line today, and I'm not ignoring the signs!"

Gustavia, never one to shy away from theatrics, straightened her shoulders and flashed a camera-ready smile. "Well, I do tend to draw in good energy."

Julie barely held back a snort. "And food truck mavens, apparently."

"Okay, okay, everybody hold tight!" Cleo turned to the rest of her customers, voice projecting with the force of someone who spoke in all caps. "I need a quick time out because this queen right here just blessed my truck. If you don't know who she is, first of all, educate yourself. Second, give me five minutes, and I promise your waffle tacos will taste even better infused with this level of iconic energy."

A few murmured grumbles came from the line, but most customers curiously took in the spectacle.

Cleo spun back to Gustavia. "You, me, livestream. Now."

And just like that, she flipped her phone camera to front-facing and beamed. "Hey, Cleo's Crew! It's your girl, Cleo, coming to you live from Oakville's first-ever food truck competition. And y'all—" she panned the camera to Gustavia, "—Look who just dropped into my line! Best-selling author, queen of magical stories for amazing kiddos, and all-around inspiration, Gustavia!"

Gustavia gave a dramatic wave. "Hey there, beautiful souls!"

Julie attempted to put some distance between herself and the spectacle.

Cleo grabbed Julie's wrist and yanked her into the frame. "And this here is her BFF." She looked at Julie expectantly.

"I'm Julie."

"Julie," Cleo parroted, "who I now also adore, but today is about this magical lady right here." She refocused the camera on Gustavia. "Tell us, Gustavia—what's your secret to creating such legendary characters?"

Gustavia gave an exaggerated flick of her braids, the charms tinkling together. "Surround yourself with amazing people, wear things that make your soul happy, and always—always—say yes to good food."

"Preach," Cleo gasped dramatically. "I felt that in my soul."

Behind them, the first true grumblings began in earnest. "Guys," Julie cut in, "People are getting impatient."

Cleo whirled, pointing a commanding finger at the grumbler. "You may not know it, but you're in the presence of greatness, and I will personally infuse your food with blessings if you chill for two minutes."

She pivoted back to Gustavia. "Okay, real talk. What brings you to my humble truck today?"

"I heard," Gustavia glanced pointedly at Julie, "your waffle tacos are a must-have experience."

Cleo gasped. "Oh honey, you heard right. One perfect taco coming right up. On the house."

As Cleo's hands flashed over ingredients, Julie whispered in Gustavia's ear. "I can't believe you're letting her hold up her whole line for this."

Gustavia grinned. "Listen, I get free food and five minutes of social media stardom. Let me have this."

Julie sighed, but she couldn't help smiling. "Just don't let her talk you into an entire Cleo and Gustavia collab."

Gustavia's eyes twinkled. "Too late. I think we're best friends now."

Cleo spun back, holding out two finished tacos, one for Gustavia and one for Julie. "Here you go. Try it and tell the people what you think!"

Gustavia took the taco with reverence, holding it up to the camera with a dramatic pause. Then, with the flair of a woman who understood showmanship, she took a slow, exaggerated bite.

For a moment, all was silent.

Then Gustavia placed a hand over her heart and whispered, "Cleo…I see the light."

Cleo shrieked with joy. "I KNEW IT! And that, my loves, is how you bless a food truck. Cleo's Crew, you better believe Gustavia officially approves, and if you're not in Oakville right now, I am so, so sorry for you. Okay, signing off, eat something amazing today, and remember: If it ain't made with love, it ain't worth the calories. Byeeee!"

She ended the livestream with a flourish, then immediately turned to the customers still waiting. "Okay. Okay. I'm back to business, but y'all know your tacos now come with a celebrity seal of approval."

As she practically danced back into her truck, Julie nudged Gustavia. "Well, that was an experience."

Gustavia chewed thoughtfully. "This is a pretty damn good taco."

Julie sighed. "Of course it is."

They stepped aside and wandered toward a bench, letting the line resume its natural order. Gustavia glanced at Julie. "I should probably be embarrassed, shouldn't I?"

Julie shook her head. "Nope. But I'm sending Kat the link to Cleo's socials."

Gustavia gasped. "You wouldn't."

Julie tapped her phone screen. "Already done."

Gustavia sighed. "Fine. But you owe me a cookie for emotional damages."

Julie just laughed. "Deal."

. . .

*T*he memory of Cleo's waffle taco lured Drew into suggesting we go back to town for brunch. I couldn't think of a single reason to resist.

"Looks like Tommy's jumping on the breakfast bandwagon." I pointed toward the sign boasting new offerings. "What do you think he puts in his Cowboy Scramble?"

"I don't know, but it sounds like a good name for a game show." The voice that answered didn't belong to my husband.

"Hey, Gustavia. Julie," Drew said, greeting our friends. "What's good this morning?"

"Cleo's waffle tacos," Julie balled up the empty wrapper from hers and tossed it in the nearest trash can, her eyes sparking with humor. "They've been blessed by Queen Gustavia. There's footage of the royal spectacle if you want to see it."

"What fun." I glanced at the newly appointed monarch, who seemed delighted with herself as usual.

Muttered curses interrupted whatever I'd have said next as the jovial pitmaster we all knew seemed to have checked out, replaced by a red-faced version of Tommy that chewed on his toothpick with such ferocity I feared for the wood's integrity.

"Come on, you hunk of junk," he grumbled, thumping the propane tank as if physical persuasion might do the trick. His calloused hands, sure and steady when basting ribs or flipping burgers, now fumbled with the valve, turning it off and back on. Going back inside, he leaned in to sniff the burner he'd just turned on, and his demeanor shifted from annoyance to disbelief.

Tommy exited the truck again and circled back to stare at the gauge on his propane tanks. Curiosity had the four of us following him.

"Anything I can do to help?" Drew offered.

"My gas lines—someone's been messing with my gas lines! This one's empty. Do you know what this means?" he shouted, his accusation hanging heavy in the summer air. It was a challenge, a gauntlet thrown down with the force of a man pushed to his limit. "Sabotage."

"You're sure it's sabotage?" I stepped forward and looked at the broken fitting.

"What else could it be?" Tommy's voice boomed as he pointed out the tool marks on the coupler connecting two tanks. "That didn't just happen by itself."

"Talk about cranking up the heat," Gustavia muttered, echoing the tension that crackled like electricity around us.

Every person within hearing distance turned their attention to Tommy's truck, their expressions a mix of shock, intrigue, and the unmistakable flavor of gossip about to simmer over. Leaving her business unattended, Cleo came over to see what the fuss was about. After a moment, Sophia and Ollie joined her. Jake watched from a distance but didn't approach.

Now, the center of a cluster of vendors, Tommy stood, his tall frame rigid with indignation, while the others—

Cleo with her arms crossed and Sophia biting her lip—exchanged uneasy glances. Ollie scratched his head with an air of disbelief.

"Looks like Tommy's BBQ isn't the only thing getting smoked today," Julie murmured, her gaze fixed on the commotion.

"You have a way with words that should be illegal." Gustavia poked Julie in the ribs, but none of us could ignore the undercurrent of tension surging through the judges drawn to the source of the fuss.

"Someone call the cops." I didn't see who spoke.

"Looks like someone already did." Drew pointed to where Zack approached with long legs eating up the ground.

Sweat, not just from the summer heat, dotted Tommy's brow as he made his statement. Zack noted the particulars and took photos. The process didn't take as long as you might think since no one in the general area admitted to seeing anything.

"You didn't lock the tank cover?" Zack asked for the second time.

"Bet your ass I will now," Tommy spat. "You done? I need to repair the damage and get to work. Good thing I keep the spare turned off until I need it. Or I'd be out of business for the day."

Because there wasn't much else to do, Zack stepped back. Tommy moved with furious purpose, grabbing tools from his kit like a surgeon prepping for an emergency procedure. His hands worked feverishly to tighten the loosened coupler, every motion underscored by his resolve not to let this setback char his chances at victory.

"Tampered lines or not, Tommy's not throwing in the towel," I noted as he twisted the valve on the second tank.

"More like he's using it to mop up this mess," Gustavia agreed, nodding toward the stained cloth Tommy kept swiping across his forehead.

The rest of the vendors returned to their customers, leaving Tommy to get on with things as best he could. Cleo had her phone in hand, so news of what happened had probably already winged its way across her accounts.

On her way past me, Sophia leaned in to speak but kept her voice low, "You know he'll blame me for this because I'm always the first one here, but I'd rather win or lose on my own merits."

I said nothing because she might be correct, but I gave her a sympathetic look.

"You other vendors aren't the only ones with a motive," Gustavia said. "Not everyone in town was happy about the decision to host this competition. It's causing traffic issues for local business owners and residents alike."

"Let's not forget local eateries," Julie piped up, her voice carrying over the crowd's din. "Becky Getchel wasn't exactly thrilled about the food truck invasion since it was taking place right in front of her diner. Could be locals trying to scare you all off."

"Could be a sore loser situation, too," Drew said, folding his arms. "Someone who didn't make the cut and isn't happy about it. Or someone who didn't like their pulled pork, as unlikely as that is. Not everyone has the same great taste as me."

"Too many possibilities," I sighed, estimating the long wait time now that a line had formed near Tommy's truck. "But now that he's got his grill going again, I wouldn't feel right ordering a waffle taco from Cleo when Tommy's suffered such a misfortune. I guess I'll find out what's in the Cowboy Scramble after all."

"Oh, honey," Gustavia leaned close, the musical tinkle arising from her person only serving as a counterpoint to the sparkle in her tone. "There's no rule against having dessert after breakfast. The taco went quite well with Ollie's eggs and bacon pizza."

"I'll take that under advisement."

Letting me a minute to say goodbye to Julie and Gustavia and finalize arrangements for the impending cookout, Drew got in line. Once they'd gone, I joined him.

"The mystery bug biting you yet?"

"Nope," I said firmly, "I'm not getting involved. This is our honeymoon, and Amethyst promised it would be ghost and mystery-free."

Amethyst was wrong on both counts, as I would soon learn.

CHAPTER EIGHT

"What do you want to do for the rest of the day?" Sitting next to me on the dock where we'd chosen to settle with our breakfast, Drew slipped off his shoes and dangled his feet in the water. "Head back to the lake house? Or maybe drive to Port Harbor? It's not Greece. Not Milos, but we could take a whale-watching tour."

Considering, I said, "That sounds fun. Why don't we plan that for tomorrow or the next day? Give me time to check out the options."

"Because today, you want to hang around here and poke your nose into the mystery of the sabotaged barbecue truck?" That Drew's voice carried neither amusement nor condemnation was one of the things that made me love him so much.

"I'd rather check out a few more shops, but if you're deep into the mystery vibe, we can chat up the locals while we're at it."

"I can admit to a certain level of curiosity." The way his eyes twinkled, I figured his level was similar to mine— not burning, but definitely simmering in the background.

"And I wouldn't mind strolling through the used boatyard at the marina."

His attempt to look innocent wasn't fooling me at all. "I knew this was coming the minute you saw that boat key on the table. You want one."

"Don't you?"

"Maybe." I laughed because he looked like a kid standing in front of an ice cream truck anticipating a yummy treat.

An hour later, Drew and I strolled down Oakville's quaint Main Street, hand in hand. Despite the forecast of possible rain, the sun was shining, the air was warm, and I put Tommy's drama behind me.

"Oh, look!" I tugged on Drew's arm, pointing at a charming storefront that would fit right into a scene from Back to the Future—the first movie. "There's the drugstore. Let's pop in and grab some extra sunscreen."

As we approached the entrance, I froze. The tourist ahead of us walked right through the figures of two older women and a man engaged in animated conversation. Ghosts. Of course. Because what's a vacation without a supernatural encounter?

"Change your mind?" Drew's voice cut through my surprise.

I plastered on a smile. "No, just...admiring the architecture," I lied, gesturing vaguely at the building. My options were to feign ignorance and walk through the ghosts like Drew was about to do, or...let's face it, that was my only option if I didn't want to get dragged into a conversation with the Oakville Haunting Society. And I didn't.

But walking through ghosts is not the most pleasant of sensations. Imagine being drenched in chilled, spider-infested bog water while creepy fingers tiptoe up your spine. Most people feel nothing more than a slight chill, but that's what it's like for me.

Still, I geared myself up to endure a major case of the heebie-jeebies and do what I had to do to keep my honeymoon ghost-free. I'd have pulled it off, too, if I hadn't heard the taller of the two female ghosts call me a trollop.

"Excuse me," my mouth said before my brain could engage. Worse, I made eye contact. Big mistake.

The ghost's eyes widened, and I could practically see the spectral light bulbs flickering to life above her head.

"Well, I'll be," the stocky ghost with the mustache exclaimed, his folksy tone echoing in my ears. "Looks like we've got ourselves a live one, ladies!"

Desperately trying to maintain my composure, I forced a smile as Drew looked at me quizzically. "Everything okay, honey?" he asked, his brow furrowed with concern.

"Er," I muttered, my eyes darting between my confused husband and the suddenly excited trio of ghosts. Great. Just great.

The shorter, plump ghost with white hair beamed at me. "Oh, dearie, it's been ages since we've had someone new to chat with! We'd have thrown a party for such an occasion in my day! I'd have baked a pie."

I could feel a headache coming on. This was not how I'd planned to spend my day. "I'm on my honeymoon," I answered Drew's question while staring down the ghost who had called me a trollop, "Wearing a pretty and perfectly appropriate sundress, enjoying a nice, ghost-free getaway with my new husband. What could be wrong with that?"

The name-calling ghost gave me an up-and-down look. "Not that appropriate, young lady. And it's quite rude to ignore one's elders, even if we are deceased."

Losing my composure, I hissed, "You called me a trollop, and now you're accusing *me* of being rude?"

"Ev?" Drew's voice snapped me back to reality. "Who are you talking to?"

I plastered on my best 'everything's normal' smile. "The ghosts of Oakville, apparently. If you want to keep shopping, I'll head over to that park with the picnic tables. I could use a little fresh air while I deal with the situation."

"I think the sunscreen can wait." Taking my hand, Drew squeezed it. "Never a dull moment with you, is there? Keeps things fresh and exciting."

"Tell me that again in twenty years," I suggested, ignoring the ghostly trio trailing behind us like excited puppies.

"Count on it."

Because I knew I could, the impromptu séance bothered me less than it might have. "I'll give the chatterboxes half an hour to tell me their tales of woe and murder, and that will be the end of it. Any cold cases in this town are Kat and Zack's problem, not mine."

Woe and Murder—excellent book title.

"We can hear you, you know," the cranky one said. "And none of us were murdered, so we're nobody's problem."

"You could have just let me walk on by."

"There's no need to get snippy, Edna," the short, stocky female ghost admonished her companion, then said to me in a placating tone, "We just want a quick chat, dear. We mean no harm."

"We're good ghosts," the male one added. "I promise."

"That's what they all say," I said, then repeated the conversation for Drew's benefit.

"Three, huh? Your new ghostly fan club."

Did I need one of those? No. I did not, but no one asked me. "The Oakville chapter."

We'd reached the relative privacy of the picnic table in the otherwise deserted park. "Who, if they're able, could do the decent thing and make themselves known to you. All it takes is a little effort."

On cue, the three spirits shimmered into view for Drew. His eyes widened, but to his credit, he didn't jump. This wasn't his first time, and he'd reached the point of being unflappable in the face of the supernatural. Mostly. Charlotte's descent into the nether regions had flapped us both pretty hard.

The ghosts, clearly thrilled at having a larger audience, began talking over each other excitedly. The oldest and shortest of the three was Iris McCann. Miss Judgie Pants turned out to be Edna Mayfield.

"I'll tell you one thing," said Howdy Pritchard, the third and youngest as well as newest of the three ghosts. "This food truck hullabaloo is the most excitement we've had since the Great Moose Stampede of '62!"

Prim and proper, Edna rolled her eyes. "Oh, hush, Howdy. You weren't even born yet in 1962. These food trucks are not exciting—they're a menace. They're attracting the wrong element to our town, and the flashy one nearly took out poor Mrs. Higgins' rosebushes."

Grandmotherly Iris waggled her brows. "Who cares about rosebushes? Did you see the hunk driving the BBQ truck? Johnny something or other, I think, is his name. If I weren't dead, I'd—"

"Iris McCann!" Edna gasped, scandalized. "Such talk!"

As ghosts went, at least these were fun ones who didn't seem to want anything from me. Kind of like Dolly back home. Drew, bless him, looked both amused and slightly overwhelmed until Iris tilted her head and gave him a measuring look. "This one's got definite hunk potential once he's aged up a bit."

Drew went from slightly overwhelmed to red-faced and embarrassed in a hot second, which I found delightful since I'd rarely seen him so nonplussed. I do love a man who blushes.

"I think he's pretty hunky just as he is," I said and patted him on the thigh.

"Get your head out of your loins, Iris," Edna warned,

her face stern and unforgiving. It was all I could do to keep from snorting a laugh. "And focus on the big picture here. We've got access to a living person."

Although Edna's delivery of the statement indicated she thought being able to talk to me was a big deal, Iris didn't seem to catch on.

"So?"

"Your elevator doesn't go to the top floor, does it?" Edna said in a cutting tone.

"Edna," Howdy said, attempting to placate his companion but sounding bored as if this was not the first time he'd diffused tension between the two ghostly women. "Be nice."

Edna bristled. "If she can't see this as an opportunity to have a say in this town, finally, I stand by my assessment."

Confused, Iris said, "Why would we need a say in anything?"

"To talk some sense into the powers that be, of course. Have you seen the state of the library lately? They've added a craft room. With sewing machines. Can you believe it? Who wants to settle down with a good book with that racket in the background? I certainly wouldn't."

"Because you're an old fuddy-duddy," Iris pronounced without hesitation. "I've always known this about you, but that's no reason to ask Everly to intervene in town politics."

"Which." I held up a hand to put a stop to the topic. "I have no intention of doing. I'm on my honeymoon and have sworn off ghostly shenanigans for the duration. But even if sewing machines in the library were enough to make me break my rule, what makes you think I'd be effective? I'm not from here. How would it look if some random woman from two hours away tried to insert herself into a situation that is none of her concern?"

Practically crowing, Howdy pointed a finger at Edna. "Girl's got smarts."

"Why can't you just appear to whoever you want to talk to?" Drew said. "Like you're doing with me right now."

It was a viable question and one I'd never thought to ask a ghost before.

"Because they know I'm dead." Edna's tone suggested Drew might not be capable of adding one and one together and getting the right answer.

"Now, do you see why we need your help? Scaring the pants off town officials isn't the way to get results," Edna said, eliciting a giggle from Iris.

"But it might be fun."

"Fun or not, I'm not the woman for the job. Why don't you talk to Kat Roman? She lives right over there," I pointed toward Kat's street. "Being local, she'd have more pull with your town officials."

Howdy shook his head. "That one. She's not like you."

"In what way?" Kat had explained her take on the difference between ghosts and spirits to me before. According to her, ghosts were made from the residual energy of souls caught on this side of the veil for one reason or another, while spirits were the souls of the dead who had crossed over. Kat connected to spirits, while I dealt almost exclusively with ghosts. While I understood the theory, it seemed that Howdy might know something I didn't about the practical side of it all.

"She doesn't vibe with us," he finally admitted.

"Vibe?" Edna sniffed. "That's hippie talk."

"How would you explain it, then?"

"You know the difference between FM and AM radio stations?" Edna picked an analogy she thought I'd understand.

And I sort of did. "I get it. It's a frequency thing. You can't tune into each other at all?"

"Not without it draining our energy." Howdy nodded, happy that I finally understood. "She can't see us until we go into the light. Maybe you should do that, Edna. Then you could get the Sheriff's wife to put an end to blasphemy in the library."

"Hey, that sounds like a good title for a mystery novel," Iris said, laughing at her joke and proving she and I thought along similar lines.

"Speaking of mysteries, did any of you see what happened to Tommy O'Malley's food truck? He's the guy Iris thinks is a hunk." Ghosts weren't allowed to discuss their own murders, but that didn't mean they couldn't rat out a wrongdoer. Especially if the issue at hand had nothing to do with them. I hoped. Also, I needed to distract Edna.

"If I'd have known there was treachery afoot, I'd have

paid more attention," Howdy spoke up first. "The first I heard of it was when the police scanner scared off all the fish."

Considering he wore a pair of waders and carried a bait bucket, I assumed Howdy's death must have had something to do with fishing. Or Halloween if he was in costume.

"You were out on the water at the time?"

"Been riding out with Jed Watson ever since he found my favorite fishing spot. Biggie Smallie hangs out near there."

"Who?" It sounded like a rapper's name.

"Biggie Smallie. Biggest smallmouth bass I ever saw. At least a pound over the state record. Got him on my line once or twice, but he always spit the hook before I could land him."

"The one that got away?" Drew said with a smile that crinkled lines at the corners of his eyes.

"Betcha," Howdy's face changed. "Day I died, I was out on the lake right at the start of fishing season. Smallies tend to hang out in the shallows if there's good cover—old rocks, logs, whatever. But they'll hunker down in a good drop-off, too. Biggie's favorite spot is about halfway down a ten-footer over on the north end of the lake."

"We rode out that way yesterday," I said, referring to the direction he'd pointed, but Howdy didn't hear me. He'd gone off into memory-land.

"This particular morning, I knew my luck was running

high. The lake was clear as glass when I picked my spot and dropped my line. It wasn't fifteen minutes before I got a strike, and by the feel of the pull, it had to be Biggie. Figuring I had plenty of time, I played out the line some. Let him think he'd got away clean with a nice shiner for his breakfast. Wasn't paying attention to the weather. The squall hit just as I stood up and gave my rod a yank to set the hook. Lost my balance and went over the side."

A single tear slid down his face while Howdy told his tale.

"The water was too cold, and I was too far from shore. For all I know, Biggie's still dragging my rod and reel behind him. Anyhow, I was out keeping an eye on Jed when the call went out. Jed's in the fire department, so he always keeps the scanner on."

"What about you, Iris? Did you see anything last night?"

"I might have if it wasn't doing my rounds."

"Your rounds?"

"Oh, you know." Iris waggled her fingers in the air. "There's the bakery and that cute little pie shop in town. Pies were never my main thing, though I did perfect my crust recipe, but I can't help poking my nose in the coolers at the bakery. Chilling is essential to making a good brioche dough."

"Do not get her started on recipes. She'll talk the ears right off your head," Edna warned.

"Like you don't yammer on about the Dewey Decimal System every other five minutes?" Iris rolled her eyes.

Noting that Edna's figure seemed blurrier around the edges, I asked what she'd been doing overnight.

Edna cleared her throat. "I did see someone skulking around on Cranberry Lane late last night."

My curiosity piqued. "Did you get a good look at them?"

"Not really, dear. These old eyes aren't what they used to be, even in death. This whole food truck thing is nothing but a craze," she offered her opinion, "and it was a stupid idea to hold a competition here. I still don't know how that came about."

Iris and Howdy exchanged knowing looks. Howdy leaned in conspiratorially, his ghostly belly jiggling. "Well, word on the street is that one of the muckety mucks in town has a nephew who wants to break into the food truck business. He convinced the board that putting Oakville on the culinary map might bring a different set of tourists out this way."

Edna sniffed. "As if a good church potluck wasn't map-worthy enough."

Iris patted a spectral curl into place. "It'll probably work. Nothing brings in crowds like the promise of over-priced street food!"

"How would you know? You died before food trucks were a thing," Edna scoffed. "You're just repeating what your great-grandson said yesterday when he brought his wife around, and she turned her snooty nose up."

"I'll have you know I served dynamites out of the Grange trailer at the county fair for fifteen years, and if that's not where this food truck craze got its start, I'll eat my left shoe. Not that we overpriced our food. It was for fundraising, not profit."

As they bickered about the true reason for the competition, I caught Drew's eye. He was grinning, clearly entertained by the ghostly gossip session. I felt a wave of affection for him, grateful for his easy acceptance of this weird part of my life.

Eventually, the ghosts bid us farewell, fading away with dramatic flair (Iris), saying he needed to get back out on the lake (Howdy), and grumbling complaints about "kids these days" (Edna), leaving us to finish our shopping trip in peace.

In a jewelry shop run by a lovely woman named Tamara, I found the cutest silver earrings with pink dangles for Jacy, an enameled necklace that screamed Neena, and a chunky bracelet in a modern style that Patrea would love. Drew found a pin in the shape of an angel that he swore would bring tears to his mother's eyes, and I snapped up a book-shaped one for my mother.

"You hungry again?" Drew said as we walked out the door. Between the ghosts and browsing shops, we'd whiled away enough time to hit the afternoon lull between lunch and the judging.

"Only as much as I am curious if there's been any news. Why don't you check in with Tommy and get that pulled pork you've been craving while I try another one of Cleo's tacos? We'll do salads from Jake, hit Sophia for dessert, and then grab a pizza from Ollie to take home for later."

"With a side of gossip?" Drew grinned.

"Adds the right touch to any meal," I grinned back and, because he was there, pulled his head down for a kiss.

"Why didn't you bring Molly?" Cleo looked past me as I approached.

"She's not a fan of shopping, so we let her stay back at the house." I cocked a brow at Cleo's disappointed pout. "I can bring her to the cabins this evening for a visit if you'd like."

That brightened her, and it had the undesired effect of ending up in a selfie with her that got posted on her socials. At least, I told myself, it wasn't a livestream this time.

"I've got skirt steak and pineapple tacos on special today. I'd love to get your opinion on them."

"I'll have two, thanks."

"Coming right up. Can I interest you in a triple choco-late brownie taco for dessert? I'm running a B2GO special today. Buy two tacos, and get one for half off. Might as well make it something sweet."

"Sure. Why not?" I'd still buy something from Sophia. "We've been shopping all day. Have you heard anything new about what happened with Tommy's truck?"

"Not a thing. Here you go." She tucked the brownie taco in a separate bag, then stuck it in with the others. I felt dismissed.

Tacos in hand, I met up with Drew just as Jake handed him a container of watermelon, arugula, mint, and goat cheese salad bathed in a honey vinaigrette. "That looks fabulous," I said to Jake, who only nodded before waiting on his next customer.

"How'd you make out with Cleo on the gossip front?" Drew asked as soon as we were in the car and headed back.

"She wasn't forthcoming, but with the judging coming up in a couple of hours, she probably had other things on her mind."

Drew eyed me with a gleam of interest. "I've got other things on my mind, as well."

It was our honeymoon, after all.

CHAPTER NINE

*B*AM! BAM! BAM!

The pounding jolted me awake. Adrenaline blasting through my system, and my heart thumping wildly, I bolted upright in bed. Beside me, Drew groaned and pulled a pillow over his head.

"What in the name of all that's holy?" I muttered, fumbling for my phone on the nightstand and hitting the button to deactivate the lock screen. Squinting in the sudden brightness, I read the time: 5:47 AM. Seriously?

I stumbled to the open window, raised voices echoing from the rental cabins next door as I peered through the curtains into the low light of dawn. Pajama and bathrobe-clad residents spilled out of the tiny houses, looking around to see what all the fuss was about. It was about Ollie, his round belly straining against a grease-stained apron, hammering on Cleo's door.

"I know you're in there. I heard you come sneaking back to your lair in the middle of the night." Ollie bellowed, his face tomato-red. "What the hell did you do to my truck?"

I groaned inwardly, so much for a peaceful morning.

"Everly?" Drew's sleep-roughened voice called from the bed. "What's happening?"

"Looks like Ollie's accusing Cleo of something to do with his truck," I replied, unable to tear my eyes away from the unfolding drama. "Want to place bets on how this ends?"

Drew chuckled, joining me at the window. "My money's on Cleo throwing a smoothie in his face."

Cleo emerged fully from her cabin as if on cue, her hair a wild tangle around her face. Despite the early hour, she'd taken time to apply a swipe of hot pink lipstick that clashed spectacularly with her rumpled pajamas.

"What is wrong with you? It's the butt crack of dawn," she said, pressing the palm of her hand to her forehead. "I was sleeping."

"You were sleeping?" Even from a distance, I could see Ollie's face redden as his voice rose at least an octave. If he weren't careful, he'd give himself a heart attack. "I shouldn't be surprised. It takes a cold heart to sabotage a man's truck and then go home and crawl into bed."

"What are you talking about?" Tommy said, his voice still carrying an edge of annoyance at being woken up so early.

"Excuse me for disturbing your beauty sleep," Ollie all but shouted, "but I took the shuttle into town to fire up my ovens for the breakfast pizza rush and discovered the Taco Witch jacked my electrical panel. It's fried."

"Have you lost your tiny mind?" Cleo snapped, jabbing a finger at Ollie's chest. "I was out with a friend last night, not screwing around with your greasy heart attack wagon."

That information seemed to hit Chase where it hurt. He looked away from Cleo and crossed his arms over his chest.

Breathing hard, Ollie shook his head. "If not you, then who?" Everyone else was here last night. You're the only one who left. It had to be you."

"What about her?" Cleo aimed a finger toward Sophia and tossed her squarely under the bus. "She could have ridden that bicycle of hers into town, couldn't she? Or any one of the rest of you could have borrowed it."

"No one did." Stepping closer, Sophia defended herself and gestured toward where the bike was secured to the stair rail. "I keep it locked. Not because I don't trust you all. It's just a habit."

"Whatever," Cleo cut her off. "I don't appreciate the accusation. You're lucky I don't have my face on right now, or I'd be filming this for my socials."

"Was that a threat?" I asked Drew hesitantly.

Before he could answer, a police cruiser pulled up, its lights flashing silently in the pale dawn. A tall, broad-shouldered man in uniform stepped out, his expression a mix of weariness and determination.

We watched Zack Roman approach the group, his presence immediately commanding attention. Even from a distance, I could see the tightness in his shoulders as he surveyed what was obviously a tense scene.

"All right, folks," the Sheriff's baritone voice carried

across the lawn. "Let's calm down and talk this through. Mr. Hensen, why don't you start by telling me what happened?"

As Ollie launched into his tale of woe, punctuated by dramatic gestures and the occasional glare at Cleo, Zack showed admirable patience. He wore a mask of professional neutrality and listened attentively, jotting notes on a small tablet. By the time Ollie was done, his voice had lowered enough that we couldn't hear everything being said.

"That," I said, turning to Drew with a wry smile, "was quite a show. Should we go over and offer Ollie our support?"

Drew yawned, wrapping an arm around my waist. "As tempting as that sounds, I vote we let the good sheriff handle things and go back to bed. Unless you're itching to play Nancy Drew?"

I hesitated, torn between curiosity and the siren call of a naked man and a warm bed. "You're right," I admitted when man-in-bed seemed the better option. "Even Molly isn't ready to get up. Besides, I doubt this is the last we'll hear of Oakville's great food truck caper."

By the time we crawled back out from under the covers, ate breakfast, and took Molly for a romp in the water, things had gone quiet next door. The shuttle bus was gone, and so was Sophia's bicycle.

As I passed where I'd left it on the table outside, my phone buzzed incessantly. Checking it, I found a flood of notifications from Cleo's social media followers.

"Looks like Cleo had a busy night," I murmured, scrolling through the posts of her whooping it up at what I assumed was the local bar. "She must have spent half the night uploading new photos. There have to be a hundred at least."

Having waited for me, Drew peered over my shoulder. "That gives her a pretty solid alibi."

I nodded but couldn't ignore the nagging doubts bubbling up inside me. "I guess. But something still feels off about this whole situation."

"Are you thinking of looking into it?" Drew asked, his tone carefully neutral.

I shook my head. "No, absolutely not. We're on our honeymoon, remember? No ghosts or mystery-solving. Just us."

But even as I said it, I could feel that familiar itch of curiosity. Judging by the look in Drew's eyes, he felt it, too.

"But you have to admit," Drew said slowly, a smile tugging at his lips, "it is pretty intriguing."

I groaned dramatically. "Don't tempt me, Parker. We are not getting involved. And we have a cookout to get ready for. Ollie will have to fend for himself."

Before pocketing my phone, I scanned through texts and emails, thinking it odd that I hadn't heard from Patrea or Neena since I'd let them know we had arrived safely. Or my mother, which struck me as even stranger.

Probably just giving us some honeymoon privacy.

CHAPTER TEN

*J*ulie had described her house as eclectic, but nothing could have prepared me for something out of a not-quite-right gothic fairytale. Hayward House came complete with ivy-covered walls, a sprawling front yard, and a vibe that suggested hidden passages, ancient portraits with eyes that followed you, and more family secrets than any single house should be able to contain.

"I could see Gustavia living here, but it's not the kind of house I'd expect Julie to own." I leaned forward to get a better look. "She's so pragmatic, and this house just isn't."

As Drew parked, I squinted through the windshield, wishing ghost-repelling spray was a thing I could keep in my purse for emergencies. Oh, who are we kidding? I'd douse myself with on the daily if it existed. Drew grinned like he was about to meet a bunch of long-lost cousins he'd grown up with while I wondered how many sage bundles and protective crystals Leandra might have whipped out to get through the evening.

"Do you think Julie knows if the house is haunted?" I asked, not exactly joking. "I mean, I know the story of her grandmother and great-grandfather's visits, but I wonder if others lurk here."

Drew smirked. "Pretty sure Kat would have mentioned something if there were."

"You know we operate on totally different levels, and you heard what the local ghosts said. She doesn't vibe with them at all. The house could be lousy with ghosts, and she wouldn't see them."

Julie met us at the door with a smile that suggested she knew exactly what I was thinking.

"Come on through. We'll say hi to everyone and get the dogs acquainted, and then, I'll give you the tour."

"It's quite a house," Drew said, staring at the bits of the interior we could see as she guided us through and into the backyard. "Everly's wondering if it's haunted."

"Not so much anymore," Julie grinned. "Not since Grams and Julius moved on. The house isn't as old as it looks, so it hasn't had time to rack up much of a ghost count."

"Good to know," I said as we stepped out onto the deck where the others gathered around the grill— Gustavia, unmistakable in her flowing skirt and jingling jewelry, sprinkled what looked like a cloud of herbs over the coals. The smoke spiraled up like a mystical offering, and I swore I could see shapes forming in it. I'd chalk it up to my overactive imagination in any other place, but here? Here, I wasn't about to assume anything.

I took Drew's hand, and together, we started toward the others while Molly flashed past us, her toenails scrabbling across the deck planks. She bounded down the steps to greet the two dogs already frolicking across the grass.

"Lola's the boxer," Julie informed me. "She belongs to me. The little white ball of energy is Fritzie. He's Gustavia's Jack Russell Terror...I mean, Terrier."

"You got it right the first time," Gustavia teased.

"Molly's in doggie heaven right now," Drew said, watching her tail swing in wild circles.

"So's Lola," Julie laughed. "You can tell because she's doing her dance of happiness. Fritzie runs rings around her, so having a friend her own size is a rarity."

Lola's happy dance consisted of twisting her body into a C shape, bouncing up with all four paws off the ground, and then rearing up on her hind legs before landing in a playful pounce. Grinning the whole time, her stubby tail wagged so fast her whole body wiggled. Meanwhile, Fritzie, as described, ran in circles around her, his form moving so quickly that he looked like a white blur.

Dragging our attention away from the dogs, we greeted the rest of the human guests. Amethyst, as always, decked out in shades of purple from head to toe, stirred something in a pot that looked suspiciously like a cauldron.

Next to her, Tyler brushed barbecue sauce across three whole chickens cut and splayed out over the grill grates. Finn, Reid, Kat, and Zack greeted us warmly, each seeming entirely at home.

"Thanks for having us," I said. "What can I do to help?"

"Nothing." Tyler grinned and flipped one of the chickens. "We've got beer in the cooler or wine on the table. Help yourselves."

"I'm taking them on a tour of the house," Julie leaned over to kiss her husband on the cheek. "How long before we eat?"

"The chickens have another fifteen minutes on this side, and then they can rest while I cook the burgers. That gives you just under half an hour."

"Plenty of time," Kat pushed off the railing she'd been leaning against. "I'm coming with."

"Me, too." Gustavia and Amethyst spoke at once.

Walking deeper into the house, I was charmed by the eclectic decor. Patrea would have a field day in the foyer alone. I'd have to bring her for a visit sometime—just to watch her head explode.

Julie beamed at us and, practically glowing with pride, led the way to what might have once been called a parlor but was now considered a living or great room. Pointing to the portrait of a man that hung over the fireplaces, she said, "That's my great-grandfather, Julius, and welcome to Hayward House. It's a work in progress."

She led us up a set of stairs that gave me staircase envy, her voice animated as she launched into Hayward family history. "This house was originally built in the Greek Revival style, but my great-grandfather, Julius Hayward, was...well, eccentric." She chuckled. "He added the Gothic wings because he liked that style of architecture. Also, most of the rooms are themed."

"Themed?" Drew wondered. "I'm intrigued."

"Eccentric is one word for Julius. Enterprising is another. He opened the house for furniture companies to use in advertising, so he got paid a nominal fee for letting them decorate how they wanted. I guess they worked out deals on the furniture, but it turned the house into a hodgepodge of styles."

"It's working out well for Julie, though." Gustavia's voice held pride in her friend. "The decor lends itself to fashion photography, so the whole house has become her studio."

"Speaking of which," Julie said, touching my arm to get my attention. "I'd like to shoot the two of you. As a wedding gift."

"Didn't you already give us a cake plate? I swear I sent you a Thank You card."

"Busted," Julie laughed. "But I want to get you in front of my camera. It's almost a compulsion."

"It is," Amethyst confirmed. "One we've all had to put up with. You might as well give in gracefully, or she'll harangue you until you do."

"I do not harangue." Feigning insult, Julie gasped theatrically. "At best, I employ gentle but persistent persuasion." She grinned. "Until I wear you down, and you give me what I want."

"Resistance is futile," Kat added. "So you might as well say yes and get it over with."

I looked at Drew, who grinned and shrugged. "Why not?"

"Okay. And thank you," I said, then revealed, "I've looked up your work, and I'm flattered to be part of it."

"Good. That's settled. Let's go on with the tour. This was the suite of rooms Julius slept in. It has the first of the stained glass windows that led us to one of the hidden compartments where he stashed a few of our family heirlooms."

"I'm guessing these aren't your average 'family albums in the attic' kind of heirlooms?" I ventured.

"Nope." Gustavia shook her head emphatically, making the bells woven into her braids tinkle. "Think old family silver, jewels, and notes from his various inventions. He put them away to keep his son from squandering his valuables. Then, he up and died without telling anyone else where to find them. Julie nearly lost the house because she didn't have the means to fix it up."

"But then, Gustavia brought her in for a reading, and Julie's grandmother came through," Kat said, her eyes twinkling with the memory. "She attached herself to Julie and brought Julius through with her. She'd crossed over before she realized he hadn't, so it wasn't an easy feat, but Estelle made it work."

"It helped that Julie and her grandmother had compatible auras," Amethyst said.

"You can see why I sympathize with your situation," Julie said. "I didn't believe in ghosts, or what Kat calls "spirit" until I had no choice. And even then, I had a hard time accepting what happened. I don't know what I would have done without my friends to help me through."

"She's buttering us up again," Gustavia teased. The easy camaraderie between the four women made me miss my friends a little. "Because we help out with product shoots from time to time, and she's landed a new client. But back to the story, Julius came through and gave Julie the first of four clues to where he'd hidden his stuff. Each clue involved one of these windows and could only be accessed during a solstice or equinox, so it took us an entire year to track everything down."

"And I thought I'd had some ghostly adventures," I said, wanting to know more.

"This is the first window." Julie directed us toward a spare, minimally furnished bedroom. The elaborately wrought stained glass faced the bed, its colors catching the late afternoon light. "Each window represents a season. This one's summer. We found our first clue hidden right in that carved frame."

She pointed to a notch in the wood, and I could almost imagine Julius Hayward snickering as he tucked something in there, knowing it would be decades before anyone found it.

"And let's just say," Kat added, her expression mysterious, "the clues didn't exactly jump out and explain themselves."

Julie rolled her eyes. "That's an understatement."

"And Julius isn't still around?" Drew asked, clearly invested.

"Oh, no," Kat assured us. "He's moved on to other aspects of the afterlife." I sensed a more remarkable story behind her casual delivery but didn't want to ask. Maybe later, I could pry out a few more details.

"At one time, this floor was used as a boarding house for war widows. That was before the furniture companies got hold of them. We've turned one suite of rooms into Tyler's office and just finished renovating another for mine. Then, there are two more that we've cleaned up and made into guest rooms. One of those has the next window."

The beautifully patterned window took center stage, with the room decorated to showcase its glowing autumn colors. Gustavia explained, "This window helped us find the second stash."

Amethyst, who had been mostly quiet, spoke as we entered a bedroom lavishly decorated in the art deco style. "This is where my husband stayed when he showed up. It's my favorite room in the house."

Wallpaper in a wide black-and-gray stripe above a simple white-paneled wainscot served as a backdrop for a large mirror in a gleaming silver frame that looked like a bird in flight. The bed's headboard echoed the wing-like shapes, as did the dresser and a pair of nightstands.

A turquoise duvet provided a splash of color to keep the room from being too stark. On the wall across from the door, the winter scene picked out in stained glass echoed the colors in the room—white snow on a black tree below a blue sky.

"The clues for this one took us down a weird and winding road." Amethyst tucked a lavender strand behind her ear, looking almost wistful. "There were a few...supernatural issues."

"More ghosts?"

"Something like that." Amethyst declined to elaborate.

"The last one is my favorite." Kat took the lead in showing us the spring-themed window. "The clues were obscure, even by Julius' standards."

Gustavia nodded, her smile sly. "It took all of us working together to figure it out. Even Zack had to pitch in." She glanced at Kat and grinned. Again, I sensed a larger story that none seemed inclined to share. Yet. I'd get the whole of it at some point.

The rest of the tour went more quickly, leaving my head reeling with decorating ideas for my place. We rejoined the men just as Tyler declared it was time to eat. Amid lively chatter and the clinking of cutlery against simple white plates, that's just what we did while getting to know each other better.

"Did Julie talk you into the photo shoot?" Tyler directed the question toward me.

"She had some help with that," I mock-glared at the women seated around the table. "But, yes, she did."

"Pay up," Kat gestured toward Amethyst.

"Nope. You had your chance upstairs. It's too late now. You forfeit the spoils."

Gustavia rolled her eyes. "It was a sucker bet, Kat, and you know it."

"It wasn't," Amethyst pulled a twenty out of her

pocket and handed it across the table. "I truly thought Everly would be the first person to stand up against Camera Annie over there."

Watching the byplay, I had no idea what it meant, only that I'd been the subject of some sort of wager. "Do I want to know what this is about?" I asked.

"Probably not," Tyler responded, his eyes glittering with amusement.

"What about a sunrise shoot?" Gustavia suggested, altering the subject slightly. "The mist on the lake would be gorgeous."

Kat nodded enthusiastically. "And you should both wear white. Not bright white, but something gauzy and ethereal that will almost blend into the mist, right, Julie?"

"A nice lavender," Amethyst suggested, "would blend in with the mist better than white."

"Not with Everly's coloring," Julie said, shaking her head. "She can pull off purple, but it would need to be more saturated than lavender to work with her hair. "

As our new friends continued brainstorming, I leaned into Drew, whispering, "What have we yupped ourselves into?"

He chuckled softly, "Let's just go with it. Have a little fun."

When talk inevitably turned to our neighbors and the food truck competition, Zack could shed no light on recent events.

"Whoever sabotaged those trucks had to know the webcams are all down now. Something to do with a server error. Otherwise, we'd have video proof. And I'd have a better shot at catching whoever's picking pockets all over town, too."

"Someone's picking pockets?" Julie stared at him. "In Oakville? That's ridiculous."

"Ridiculous or not, it's a thing," Zack countered. "For the past few days, anyway. This competition might benefit the local merchants, but it's made my life harder."

By the time the sun disappeared over the horizon, Molly had run herself out, was draped across my feet, snoring away, and we'd become comfortable enough to join in some of the teasing banter that rocketed around the group.

"It's getting late," Zack looked at his watch. "And I'm on duty tomorrow."

"We need to head out as well," I said, realizing it was nearly eleven and the evening had flown by. "Thank you all for a lovely evening. We've had a great time."

Before we left, we solidified plans for the photo shoot in three day's time, and somehow, I let myself be maneuvered into a shopping trip to pick out camera-suitable attire.

The rental cabins were quiet as we approached, starkly contrasting the earlier commotion. Drew slowed the car, his gaze sweeping over the area.

"Looks like things have settled down next door," he observed as we went inside.

"For the time being, anyway." I let him lead me upstairs.

CHAPTER ELEVEN

*T*he cool lake water still dampened my skin as I peeled off my swimsuit and tossed it over the shower curtain rod to dry. Drew, already changed into dry clothes, lounged on the bed, his muscular frame stretching luxuriously as he watched me with a playful glint in his blue eyes.

"You know," I said, slipping on a soft cotton t-shirt, "I could get used to mornings like this. The lake was so peaceful, it almost felt magical."

Drew grinned, his chiseled jaw relaxing into an easy smile. "A nice slice of serenity before the chaos begins."

I snorted, pulling on a pair of shorts. "Chaos? In our blissful newlywed bubble? Perish the thought."

"Hey, you never know," Drew teased, sitting up. "With your uncanny ability to attract trouble, we might—"

A sudden commotion from next door cut him off mid-sentence. Raised voices and what sounded like a slamming door echoed from the direction of the rental cabins.

Drew and I exchanged a look, eyebrows raised. So much for serenity. At least we were already awake this time.

"What do you think that's about?" I asked, moving toward the window.

Drew joined me, his warm presence at my back as I twitched the curtains aside to peer out at the cluster of tiny houses next door. "Looks like today's episode of Food Truck Island has started. I wonder who's changing alliances today," he murmured.

I couldn't hold back a snort, "In this week's challenge, contestants must smoke a brisket while sabotaging their opponents' sauce recipes."

The scene unfolding before us certainly seemed like a bizarre theater production as Tommy O'Malley's voice cut through the morning air, sharp enough to make me wince.

"Cleo! Come on, we're gonna be late!" he bellowed, pounding on Cleo's cabin door with enough force to rattle the tiny structure. "The judging starts in three hours, and I need every minute I can get. I'm leaving with the shuttle in five minutes! Get your butt out here!"

I leaned closer to the window, my breath fogging the glass. "Uh oh, someone's not ready for their close-up," I muttered.

Drew's breath tickled my ear as he leaned closer. "No kidding, and it looks like Tommy's ready to vote her off the show."

We watched as Tommy, sans his usual easy-going manner, paced in front of the cabin, compulsively running his hand through his hair until it stood up every which way. Every few seconds, he'd glance at his watch, his agitation visibly growing.

"Ten bucks says Cleo's still in bed," I whispered, my inner snark coming out to play. "Probably dreaming of Instagram likes and TikTok fame."

"Two minutes, Cleo!" Tommy shouted again, his voice cracking slightly. "After that, I'm leaving you here."

"Leave her anyway," Ollie yelled. "It's what she deserves."

"You have to give Tommy points for trying so hard when Cleo's absence would only increase his standing in the competition. Maybe the sabotage screwed up his alliance with Ollie, and now, he's trying to cozy up to Cleo."

We were living next door to the live version of a reality television show, and I was there for all of it.

Drew shook his head slightly. "He'd be better off if he hooked up with Jake and Sophia to form an opposing faction. If you ask me, Jake's the dark horse in this thing, and Sophia has more going on under that sunny facade than you expect. Should be interesting to see how it all plays out."

As if on cue, Tommy let out a string of expletives colorful enough to make a sailor blush. He gave the door one last emphatic knock before throwing his hands up in defeat.

"Fine!" he yelled. "We're leaving without you! Don't blame me when you miss the judging."

A new player entered the scene just as I considered making some popcorn for the show. Chase, his dark hair even more tousled than usual, burst out of his cabin like a man on a mission. He shouldered past Tommy with surprising force for his slight build, sending the larger man stumbling.

"Whoa," I breathed, pressing closer to the glass. "This is getting intense."

Chase reached Cleo's door and rapped his knuckles against it, his movements urgent but gentler than Tommy's assault. "Cleo!" His voice contained a mix of concern and determination. "Are you okay in there? It's Chase. I'm sorry about...we need to talk. Can I come in?"

Tommy, regaining his balance, snorted derisively. "She probably spent the night with some guy she picked up in a bar. You're wasting your time, lover boy. She's not worth it."

Where had this vitriol come from? Until now, the worst he'd said about Cleo was that she was a cutthroat competitor. That wasn't the same as maligning her reputation.

Chase whirled on Tommy, his usual laid-back demeanor vanishing. "You don't know anything about her that you haven't seen online," he snapped. "Cleo's a lot more than her social media persona. She's...complicated. Misunderstood."

"Oh please," Tommy rolled his eyes. "I've seen her type before. All glitz and no substance."

"Who dumped you, Tommy?" I wondered.

Behind me, Drew chuckled. As a recent reality show convert, he didn't get as invested in them as I did.

Chase's voice lowered, taking on an edge I hadn't heard before. "You're wrong about her. Cleo's got more talent and drive in her little finger than most people have in their whole body. Just because she markets herself along with her food doesn't make her shallow. And I know for a fact she was here last night."

As Chase stepped between Tommy and Cleo's door, I found myself grudgingly impressed. "Well, well," I said to Drew, "looks like Prince Charming's found his backbone."

Drew chuckled. "Think it'll be enough to win the fair maiden's heart?"

I snorted. "Please. The only heart Cleo's interested in is the one that shows up when you like her posts. And she's done with him. You can tell by how she doesn't even glance at him most of the time. She's the disruptor of the show."

"The one who's out for herself and doesn't form alliances."

I grinned, warming to the theme. "Ollie would be the gruff but lovable mentor. But only when it comes to food. He's the one doling out sage advice about optimum cooking temperatures and whether sea salt is better than iodized."

"That makes Sophia the ingénue. And Jake the loner."

Things next door had gone quiet for a moment while Chase knocked again and waited for Cleo's response.

"And Tommy's everybody's favorite uncle. Or he was

until now, I suppose," I said, just as Tommy's voice rose again in frustration. "He keeps this up, he'll turn into the one everyone loves to hate."

As if on cue, Ollie's voice cut through the commotion when he yelled from the shuttle where he and Jake waited. "Tommy! Get a move on. We're burning daylight!"

"That puts Chase in the role of outsider or, possibly, mediator," Drew said. "But with an ulterior motive. He doesn't care about the competition, just the one competitor."

I nodded along. It was sweet, really, how fiercely Chase defended Cleo. Having been exposed to her—mainly through her online presence—I didn't think she was the type to jump into a second-chance romance, but you couldn't blame the guy for trying.

Tommy's face had turned an alarming shade of red, his frustration practically radiating off him in waves. "Whatever," he spat, throwing his hands up in exaspera-tion. "I'm done waiting around. If Princess Cleo can't be bothered to haul her butt out of whatever bed she hopped into, that's her problem. I've got a competition to win."

Poor Cleo. Whether she deserved it or not, it seemed she had quite the reputation to contend with.

As Tommy stormed off toward the shuttle, Chase called after him, his voice laced with scorn, "Leaving without her won't win you a damn thing. I'll give her a ride to town when she's ready."

Drew nudged me gently, his breath warm against my

ear. "Speaking of lovable characters, check out Prescott," he murmured.

I followed his gaze to Chase's dog. Tongue hanging out, practically ignored by his owner, Prescott strained at his leash, tail wagging furiously as he looked longingly in the direction of our lake house.

"Looks like someone's eager to see his new friend," Drew chuckled. His blue eyes lit up with that boyish enthusiasm I loved so much.

I smiled. "Poor guy. Probably desperate for some canine company after all this human drama."

"Maybe we should suggest a play date with Molly? It might be nice to have some peaceful dog energy to balance out the daytime drama next door. I could ask Chase if it's okay to take him on walks with Molly."

I grinned, picturing Molly's reaction. She must miss her regular trips to the dog park to hang out with canine friends.

"That's a great idea," I said. "It might help take Chase's mind off things too."

We watched Chase trudge back to his cabin, Prescott in tow, and his shoulders rounded in defeat. He looked back at Cleo's cabin with naked longing. No one could have slept through the racket Tommy made, so it seemed pretty clear she wasn't there. The question that nagged at me was this: why, if she was serious about winning, would Cleo spend the night before an important judging with some random hookup? Call it intuition, or maybe just an overactive imagination, but something about this whole situation felt...off.

"Hey," Drew said softly, pulling me from my thoughts. "What's going on in that beautiful head of yours?"

"Something seems weird, but it's probably just me seeing mysteries where none exist." I shook my head, trying to dispel the nagging worry. "I'm sure it's nothing."

The shuttle's engine roared to life, drowning out the last of Tommy and Ollie's bickering. They peeled off, leaving a dramatic cloud of dust in their wake.

"Well," I said, turning to Drew with a wry smile, "there goes our daily dose of lakeside drama. Whatever will we do for entertainment now?"

Drew chuckled, wrapping an arm around my waist. "I'm sure we can find some way to occupy ourselves, Mrs. Parker."

I leaned into him, savoring the warmth of his touch. "I'm sure we can. Did you still want to go to Port Harbor? Or just take the boat for a spin into town. We haven't hit the art gallery or that cute little pottery place yet."

"Only if we can stop at the wine cork museum." He'd seen it the day before and decided it had to go on the to-do list.

"Sure, but do you mind if we don't do the food trucks today? I could really go for a lobster roll from the Salty Seagull." If they were half as good as the photo on the side of the building looked, we couldn't go wrong. The combination sit-down and takeout spot had been packed the day before, so the food must be good, and I'd had enough food truck drama for one day.

Drew's face lit up. "Now you're speaking my language. Boat ride with my two favorite girls and seafood? Count me in."

Later, we made our way down to the dock, Molly bounding ahead of us, her tail wagging so hard I thought it might fly off. The simple joy of spending time with both of my favorite people made me glad I hadn't taken my mother up on her offer to keep Molly for the duration. Thinking of her reminded me that I still hadn't heard from her. I made a mental note to call or message her later.

"Watch your step." Drew offered me his hand as I stepped over the side. Her first-time jitters long forgotten, Molly jumped in after me, rocking the boat with her excitement.

"Easy there, girl," I laughed, steadying myself. "We're all going for a ride, no need to leave us behind."

The cool breeze off the lake tousled my hair as we pulled away from the dock, sending unruly red curls flying in all directions. I caught Drew stealing glances at me, a soft smile playing on his lips.

"What?" I asked, suddenly self-conscious.

"Nothing," he said, his eyes twinkling. "Just thinking how beautiful you look with your hair all wild like that. Like a fierce mermaid."

I snorted but felt a blush creeping up my cheeks. "What you call wild, I call too lazy to bother with a blowout. Besides, we're on vacation."

The boat cut through the water for a pleasant half hour, sending up a fine mist that sparkled in the sunlight. Molly sat at the bow, her ears flapping in the wind, looking like the figurehead of our little vessel.

"You know," Drew mused as we neared the town docks, "Greece would have been nice, but I'm just as happy here. This would be a good second option if we don't find lakefront property near Mooselick River. I know it's a bit of a drive, but I like the area."

The idea sent a little thrill through me. "Let's see if we survive two weeks first, shall we?" I teased. "But it couldn't hurt to look if you see any For Sale signs."

As we pulled into the town's small marina, the peaceful bubble we'd been floating in promptly burst. The first thing I noticed was Cleo's distinctive food truck. Her face splashed across the side, making it impossible to miss. But instead of the usual bustling activity and mouthwatering aromas, it sat silent and shuttered.

The competition was in full swing in the town square —minus Cleo. Under a tent that hadn't been there the day before, a scowling Ollie pulled a large pizza from a portable oven. Under another, three judges sampled the first entries of the day.

Drew glanced over at me, his brow furrowing when he followed my gaze. "Maybe she's running late?"

We made our way past the competition area, the knot in my stomach tightening with each step. The absence of Cleo's bubbly energy and camera-ready smile was glaring.

"I have a bad feeling about this," I said, scanning the

crowd. "According to everything she posts, Cleo lives for these events. There's no way she'd miss a judging unless something was seriously wrong."

Drew squeezed my hand. "Let's not jump to conclusions. Maybe she's just..." he paused. "I've got nothing. It's definitely weird."

"Hey, Ollie!" I called out. "What's cooking?"

"Smells fantastic." Drew sniffed the air. He'd better not be rethinking his lunch choices. I still wanted that lobster roll.

"Brie, pancetta, and pesto pizza. It's gonna blow the judges' minds! Be better if I had my own setup, though. This oven's okay, but it's not like mine."

"Still no sign of Cleo?"

He looked up from working a round of dough, his face darkening. "Haven't looked for her and couldn't care less if she shows up or not. I've been too busy trying to make things work after what she did to my truck."

"It's still weird that she'd forget about the competition."

"Maybe she grew a conscience and that's why she's not here. Or else the judges kicked her out for sabotage, and she's hiding her face until the contest is over. This isn't the first time something like this has happened, and what's the common denominator? Cleo, that's what."

Since there seemed nothing else to say on the subject, we left him to his pizza-making and made our way to the Salty Seagull where the lobster rolls lived up to their hype.

The cork museum did not, but it got full marks for being highly campy, and I found an incense burner at the pottery shop that I knew Momma Wade would love, so the shopping trip wasn't a total loss.

CHAPTER TWELVE

*B*ack at the lake house, we'd just tied off the boat when a brown and white blur zipped across the lawn, heading straight for Molly. I barely had time to blink before Prescott, Chase's beagle, was upon us, his tail wagging so fast it was practically a propeller.

Molly's ears perked up, her chocolate fur bristling with excitement, her butt wiggling with joy. The two dogs circled and sniffed each other like long-lost pals.

"Well, hello to you too, Prescott," I laughed, watching as Molly barked playfully and took off running, the beagle hot on her heels.

Drew chuckled beside me. "I guess our quiet afternoon just got a lot more interesting."

Chase came jogging into view as if on cue, slightly out of breath and looking sheepish. His well-worn t-shirt clung to him in a way that suggested he'd been chasing his four-legged friend for quite some time.

"I am so sorry," Chase panted, stopping near us. He leaned against the dock post, trying to catch his breath. "Prescott caught a whiff of something and took off. I swear, that nose of his will be the death of me."

I bit back a smile, amused at Chase's attempt to look casually cool while gasping for air.

Drew waved off Chase's apology. "No worries, man. Prescott's welcome anytime. Besides," he gestured to where the dogs were now engaged in an enthusiastic game of chase, "I think Molly's enjoying the company. We were planning to set up a doggy play date, anyway. Now is as good a time as any."

I nodded in agreement, watching Prescott trailing behind Molly, his floppy ears bouncing with each step. "They certainly seem to be having fun. Looks like he put you through your paces, though."

Chase straightened up, trying to smooth down his shirt in a futile attempt to look more put-together. "Keeping up with Prescott is a workout."

"Well, since you're here," Drew said, indicating the deck chairs with his chin, "why don't you sit down and join us for a bit? We were just about to crack open some lemonade. I'll bring out an extra glass."

"I don't want to intrude on your honeymoon."

"You're fine. Let the dogs play," I said. "Molly loves making new friends." I didn't say that he looked like he could use a friend, too.

Not that Prescott was paying attention to Molly at the moment. He'd abandoned the romp to pad back onto the dock and sniff the side of the boat. Probably because Molly had been in it.

Worry lines creasing his forehead, Chase accepted the glass of lemonade Drew handed him, his movements jerky as if the motion cost him something. I didn't think I'd ever seen a man so tightly wound. It made me want to pry.

"So, Chase," I began, aiming for casual but probably landing somewhere between nosy and concerned, "have you heard anything from Cleo?"

Chase's shoulders tensed, and he took a long sip of lemonade before answering. "No one has. It's like she just...vanished."

I felt a prickle of unease crawl up my spine. "You're worried for her." It wasn't a question.

"So much!" Chase exclaimed, his casual facade crumbling. He ran a hand through his hair, making it stand up even more. "She wouldn't just take off without telling anyone. And her food truck? It's her baby. There's no way she'd abandon it, especially not in the middle of a competition. Cleo lived...lives for that type of thing,"

Drew's glance strayed to mine, and he lifted a brow at Chase's correction.

I chewed my lip, my mind racing. Cleo was ambitious. Driven, even. I didn't know her well, but a cruise through her Instagram account was enough to show that leaving her business behind didn't fit her personality. "Have you spoken with whoever owns the cabins? Someone should go in and check. Maybe she's not feeling well and needs help."

Chase shook his head, his eyes dark with worry. "I already called. The owners run this like an Airbnb, so the keys are in a lockbox next to the door. They wouldn't give me a code since I'm not family." He made air quotes.

"I see."

"She wouldn't abandon her truck. Something's not right. I can feel it in my gut." The bitter note when he mentioned her truck made it reasonably obvious her dedication to it had been a point of contention.

"Anyone have it out for her?" Drew asked. "A rival, or maybe an online fan?"

"This guy stalked her a year ago, but he wasn't dangerous or anything."

Drew and I exchanged a look. "Stalking sounds plenty dangerous to me," I said.

"It wasn't like that." Chase shook his head. "He wasn't stalking *her* so much as trying to figure out the secret ingredient in her fish taco batter. He followed her to three competitions and bought about fifty tacos before he realized it was turmeric."

"Okay. That sounds fairly tame, as stalkings go. Anyone else?" I didn't point out that he'd followed her here, which, by definition, could make him a stalker, too.

"Not unless someone latched onto her in the two weeks since we split up. I'm telling you, something's happened to her. She wouldn't leave her truck unattended."

People did all sorts of things—good things, bad things, weird things, and frequently unexpected things—often in the pursuit of love or even the chance of it. I doubted Cleo was as predictable as Chase made her out to be. But people see what they want to see.

"Listen," he said, "I should get back. I want to be

around if she shows up or the cops need to talk to me again. Come on, Prescott."

Whatever scent he'd detected had Prescott mesmerized. Chase finally had to clip on his leash and tug to get the dog to follow him back toward the rental cabins.

Once they'd disappeared down the gravel path, I turned and pulled Drew to his feet. "What do you think? About Cleo, I mean."

Drew's brow furrowed. He squeezed my hand. "I honestly don't know, Ev. Chase seemed genuinely scared, but it could be a case of his heart being tangled up with his head."

I flopped onto the porch swing, its gentle creak matching my sigh. "I know. And I can't help but feel like we should do something. But..." I trailed off, gesturing vaguely at our idyllic surroundings.

Drew settled beside me. "But it's our honeymoon," he finished, a hint of understanding in his voice.

"Exactly!" I exclaimed, feeling a rush of guilt even as the words left my mouth. "Is it awful that I'm torn between wanting to help and wanting to just...be here with you?"

"Not awful," Drew assured me, his thumb tracing soothing circles on my palm. "Only human. It's your nature to fix things. That's how Martha keeps dragging you into town business. And I get it because I'm the same way. It makes us feel fulfilled. And it's a good thing—until it's not. I mean, I stopped to help someone change a tire not so long ago, and look how that turned out."

That bit of Good Samaritanship had landed him in jail with a murder charge hanging over his head. If Drew never wanted to help another person, I'd fully understand. But I also figured changing his fundamental nature would take more than one bad experience.

I leaned into him, savoring his steadiness. "Maybe I'm overreacting. We don't know for sure that anything's wrong, right? For all we know, she's posting pictures from Cabo because she fell in love and took off with the man of her dreams."

Even as I said it, my free hand was already fishing my phone out of my pocket. I pulled up Cleo's Instagram, scrolling quickly through her feed.

"Nope," I muttered, frowning at the screen. "She's definitely not in Cabo. She hasn't posted since yesterday."

Drew peered over my shoulder. "What was it?"

"Just a picture of a fish taco. Caption says, 'Catch yours in Oakville!' Nothing since then."

I switched to her Facebook and then Twitter and found similar radio silence. Even more concerning were the comments piling up on her latest posts:

"Cleo, where are you?"

"Getting worried, girl. Where you at?"

"Has anyone heard from Cleo? This isn't like her..."

I felt my resolve crumbling like a sandcastle at high tide. "Drew," I said slowly, "I think we might need to look into this. Just a little. To make sure she's okay. The last thing I need is her ghost showing up to ruin my week."

Drew nodded, squeezing my hand. "What's the plan?"

I looked up at him, overwhelmed with love and gratitude. "You're not upset?"

He grinned that crooked smile that never failed to make my heart skip. "Upset that my wife is compassionate and brave? Never. Besides," he added with a wink, "I didn't marry you expecting a quiet life."

I took a deep breath, setting my phone down on the coffee table. The worry for Cleo gnawed at me, but as I gazed at Drew, I felt a surge of determination.

"No," I said firmly, more to myself than to him. "You know what? We're on our honeymoon. Cleo's an adult, and she's not our problem. Zack and Kat have experience with missing persons. They don't need us, and we deserve this time together."

Drew raised an eyebrow, surprised. "Are you sure? It won't bother you not to help?"

I nodded, hoped I meant it, and squeezed his fingers. "I'm sure. You're right. I do want to help. But I want time with you more. We've been through a lot to get here, and I won't let anything ruin it."

As if on cue, my phone began to buzz. I glanced at the screen, seeing Gustavia's name flash across it.

"Speaking of ruining things," I said, answering the call. "Hey, Gustavia. What's up?"

Gustavia's voice exploded through the speaker, bright and bubbly as ever. "Look, I know this is your honeymoon and all, but I'm calling with an invitation you absolutely cannot refuse! I hope."

I couldn't help but laugh. "Oh really? And what might that be?"

"We decided we're doing karaoke night at The Rusty Anchor and thought you might want to tag along. It'll be fun," she wheedled. "It's a live band. Not one of those silly machines."

I glanced at Drew, who was watching me with amusement. "Karaoke night?" I repeated for his benefit.

"I'm in if you are," he said in a low tone so Gustavia wouldn't hear him.

"I'm not taking no for an answer," Gustavia warned. "We'll have fun. I promise."

I sighed, but I could feel my resolve weakening. It did sound fun. "Okay. We'll be there. But Gustavia?"

"Yes?" She dragged the word out long, and I could hear the smile in her voice.

"If you try to get me to sing, I swear I'll sic every ghost in Oakville on you."

Gustavia's laughter rang out. "No promises, sweetie. See you tonight!"

As I hung up, Drew was grinning at me. "Karaoke, huh? Sounds like a perfect honeymoon activity to me. I can't wait to hear you sing."

I groaned but couldn't keep the smile off my face. "You heard what I just told her. That will not be happening."

"Have you met Gustavia? Ten bucks says she talks you into it."

"Have you caught the betting bug from Kat and Amethyst?" I teased.

He shook his head but kept on grinning. "No, but my money's on Gustavia all the same."

Feigning a fatal wound, I slapped my hand over my heart. "Barely married a week, and you're already taking sides against me."

He laughed at my theatrics and then made a concession. "I'll tell you what, if you end up singing, I'll sing. How's that?"

"You don't even sing in the shower. How does this translate into betting against me?"

"It doesn't."

Somehow, he'd flipped sides, but I couldn't pinpoint how or why. "Okay. I guess we have a deal."

Drew pulled me close, pressing a kiss to my forehead. "That's my girl."

I was about to kiss him when a sudden rumble of thunder made me jump. Before we could call Molly out of the water, fat raindrops pelted the deck, making me thankful we'd been sitting under the awning.

"Well, at least we made it back before the storm started," I sighed, watching the previously sun-drenched landscape transform into a watery blur. Thunder being her least favorite thing, Molly raced past us and skidded to a halt in front of the lake house door. She looked back at me with naked pleading in her eyes. "Better get Molly dried off."

Once we had, she refused to settle, staying plastered to my side as I stood looking out the windows at the lightning flashing over the lake.

Drew wrapped his arms around me from behind. "I love a good storm over water. Brings back memories of summers on the lake. Granted, our accommodations weren't quite as impressive, but this does give me an idea."

I raised an eyebrow. "Oh? And what might that be, Mr. Parker?"

"Board games." He grinned, already moving toward the cabinet of them. "I'll pick one out. You make the popcorn."

His enthusiasm made me smile. "Okay, I'm in. But if you think you're getting me to play the strip version, think again. It's bad enough we'll be eating our popcorn with a side of damp dog. I'm not getting naked with her in thundershower mode."

"Fine. Take all the fun out of it." His cheerful tone belied the sentiment.

As Drew rummaged through the games, I tossed a bag of popcorn into the microwave and changed into lounge-around-the-house clothes. The rain outside intensified, creating a soothing backdrop to our impromptu gaming date.

"You know," I mused, rolling my second Yahtzee, "For us, this is very honeymoon-esque, and I love it."

Drew settled beside me, his warmth a comforting presence. "See? Who needs sunshine when you've got popcorn and...is that my shirt you're wearing?"

I grinned innocently. "Maybe. It's comfy. Sue me."

We were halfway through Parcheezi when a familiar chill slipped across my skin. Oh no. Not now.

"Well, well, well! Ain't this just the coziest little setup I ever did see!"

I groaned internally as Howdy materialized, his ghostly fishing hat slightly askew. "Howdy. Now's not the best—"

But it was too late. Iris and Edna shimmered into view on either side of him. A glance at Drew confirmed they'd taken the trouble to show themselves to him.

"Oh, how darling!" Iris cooed, her grandmotherly face beaming. "It reminds me of when my Harold and I used to—"

"Now, Iris," Edna interrupted primly, "let's not get carried away with nostalgia. You dragged us out here to discuss important matters. Stay on topic."

I shot Drew an apologetic look. He just smiled and shrugged, used to these supernatural interruptions by now.

"Let me guess," I sighed, setting down my glass of wine and letting my sarcastic side out. "You've decided there's too much water in the lake, and you want me to have a word with the proper authorities to see what they can do about it."

"Don't be ridiculous." Edna looked at me like I was something she'd stepped in near the dog park.

Iris gave Edna the same look. I had to clamp my lips to keep from smiling.

"It's about that missing girl." Howdy got to the point. "The one who chirps at her phone all day."

Now, I did snort. That was as good a description of Cleo as anyone would ever hear.

"That handsome Sheriff was in town all morning. Papering businesses."

"You mean canvassing, Iris." Rather than rolling her eyes, Edna let the firm set of her lips show exasperation. "It's called canvassing when policemen go door to door."

"Police officers, Edna." Iris refused to be chastised. "Not police*men*. That's sexist."

"Police officers," Edna emphasized her use of the term, "canvas the area when they're investigating. Haven't you ever read a crime novel?"

The energy generated by their bickering caused the hairs on my arms to stand up, sending prickles across my skin. "That's enough," I said.

"She's right," Howdy backed me up. "You're not helping anything by sniping at each other."

"Who asked you?" Iris rounded on him, her hands planted on ample hips. "My great grand-niece is missing, and canvassing isn't enough. We need action. We need a plan. And we need someone who can serve as our communications expert."

It didn't take much effort to figure out who she meant.

"You'll do it, won't you, Everly?" Iris turned pleading eyes on me.

"How? I'm not the police. I'm not from around here, so

I wouldn't know where to look for her. For all we know, she's shacked up with someone she met online or at the bar in town. There's no proof anything happened to her. Let Zack do his job; I'm sure all will be revealed in no time."

I was not sure of any such thing.

If you've never seen a ghost's eyes burn with fervor, it's an uncanny experience. "I have no intention of getting in his way, but you will help find my niece, or I'll haunt you like you've never been haunted before."

"You think you're the first ghost to make that threat?"

"I don't know about being the first, but I'm the one who's making it now, and I wonder what kind of honeymoon you'll have with me standing at the foot of your bed every night."

"That's a horrible thing to say." Edna turned on Iris. "You wouldn't dare intrude like that."

"Wouldn't I? Just watch me." Iris stood her ground, defiance evident in the angle of her chin. "And if that isn't enough, I've got more."

One time, a pissed-off ghost rearranged all my furniture. Iris settled on upending the popcorn bowl over the Parcheezi board while offering me a thousand-yard stare.

Whatever response she expected, all she got was a raised eyebrow. I'd seen worse, and isn't that just sad?

"Okay," Drew said loudly enough to get everyone's attention. "That's enough. You don't need to threaten anyone, Iris. Everly's not refusing to help. She's merely stating the facts. We're not equipped to take on a missing person's case. But that doesn't mean we won't do what we can."

That calmed Iris down a bit.

"Drew's right," I confirmed. "But I have no idea where to start."

"The first step," Howdy said, his voice rising as he set down his bait bucket. "Is to scope out the poor girl's cabin. Look for evidence. Search for clues."

Almost in unison, Drew and I held our hands up.

"That would be breaking and entering," Drew said. "Plus trespassing."

"Not to mention evidence tampering if there is any." I chimed in. "If we get caught, we'll end up in jail. How much help would we be, then?"

Having flipped back from vengeful to cheerful, Iris waved his protest away. "No one asked you to break or enter. Howdy meant the three of us. We're ghosts, dear. Trespassing is our specialty. Besides, who else will know? All I'm asking is that you pass whatever information we find to the hot Sheriff."

"Hot?" Edna glared at Iris.

"It means he's good-looking," Iris said without a shred of repentance. "And, boy, is he ever."

"Focus on the task at hand," Edna advised. "And get your mind out of your panties."

Before I could process Edna's remark and form a complete sentence, the three spectral busybodies had already floated through the wall. I groaned, pinching the bridge of my nose.

"That was interesting," Drew said softly, his eyes alight with humor.

"Interesting is one word for it."

I didn't have time to come up with another one before the ghosts returned.

"Her phone's still plugged in, and there's a half-eaten taco on a plate on the table," Howdy informed us. "Along with a bottle of painkillers and an empty water glass."

My stomach twisted. "She wouldn't leave her phone behind. Not with her social media following."

Howdy had more to add. "I took a look at her phone."

"You touched her phone? Good way to obscure evidence that might help the police find her."

"Relax," he said, smirking at me. "You sounded like Edna for a minute there. I didn't have to touch the phone exactly. It runs off electricity, sort of. Electricity is easy to manipulate. It's why we use it to communicate with the living."

Well, that explained the trope of lights turning on and off at haunted houses, I supposed.

"Anyway, her last text said she'd heard a noise outside and was going out to see what it was. That's helpful, right?"

"It is. Did you check the timestamp on the text?"

Howdy snapped his fingers. "Well, shoot. I didn't think about that. I'll do it now." He winked out.

"But," Edna added her two cents worth. "There are clothes strewn all over the bedroom. Could be signs of a struggle."

"It was one top and a skirt, Edna," Iris said, shaking her head. "Looked to me like she'd come home and changed into something more comfortable. Probably had a headache and took the painkillers out of her purse, which is still sitting open on the table."

"10:25." Howdy popped back in with the news.

I ran my fingers through my hair, my earlier resolve crumbling. "This isn't good. This means Cleo didn't just up and leave. Something else happened. I'll tell Zack about this at karaoke tonight. At least he won't be surprised by the source of my information."

Iris clapped her spectral hands together. "Ooh, karaoke! Can we come?"

I smiled despite myself. "I don't see how I can stop you." I'm a ghost whisperer, not a ghost wrangler.

CHAPTER THIRTEEN

*T*he moment we stepped into The Rusty Anchor, a wall of sound hit me. Laughter, chatter, and the less-than-dulcet tones of someone murdering "Sweet Caroline." I squeezed Drew's hand, my earlier worries momentarily pushed aside by the infectious energy.

"Everly! Drew!" Gustavia's voice cut through the cacophony. She came up from the side, hugged me, and then led us to a table near the front, her smile as bright as her bedazzled top. "You made it!"

I slid into a chair facing the stage, Drew's arm settling comfortably around my shoulders. "Wouldn't miss it for the world," I said, eyeing the lyric screen with mock suspicion. "As long as no one expects me to sing."

Zack, nursing a beer, leaned in. "Come on, Everly. Where's your sense of adventure?"

I snorted. "Safely tucked away with my dignity, thanks."

The table erupted in laughter, and I felt a warmth that had nothing to do with the crowded bar. These were good people. The kind that made you feel safe and welcome from the start—almost like family. Even with the nagging worry about Cleo, I let myself be swept up in the moment.

We laughed and listened to good and bad singers until Gustavia nudged Julie with her elbow. "Shall we?"

"Why, yes. I think we shall." Julie rose. As if on cue, Kat and Amethyst stood as well.

The entire bar erupted. Chanting and clapping accompanied the four women to the stage. I sat back and prepared to enjoy the show until Amethyst whirled around. The next thing I knew, she had me by the arm, and I was halfway to the stage. I'm not sure how she managed to get me out of my seat. I think she might be magic.

Trying to tug my arm away, I leaned in and said in her ear, "I don't sing."

"Everyone sings, but you don't need to. You can be our backup dancer. Don't tell me you can't dance. You've got former cheerleader written all over you."

"Fine." I gave in. "I'll dance, but that's it."

Words cannot describe my surprise when the backup band vacated the stage, and my companions took their places. The tambourine Kat handed me might as well have been a snake the way I held it.

"Don't worry, you'll have fun. Just keep the beat, and you'll be fine," she assured me as she took her place at the keyboard. Amethyst nearly disappeared behind the massive set of drums while Gustavia slipped a guitar strap over her head. It seemed that Julie was the bass player and the lead singer.

I felt like a duck swimming in a pond full of swans as Amethyst counted down the beat. Still, what faces I could see in the crowd seemed encouraging, so when they launched into "Since U Been Gone" by Kelly Clarkson, I pretended I had the first clue what I was doing and played along.

Despite my misgivings, I had a blast. Toward the end of the second encore, Julie handed the bass off to its owner so she could concentrate on her singing and dance with me. By then, I felt comfortable enough that when she stuck the mic in my face, I belted out the last two lines of "I Love Rock and Roll" with her.

"Okay, that was fun," I admitted when, flushed and energized, we returned to our seats amid thunderous applause. "Do you do this every week?"

"Once a month, anyway," Gustavia winked at me. "You're welcome to join anytime."

"I guess I'm up next," Drew said, pointing to the copy of the song list. Every table had one.

I nudged him playfully. "You don't have to. What I did can barely be described as singing. You're off the hook so long as you remember I was the bigger person."

Drew's eyes twinkled with mischief. "Oh ye of little faith," he said, standing up. "Prepare to be amazed, Mrs. Parker."

"By all means, Mr. Parker."

As he made his way to the stage, I turned to Zack, my voice lowering. "Hey, I need to talk to you about Cleo. There's something—"

But the words died in my throat as the opening chords of "Can't Help Falling in Love" filled the air. I spun around, my jaw dropping as Drew's rich, velvety voice caressed the lyrics.

"Whoa," I whispered, unable to tear my eyes away from my husband. The man I thought I knew everything about suddenly revealed a whole new side of himself. And I liked it.

As Drew crooned the final notes, the bar erupted in applause. He gave a little bow, his eyes finding mine in the crowd. The look he gave me sent electric sparks shooting across my skin.

He sauntered back to our table, grinning. I pulled him down for a kiss, ignoring the catcalls from our friends. "Why didn't I know you could sing like that?" I asked, genuinely curious.

Drew shrugged, a faint blush coloring his cheeks. "One of my many hidden talents."

As our friends showered Drew with praise, I felt a familiar tug at my heart. This man never ceased to surprise me, and I loved him all the more for it. We had a lifetime ahead of us. Plenty of time for me to discover the rest of his secrets.

I was about to resume my conversation with Zack when something across the room caught my eye. My jaw dropped faster than a ghost through floorboards.

"Don't look, but Sophia's here," I whispered, nudging Drew. He looked because that's what people do when you tell them not to.

There she was, in the last place I expected to see her— practically glued to Chase's side, her hand resting on his arm while she laughed at something he said. Chase, for his part, looked caught between discomfort and politeness, his eyes darting around the room as if searching for an escape route.

"Well, that's...unexpected," Drew murmured, his eyebrows raised.

Watching her, my eyes narrowed. "She has to know he's still hung up on Cleo. Can't she see he's not into her?"

As if the scene wasn't bizarre enough, my gaze shifted several feet to the left and landed on Jake engaged in an intense discussion with a tall, stern-looking man in a crisp suit that screamed, 'I don't karaoke.'

"And who's Mr. Serious talking to Jake?" I wondered aloud.

Drew leaned in, his breath tickling my ear. "You know, for someone who said she wasn't going to get involved, you're awfully interested in everyone's business."

My cheeks flushed. "Do you want Iris standing over our bed every night? Because I don't."

"She can watch if she wants to," Drew chuckled. "It won't cramp my style one bit."

It would certainly cramp mine.

I tried to focus on our friends' animated chatter, but my eyes drifted back to the odd tableau across the room. Sophia's overly enthusiastic gestures, Chase's awkward stance, Jake's tense shoulders, and the way he kept shaking his head—it was like watching a real-life soap opera unfold.

"Weren't the ghosts supposed to be here?" I scanned

the room but didn't see them. "They'd make perfect spies."

Silly ghosts. Always hanging around when you didn't want them but nowhere to be found when they could be useful. Chase had shrugged Sophia off, and Jake had gone by the time Iris and her cohorts showed up. Too little, too late.

The ghosts stood in the back, but I felt Iris watching me the entire time. And so, during the band's next break, Drew and I followed Zack to the bar and waited while, as designated driver, he ordered a soft drink.

"I need to talk to you about Cleo Martin. You know she's missing, right?"

"Yes. I know she wasn't at her truck today. Unfortunately, until someone files a report, I can't do anything in an official capacity other than keep an eye out for anything strange."

"Speaking of strange." I steeled myself for the conversation ahead by telling myself I hadn't done anything wrong. "I've got some ghostly gossip that has to do with Cleo and her cabin."

"Ghostly gossip?" Zack's eyebrows shot up. "What does that even mean?"

Given his wife's unique abilities, Zack wasn't surprised to learn that his town was haunted by a benevolent, albeit nosy, trio of ghosts.

"Relax, Officer Roman," I said, holding up both hands. "I didn't ask them to go snooping. One of them's a relative of Cleo's, so my incorporeal friends took it upon themselves to do a little recon."

He pinched the bridge of his nose, a mix of exasperation and resignation washing over his face. "Of course they did. Why am I not surprised?"

I couldn't help but smirk. "Hey, you married a medium. Supernatural shenanigans come with the territory."

"Don't remind me," Zack muttered, but I caught the hint of a smile. "All right. Lay it on me. What did our ghostly informants uncover?"

As I relayed the information, I watched Zack's face. His professional mask slipped on, but I could see the wheels turning behind his eyes. Part of me wanted to apologize for the paranormal interference, but honestly? If it helped find Cleo, I wasn't about to look a gift ghost in the mouth.

"I know it's not admissible evidence," I finished, "but I thought you should know."

Zack sighed, running a hand through his hair. "I appreciate the information, Everly. I just wish your spectral friends would leave the investigating to the professionals."

I snorted. "Yeah, good luck with that. Telling ghosts not to be nosy is like asking water not to be wet. At least they didn't leave fingerprints around to contaminate the scene."

"Fair point," he conceded, a wry smile tugging at his lips. "I suppose I should be grateful they're on our side."

"Iris is determined to do her part to save Cleo. Since

you probably can't accept a police report from a ghost, she's decided her part includes blackmailing me into helping her any way I can."

Zack's expression sobered. "Blackmail is a crime."

"You want to arrest a ghost, be my guest. In the meantime, I'm just passing on what they told me. It's concerning, isn't it? Cleo wouldn't leave without her phone. Or her purse. It has to mean something. At least enough to bypass the...what is it? Forty-eight hour waiting period."

"That's a fallacy perpetuated by TV shows and movies. When there's compelling evidence, a person can be declared missing immediately. Unfortunately, Cleo's parents don't live in town anymore. The Martins moved two, maybe three years ago. I think they're in Ogunquit now."

"What happens next?"

Zack accepted his order from the bartender, and we headed back to the table, his gaze settling on Kat. "I'll contact her family and use whatever means I have at my disposal to find her. Lousy way to spend a honeymoon."

Overhearing the tail end of our conversation, Kat offered a warm smile. "Speaking of your honeymoon, have you decided what to wear for your photoshoot?"

I groaned dramatically. "Don't remind me. I only brought two white, or even white adjacent, articles of clothing with me. A battered old T-shirt I throw over my swimsuit sometimes and a shorty nightgown with hearts and kisses sprinkled over it. My options are 'shipwreck survivor' or 'pajama party gone wrong.' Neither exactly screams 'romantic moment in the mist.'"

"Oh honey," Gustavia said, her eyes sparkling with mischief, "we can't have that! You need something fabulous!"

Julie snorted. "Preferably something that won't blind me through the camera lens."

"You know what this means?" Kat clapped her hands and sang out, "Shopping trip! Tomorrow morning good for you? I don't have any readings lined up, so I'm free."

"Can I come, too?" Gustavia bounced in her seat. "I can write later in the day."

"I have proofs to send out to a client, but I can do that tonight and clear my morning as well," Julie said.

"You're not going without me," Amethyst said, "I'm free tomorrow. We'll hit the consignment shop in town. They have the most amazing vintage pieces."

As much as I'm not a fan of clothes shopping, their enthusiasm was infectious. Maybe a little retail therapy was exactly what I needed to take my mind off missing persons and meddling ghosts. Zack was on the job now. I could let Cleo be his problem.

"All right," I conceded, raising my hands in mock surrender. "I submit to your superior fashion wisdom. But I'm warning you now—I have no problem with vintage, but if anyone tries to get me into a muumuu, a jumpsuit, or a sweater vest, I'm calling the whole thing off."

"Don't worry, Ev," Julie grinned, patting my arm.

"We'll find you something that says 'blissfully wedded' without veering into 'fashion disaster.'"

I chuckled, a mix of excitement and trepidation bubbling in my chest. "I should probably warn you that no matter what I wear, the lake mist will turn my hair into something resembling a frightened porcupine."

Undaunted, Kat tilted her head and wrinkled her nose as she looked at me. "I think you should lean into it. Go all curly and wild. It'll be romantic."

"While you're out playing dress up," Zack added, his tone shifting the conversation to serious, "In my capacity as a concerned citizen, I'm following up on the theory that Cleo Martin might have gone into the water."

My stomach twisted. I'd known it was serious, but hearing the possibility of her death stated so bluntly made it all too real. "Do you think that's what happened?"

"It's one possibility. I've tapped a few of the locals with boats to do a surface scan while I dive the cove. It's just me, so it'll take a while."

"You got gear? I'll dive for you." Drew offered to help.

"Gear, I've got. But since this could become an official search by then, I'd need someone certified for search and rescue," Zack said, regret tugging at the corner of his mouth.

Drew raised his hand. "Right here. Certified through the military, and I've kept up my credentials since getting out."

"You got any time tomorrow, Finn?" Reid said. "I don't

dive, but I can drive a boat, and two sets of eyes are better than one."

"I was supposed to install a new door at the VFW, but I can put it off."

As we finalized plans for the next day, part of me genuinely looked forward to some carefree time with the women. Another part dreaded the inevitable fashion show I assumed would be part of my shopping experience.

And a third part worried about Cleo and what Drew might find. It was looking more and more like our honeymoon would include a side of mystery—and not one that involved how many margaritas I could drink before Drew had to carry me to bed. I suppose I shouldn't have been surprised.

CHAPTER FOURTEEN

*T*he following day dawned bright and early—too early if you asked me. I groaned as Drew's alarm chirped, disturbing my blissful slumber.

"Morning," Drew murmured, pressing a kiss to my forehead. "Zack should be here soon. Molly's had her breakfast and a good run, so she should be all set until one of us gets back."

I cracked open an eye, taking in his sober expression. "You'll be careful, won't you?"

He nodded, already dressed in the swim trunks he'd wear under a wet suit. "Always. Have fun shopping. Try not to worry, okay?"

"No promises," I mumbled.

Reluctantly, I dragged myself from the comfort of our bed, eyeing my reflection in the mirror with trepidation. As predicted, my hair had staged a full-scale rebellion overnight. Fantastic start to what promised to be an interesting day.

Not long after I'd eaten and had my coffee, a rapid series of knocks at the door announced the arrival of my enthusiastic shopping squad. I took a deep breath, steeling myself for the whirlwind to come. "Here we go," I muttered to Molly, who danced at my feet and reached for the doorknob. "Into the fashion fray."

Lively chatter on the ride into town helped dispel thoughts of what Drew might discover if Cleo had somehow managed to end up at the bottom of the lake. But I lost my breath when we walked into Oakville's best consignment shop and saw the Technicolor explosion of vintage finds. This was the place where questionable fashion choices went to live, but I hoped to find a few gems in the mix.

"Well," I mused, lifting a brow at a neon green sequined jumpsuit, "if we're going for 'blinding the competition,' I think we've found our winner."

"I'd wear that," Gustavia fingered the material, then checked the size. "Too small."

"Thank you, guardian angels of fashion," Julie muttered.

"I heard that," Gustavia said, giving Julie a mock glare.

Kat's eyes lit up as she darted between racks. "What was it you said you didn't want?" She held up a floral muumuu that looked like it had been fashioned from my grandmother's curtains.

I raised an eyebrow. "To not camouflage myself as a sofa."

Julie snorted, already arm-deep in a bin of scarves. "Come on, where's your sense of adventure?"

"I think I left it back in bed with my dignity," I muttered, smiling at their enthusiasm.

Amethyst emerged from behind a mannequin, brandishing what appeared to be a leather miniskirt. "Now, this has potential!"

I eyed it skeptically. "For whom, exactly? Biker chic isn't really my style."

"Don't knock it 'til you've tried it," Gustavia said, adding it to the growing pile in my arms.

As they herded me toward the changing rooms, I caught sight of my reflection. My hair, still in open rebellion, now sported a jaunty feather clip courtesy of Julie, who treated me to a mischievous grin.

"I draw the line at feathers." My protest was weak, at best.

"You sure do have a lot of lines," Julie said.

"Not today!" Kat declared, shoving me gently toward a curtained cubicle. "Only fabulous transformations. Try the leather skirt with that vintage top."

"It has shoulder pads."

"I know."

I sighed dramatically but couldn't keep the smile from my face. "Fine, but if I come out looking like a rejected extra from an '80s music video, I'm blaming all of you."

The laughter that echoed through the store warmed my heart, even as I eyed the leather skirt with trepidation. This was going to be one for the books—assuming I survived it.

Shaking my head, I stepped out from behind the curtain, looking exactly as ridiculous as I'd expected. The skirt barely covered enough thigh to be considered fit for public consumption, while the aforementioned shoulder pads turned my upper silhouette into a big old box.

"That is not cute," Kat said, shaking her head when she saw me.

"You think?"

Gustavia swung around the corner and into my line of vision, wearing a faux fur coat in neon pink. I should not have been surprised. "Try the prom dress next," she ordered before disappearing again.

The prom dress had poofy sleeves, which Julie declared wrong on all counts. I wholeheartedly agreed and shucked it off my body as quickly as possible before moving on to the next item. I'm not sure how many outfits I tried on after that. The next hour was a blur.

"I think that will do it," Amethyst finally said, dragging me to the counter to pay for my purchases, which included two dresses, white jeans, a blouse with long ruffled sleeves Kat had declared the find of the day, and an item Gustavia was calling a shawl, but looked more like a tablecloth to me. For Drew, we'd picked out jeans bleached to a blue so pale it was nearly white, a linen tunic, and a crisp button-down shirt.

As we exited the store, our arms laden with outfits for the photo shoot, Amethyst turned left while the rest of us headed toward the car.

"I think someone's trying to tell us something," Kat said with a grin.

"Something smells amazing," Amethyst called back over her shoulder.

Julie's eyes lit up. "Food truck lunch. I'm in."

My thoughts immediately went to Cleo.

"Good idea," I said, trying to keep my tone light. "I wonder if there's any news about Cleo."

We stashed our bags, then followed the aromas of sizzling meat and exotic spices to the food truck area. Ollie was still working out of the tent since his truck wasn't ready yet. The line for his pizza snaked around the corner.

I scanned the area, hoping to glimpse Cleo's distinctive fashion sense or hear her enthusiastic voice calling out to potential customers. But her truck stood silent. Shuttered, still.

"Still no sign of her," I murmured, more to myself than anyone else.

Kat squeezed my arm. "I'm not sensing her in spirit if that helps."

I nodded because it did. A little. "I haven't seen her, either. I'm trying to take that as a good sign."

"Everly!" I cringed at the sound of Tawny's voice and prepared myself for the inevitable as she launched herself at me and flung her arms around my neck. "I'm devastated. Simply devastated."

"This is Tawny," I introduced her to the group before I realized that, being local, my companions probably already knew her. "She's a fan of Cleo's." Also unnecessary since she wore a tee emblazoned with the words *Justice for Cleo* across the front. It had only been a day and a half. Was this already a thing?

"A bunch of the Collective are planning to join up with some of us locals and search for her later."

"The Collective?" I asked before I could stop myself.

"The Cleo Collective. It's what we call ourselves. You should come." Tawny grabbed my hand and would have dragged me away if I hadn't dug in my heels. "I'm asking everyone to help. Even the other vendors. Say you'll come."

"I'm sorry, Tawny. I'm here with friends. I can't just take off. You understand."

Given the attempt to burn me to death with only a look, I concluded she did not.

"I understand you don't care enough about Cleo to help find her. That's just pathetic. Are you jealous? That's the only reason I can see why you wouldn't at least try."

Behind me, I heard Gustavia let out a quiet snort.

"Even her rivals have agreed to help." Tawny waved a hand toward Tommy's truck. "Mr. O'Malley has offered to drive us to Lookout Point in the shuttle. But I guess you don't care about that, either."

Turning on her heel, Tawny flounced off toward Tommy's truck, ostensibly to finalize plans for their trip.

"That was—"

"Dramatic," Gustavia finished my sentence. "But Tawny idles at drama, so it's typical of her. Not that I'm making light of Cleo's disappearance. Just Tawny's reaction."

"Let's eat, and then we'll go see if the guys found anything," Amethyst said.

Unable to decide on just one, we split up and stood in the various lines to sample food from each truck. "Vegetarian pizza for me, please," Gustavia reminded Amethyst, who waggled her fingers over her shoulder as she walked toward the tent.

Curious to see what she had to say for herself, I smiled at Sofia when I finally made it up to her window. "Business looks good today." She did not smile back.

"It's because of Cleo. A bunch of her followers showed up this morning. They think we've done something to her, so they're buying our food, doing things to make it look horrible, and posting nasty reviews on their social media accounts. It's awful."

Shocked, I spun to watch a young woman seated at a nearby table pull out several hairs and plant one in her pastry while her two friends egged her on.

"That's absolutely horrible," I said, pulling out my phone and quickly recording them in the act. I'd intended to nudge Sofia into a conversation about Chase, hoping to clarify what I'd seen happening between them the night before, but it didn't seem like the right time.

"I'm considering pulling out of the competition," she admitted. "I only do these because they're fun. This is definitely *not*. Between people's trucks being sabotaged and Cleo going missing, I don't want to be here anymore. Did you hear the Sheriff thinks she might have drowned in the lake?"

"I did. Drew's out diving with him right now. He's certified for search and rescue."

Sophia shuddered as she filled a bag with sweet treats I no longer had a taste for. "I hope they don't find her," she said. "Well, I hope they do, but not like that."

Nodding my agreement, I paid for the pastries and rejoined my friends. Sophia's news had cast a pall over my mood—one that enjoying a meal in good company only partially lifted.

"This pizza is incredible," Gustavia folded a slice, bit in, closed her eyes to savor the tastes and textures, then tore off a piece and handed it to me to taste. "Who would have thought to put figs and grilled eggplant together?"

It was great pizza, but the crust texture wasn't quite the same as with his regular oven. I'd still rank it among the best pizza I'd ever eaten, but it wasn't up to Ollie's regular standard.

"Ollie's a genius, but so is Tommy. These burnt ends are the best I've ever had," I said. "I probably should have followed Julie's example and gone with a salad, though."

"Can you imagine if they hooked up and made a burnt ends pizza?" Julie wondered as she popped a forkful of roasted beet into her mouth.

Reaching over, Amethyst snagged a piece off Gustavia's plate, picked off the eggplant, and held the slice out to me. "End me," she said, nodding toward my plate. Shrugging, I obliged, deposited hunks of meat on top, and watched her bite in. "So good."

She passed the slice around, and those who tried it were compelled to agree.

Once we finished eating, we meandered toward the

judging tent, the white canvas structure a hub of activity and hushed conversations.

"Let's watch for a bit," I suggested, gesturing to a spot near the tent's entrance. "I'm curious to see who's winning."

According to the judging roster, Ollie had lost his top standing. Tommy's barbecue now held the lead, pushing Ollie to second place. Maybe the ovens were the reason, but Tommy's food was excellent, so maybe not. Sophia's pastries and breakfast offerings were in third place, followed by Jake's salads in a close fourth. Sadly, Cleo's tacos were now dead last.

As we settled near the back, snatches of conversation drifted our way. A pair of women with matching sun visors leaned close, their voices carrying over the din despite their attempts at discretion.

"I heard Cleo was sleeping with two of the other vendors," one whispered, eyes wide. "And her ex followed her here to try and get back together. Can you imagine? Talk about spicing up the competition!"

I nearly choked on my brownie. "That's ridiculous," I muttered to Kat, who sat beside me. "Tommy and Ollie both disliked her, leaving Jake and Sophia. From what I saw last night, Sophia's into men. Chase, in particular, and Jake barely talks to anyone. He doesn't strike me as Cleo's type. Or, she his."

Across from me, Gustavia shrugged, a knowing smile on her lips. "Could be he presented a challenge. Or a way to spite her ex. "

"I honestly don't think she cared enough to bother. Or at least, that's how it looked to me."

The conversation at the other table continued when a lanky man in a Bite Me t-shirt said, "Have you noticed the pickpocketing stopped once she'd gone? Maybe she skipped town with everyone's wallets!"

I'd forgotten about that. Poor Zack. The competition had put a lot on his plate, and not just foodwise.

I felt my eyebrows climb toward my hairline and quickly pulled them back down. The accusation seemed absurd. How could Cleo have been picking pockets while serving tacos from her truck? The short answer was—she couldn't. The thief must have moved on. The timing was nothing more than a coincidence.

She probably hadn't been picked up by aliens or hauled off to Facebook jail, which wasn't even a real thing, but those were two more speculated possibilities.

"People talk too much," Amethyst said, her tone carrying disgust. "And mostly out of their butts."

As we piled into Kat's SUV for the drive home, my mind was a whirlwind of conflicting thoughts. I turned to Kat, unable to contain my curiosity any longer.

"So, about your psychic abilities," I attempted to sound casual. "Didn't you tell me you use it sometimes to help Zack with police cases? Like, say, finding missing people?"

Kat's eyes met mine in the rearview mirror. "Sometimes," she admitted. "But only when he asks. He likes to exhaust traditional methods first."

"But why not use every tool at your disposal? Zack seems like the open-minded type." When I told him about the ghostly trio, he hadn't batted an eyelash.

Kat sighed, her fingers tapping a gentle rhythm on the steering wheel. "It's complicated. He worries that relying on my talents might blur the lines between the letter of the law and what's convenient."

"That makes sense, I suppose. I've learned more about the law and chain of evidence than I ever expected to know over the past year or so."

"Zack has a certain level of sensitivity, too. He calls it intuition, but it's more than that. If I don't trust and respect his process, how can I expect him to trust and respect mine? But if he asks, I'll help. I always do."

As we drove past the sparkling lake, I couldn't shake the feeling that we were missing something crucial. The gossip, the disappearances, the thefts swirled together in my mind like a murky soup of mystery. And despite my best intentions, I was already more than knee-deep in it.

The afternoon sun glinted off the lake's surface, dazzling my eyes. We'd been boating and swimming in that water for days, but knowing the placid lake could have swallowed Cleo whole made it seem sinister despite its beauty.

"I hope the guys found something," Julie muttered, voicing what we were all thinking when we pulled up next to Jack's cruiser.

"I hope they didn't," Gustavia said. "This is a case of no news is good news, right?"

After stashing the bags in the bedroom, we gravitated toward the big windows overlooking the lake.

As if summoned by my thoughts, Drew's blond head broke the surface near the dock. He climbed up the ladder in his rash guard and trunks, looking like some romance novel Adonis. If the situation hadn't been so serious, I might have wolf-whistled.

"That one packs a punch," Amethyst said, then laughed when her friends shushed her. "I'm only looking."

Zack came out of the water, ignored the ladder, hoisted himself onto the dock, and accepted Drew's hand-up.

"Come on," I said, leading the way to the door. "Let's see what they've found."

"Anything?" I called, already knowing the answer from the set of Drew's shoulders. I handed him a towel, my fingers lingering on his momentarily. His skin held a chill from the cooler water at the lake's depths, and I suppressed a shiver that had nothing to do with the temperature.

He shook his head, water droplets flying from his slicked-back hair. "Nothing." Noting my forced smile, he said, "But that's a good thing. Means she might still be alive."

I bit my lip and nodded my head. The mystery of Cleo's disappearance seemed to deepen with each passing hour. Where could she have gone?

We lapsed into an uneasy silence, broken only by the

lapping of waves against the dock and the distant hum of boat engines.

"I don't get it." Julie finally shook her head. "How can someone just vanish without a trace?"

Before anyone could answer, the sound of an approaching boat caught our attention. I squinted against the late afternoon sun. A red runabout skimmed the water's surface, heading straight for our dock. As it drew closer, I recognized Reid's dark hair, Tyler's easy posture, and Finn at the helm, their faces grim with what couldn't be good news.

The boat slowed as it approached, and Tyler expertly maneuvered it alongside the dock. Reid tossed us a rope, which Zack caught and secured.

"You found her?"

Tyler ran a hand through his dark hair, frustration evident in every line of his body. "We didn't." He turned to Zack and named off a few of the boaters who had joined the search. "Between us, we covered damn near every inch of the lake, talked to pleasure boaters and anyone within yelling distance on the shore. No one's seen a trace of Cleo."

Reid turned to Zack, his gray eyes serious. "What about you?"

"She's not in the cove." Zack slipped off his tanks, his brow furrowed. "It doesn't make sense. If she'd drowned, we should have found...something by now."

Her bloated corpse is what he meant, but he was trying to spare us the visual. Picturing Cleo's vibrant smile, her infectious laugh, and the thought of her lying cold and lifeless at the bottom of the lake made my stomach churn.

"If I had something of hers, I'd try to tune in," Kat offered, but Zack shook his head.

"Not yet."

I closed my eyes, reaching out with my senses in case I might catch a glimpse of Cleo's spirit. But there was nothing—no whisper, no flicker of otherworldly energy. Just the lapping of the waves against the dock and the faint calls of birds in the distance.

"I'm not getting any sense of her, either," I said as a blur of brown and white fur darted past me, nearly knocking me off balance. "Whoa, Prescott!" I yelped, steadying myself against Drew.

The beagle bypassed Molly, who'd run to meet him, and aimed straight for our rental boat again as if it were some form of doggy ambrosia.

"He sure seems to love that boat," I breathed, torn between amusement and concern.

Drew's arm slipped around my waist. "We'll have to take him for a ride," he murmured.

I leaned into him, grateful for his solid presence, and watched Chase dash across the yard, slightly out of breath.

"Sorry. He got away from me again." He padded down the dock, snapped a leash onto Prescott's collar, and glanced at the diving gear. "What's going on?"

"When someone goes missing around here," Zack

explained, "we generally check the lake. It's all too easy to go for a swim and get in trouble."

"At night? In pond water by herself? Not a chance." Chase shook his head. "Cleo's strictly a pool person. No way she'd swim in the same water with fish."

Unless someone helped her into the water, I thought but didn't say out loud. "They didn't find her if that makes you feel better."

"It doesn't." Chased turned to Zack. "And neither does watching you waste a day looking for her in the last place she'd be."

I watched Prescott continue his frantic investigation of the boat, my mind working through the order of events.

"Chase," I said slowly, turning to face him. "Are you absolutely certain she was in her cabin last night?"

Chase's brow furrowed, his casual demeanor slipping. "Yeah, I'm sure. They all came back in the shuttle. Everyone went inside to shower and change like always. Tommy lit the fire because it wasn't raining, and one by one, they came out to sit and have a drink—except for Jake. He doesn't socialize."

"Your cabin is nearest the driveway. Would you hear if a car like yours pulled up?" Drew asked his arm still protectively around my waist. Chase drove an electric car that could hardly be heard at low speeds. Someone else in town might have one.

"Tires still make noise on gravel roads." His tone indicated it was a stupid question. "I can hear Sophia's bike when she rides out in the morning. I'd have heard a car. You probably would, too."

"If we'd have been here—in the bedroom with the windows open, maybe," Drew responded. "We can hear some—not all—of what goes on next door. Not that we've been eavesdropping. Much."

Zack ran a hand through his hair in frustration, then pointed out, "Cleo could have walked far enough to catch a ride without anyone knowing."

"Why would she need to sneak away? She's a grown woman who does what she wants." The implication being that what she wanted hadn't been what Chase wanted, but we already knew that.

"Well, fairies didn't take her up," Amethyst said. Looking at her—pixie-sized with purple hair, wearing a gauzy number also in...you guessed it...her signature purple, you might take her for the queen of fairies and, therefore, an authority on the subject.

Chase didn't see her that way.

"Something happened to her. I don't know how or why, but that's not my job." Emotion choked his voice when he gave Zack a pained look and pointed to the diving gear. "It's yours, and that's not how to do it."

"Come on, Prescott." Chase clipped on the dog's leash, tugged gently to get him to stop sniffing the boat, and walked away. His slumped shoulders and the way he hung his head painted a picture of a disheartened man.

"If he had anything to do with Cleo's disappearance, I'd eat a hamburger," Gustavia declared. "He loves her."

"That's a strong statement from an avowed vegetarian," Zack teased his sister, then turned serious. "But people do horrible things to those they profess to love. If they didn't, I wouldn't have a job."

And I wouldn't have had to track down several killers. I only hoped I wouldn't have to add Cleo to my ghost roster before the week was out.

CHAPTER FIFTEEN

*T*he insistent buzz of my phone alarm dragged me from a fitful sleep. I groaned and fumbled to silence it, then cracked open one eye. The soft light of dawn had barely begun to filter through the curtains. Beside me, Drew stirred, his arm tightening around my waist.

"Is it morning already?" I mumbled, my voice thick with sleep. We'd planned to go to bed early the night before, but one thing led to another, and we'd stayed up later than we should.

Drew chuckled, pressing a kiss to my shoulder. "Afraid so, supermodel. Rise and shine."

I rolled my eyes but couldn't suppress a smile. "I could hate you for waking up nearly camera-ready. You know, if I didn't love you so much."

How the man could roll out of bed fully alert, run his hands through his hair, and end up looking hot was both a blessing and an annoyance to me.

"Your glam squad will be here any minute," he said on his way to the bathroom.

As if on cue, a cheerful knock echoed from downstairs, followed by an enthusiastic bark from Molly. Hearing bright voices on the other side of the door, I groaned again. "How are they so peppy this early?

Drew chuckled, planting a kiss on my forehead. "Coffee, I'm guessing. Lots of it."

I swung my legs out of bed, my stomach doing a little flip of excitement and nerves. "Let's go greet them before they decide to come up here and drag us out."

We stumbled downstairs to let them in. While my brain struggled to work, Julie, Kat, Gustavia, and Amethyst bustled around the kitchen, armed with too many makeup and garment bags. The rich aroma of fresh coffee filled the air.

"There's our star!" Julie exclaimed, thrusting a steaming mug into my hands. "Courtesy of Sophia's food truck. We thought it would help get you camera-ready."

I laughed, returning the hug. "As ready as I'll ever be, I guess."

"Being the center of attention is fun, and don't you forget it," Gustavia winked, unpacking an alarming array of hair tools and ignoring my quirked brow.

Amethyst flipped open the top of a professional-looking makeup case. "Don't worry, we'll make sure you look fabulous. Good thing we brought product to tame that bedhead, though."

"Hey!" I protested, self-consciously patting curls that, to their detriment and mine, hadn't seen a blow dryer in days.

Kat stepped in, ever the peacemaker. "Ignore her, Everly. You look lovely. Now, let's get started, shall we?"

"So," I ventured as Gustavia rubbed something into my hair, her fingertips soothing as they scraped along my scalp, "any news about—"

"Uh-uh," Julie cut me off gently. "Today, we focus on positive things. The rest can wait a few hours."

I sighed, knowing she was right. "Fine. Work your magic, then."

A half hour flew by in a whirlwind of mascara wands, hair sprays, and outfit changes. Laughter filled the room as we swapped stories and playfully bickered over color choices.

I caught Drew's eye while he watched the scene with amusement, sipping his coffee.

"Having fun there, spectator?" I called out.

He grinned. "Immensely. It's not every day I get to watch my wife being primped and preened like a show poodle."

I stuck my tongue out at him, making him laugh harder.

"Okay, people!" Julie called out, camera in hand. "Let's take this show outside. The light is perfect!"

As we filed out onto the deck overlooking the lake, I had to admit she was right. The early morning sun painted the sky in shades of gold and pink over the atmospheric mist still clinging to the lake's surface.

"Oh, this is going to be gorgeous," Julie murmured, her photographer's eye already framing shots.

For the next hour, Drew and I posed and smiled, trying to follow Julie's directions while also attempting to look natural. It was harder than I'd expected, so it took a while before I loosened up and began to have fun with it.

"That's perfect!" Gustavia cheered as I stood ankle-deep in water and struck what I hoped was a sultry pose while Drew stood next to me, his gaze trained on my face.

"Just Everly now," Julie directed, snapping away. "Give me mysterious! Now playful! Now... pretend you're a cat who just discovered opposable thumbs!"

I burst out laughing. "What kind of direction is that?"

"The kind that gets genuine smiles," Julie retorted and nodded to Gustavia, who nodded back in what could only be described as a conspiratorial manner.

"Almost done," Gustavia murmured as she guided me to stand in front of a sloped rock jutting out of the water. "If you could just bend forward."

I did as asked, then sputtered, "What the hell, Gustavia?" when she dumped water over my head.

"Don't move yet," she kept a hand on my back when I would have straightened up. "Wait until Julie says go, and then, in one swift motion, whip your head up and arch your back."

"I'll look like a drowned rat," I muttered as she splashed away from the shot and left me standing in a weird position, the ends of my hair dangling in the water until Julie yelled out my cue. Water arced and glittered in the sun that was just breaking through the mist.

"Got it. Gorgeous. Moving on."

Like smoke, Gustavia wafted up again.

"This is the next to last set, and they will be spectacular. Trust me!" She gave me no choice as she settled me on the rock, nudging my body into position, then directing Drew to stand in the knee-deep water, his face turned up toward me like a supplicant.

"That's perfect," Julie said, waving Gustavia back. "Okay, Everly. For this last set, I want you to be a mermaid luring Drew to his doom! You have all the power. You're everything he wants and needs. Feel his hunger. Glory in how much he wants you. And go."

I did my best. Drew, of course, nailed it.

"Less constipated, more come hither," Amethyst advised, earning herself a glare from me and a snort from Drew.

"Pissed off mermaid. I can work with that." Julie clicked off several shots and then asked me to try the sexy face again.

"One second," Drew held up a hand, then leaned and whispered something scandalous in my ear that did the trick.

"Hold," Julie shouted and clicked off a few more shots. "Okay, keep going. You're amazing."

"Nothing but the truth," Drew said, catching my gaze and holding it."

"Fantastic." Julie moved around to get a different angle. "Tilt your head to the right, Everly. Not that much. I just want you to cheat your face toward the sun. A bit more. Perfect. Now, look at me. Let your eyes pierce through the camera."

Julie kept up a running commentary as she continued

to shoot. "Okay, Drew. She's got you in her thrall. You're helplessly awash in her allure. Move toward her. Slower. Slower."

More clicking.

"Eyes on his, now, Everly. Give me intensity."

Julie's voice faded as my eyes locked on Drew's, and he continued forward, his hand on my foot, then my ankle, then my calf. He climbed that rock like a man compelled and laid his lips on mine.

"Okay, you two," Amethyst's voice cut through the fog that had filled me at the intensity of the kiss. "Get a room."

I blushed. But then, so did Drew, so we'll call that a wash.

For the final series, Julie called for an outfit change. Gustavia's eyes lit up with mischief. "Ooh, I have an idea! Drew, why don't you and Everly swap tops for the next set?"

I blinked, looking down at my flowing blouse. "What?"

Drew raised an eyebrow. "You want me to wear that?"

Gustavia nodded enthusiastically. "Yes! It'll be fun and edgy. Trust me, I have an eye for these things. Just the shirt, Drew. Everly. Lose the skirt, too."

Before I could protest, Drew was already unbuttoning his shirt. "Why not? I'm always up for a challenge."

As I swapped my outfit for nothing but his shirt, I had to laugh at the sight of Drew in my delicate blouse, the fabric straining across his broad shoulders.

"I don't know," I teased, striking a pose in his button-down that hung more than halfway down my bare thighs. "I think I wear it better."

Drew struck a pose, flexing dramatically and causing a button to pop off.

I doubled over laughing until my sides ached. "You look ridiculous!"

"He really does," Julie agreed. "Shirtless would be better."

"I beg to differ. I feel pretty," he declared but obligingly shucked off the wispy top, proving Julie right.

To my utter annoyance, she wouldn't let us look at any of the shots until she'd had a chance to edit them. Instead, we helped Julie pack up her equipment.

*B*ack inside the house, my phone buzzed so insistently that it vibrated across the table. I picked it up expecting a message from my mother but instead found a flurry of notifications from Cleo's social media accounts.

"Uh oh," I muttered, scrolling through the messages.

Drew paused mid-pose. "What's up, babe?"

"It's Cleo's followers again," I said, my shoulders going tense. "She has an army of them, and they're asking if I know why she's gone radio silent. They're upset because she hasn't posted."

Julie repacked her camera in its case, concern etching her features. "Won't be long before word starts to spread."

I chewed my lip, torn between not wanting to get involved with her online presence and deciding what information Cleo might wish her fans to know. "Should we say something?"

Before anyone could answer, a familiar voice called out, "Oh, honey! I hope I'm not interrupting!"

I turned to see our other neighbor, Effie Paulson, bustling toward the open doors, her floral dress billowing in the breeze and her oversized purse swinging from her arm. She carried a towering plate of what looked like blueberry muffins.

"Effie!" I called back, plastering on a smile. "You're not interrupting at all. We just finished a photo shoot."

Effie's eyes widened as she took in Drew's shirtless form. "Oh my, aren't you all having fun!" she exclaimed, her face turning pink. "I wanted to return something to you, and I thought I'd bring over some of my famous muffins."

She passed the plate to Drew, reached into her purse, and pulled out a small plastic disc. A closer look revealed a gambler's anonymous token.

"Sorry, Effie, but this isn't mine. Where did you find it?"

Her rosy flush deepened. "Oh, dear. I must confess I stepped out onto your dock earlier to watch the fun. Whatever must you think of me?"

I waved her protest away, handed back the chip, and offered her a smile. "I'm sorry, but this isn't mine or Drew's, and you're welcome to visit our dock anytime.

Though I can't complain if it got us a batch of guilt muffins."

Tickled, Effie smiled up at me. "They're not guilt muffins. Baking always cheers me up when I feel down, and I made extra."

I caught the flicker of concern in her eyes. "Is everything okay, Effie?" I asked gently.

She waved a hand dismissively. "Oh, it's nothing to worry about, dear. Carlton's just been feeling a bit under the weather since yesterday. But you know men, always making a fuss over a little tummyache."

I felt a pang of worry for the older man. "I'm sorry to hear that. Is there anything we can do to help?"

"Bless your heart," Effie said, patting my arm. "You're such a sweet girl. Now, why don't you introduce me to your friends?"

Halfway through the introductions, Molly let out two sharp, warning barks. Glancing out the window, I noted Zack's off-duty SUV pulling down the drive.

"Looks like you'll get to meet Kat's husband, too."

"Uh oh." Kat watched him alight from the vehicle. "He's got his official face on."

"Official face?" Effie's brow furrowed in confusion.

"Kat's married to the sheriff. He's investigating Cleo's disappearance," I explained.

Effie's eyes widened, her hand covered her mouth, and she headed toward the door that led out to the deck. "My lands, what a shame. I'll just get out of your way, then. He has more important things to worry about than meeting an old fusspot like me. I'll just slip out this way. Poor Carlton's probably worried about me by now, anyway."

Effie went faster than a woman her age should be able to move, just as Zack knocked on the front door. I barely had time to think her actions odd before Drew let him in.

"Any news?"

"Some," he said, pulling an evidence bag containing a cell phone from his pocket and handing it to Kat. "We officially opened Cleo's case this morning. I figured I'd get your take on this."

"Of course." She accepted the bag, sat at the table, and waited for the rest of us to follow suit.

I don't mind admitting that I found the process fascinating. She repeatedly turned the bag between her hands, her eyes unfocused. Moments passed, stretching out until the tension rose in me before she handed it back.

"She's not in spirit," Kat said, eliciting a collective sigh of relief. "But all I see are dark shadows. I wish I could be more helpful."

Zack laid his hand over hers and squeezed gently. "Knowing she's alive is more than I had a minute ago. "Don't beat yourself up over it."

"This is good news, though." Gustavia's smile hit lower on the wattage scale than usual. "It means there's hope."

"It does," Zack agreed, turning to me. "Maybe you and Drew can help me out with some information. What can you tell me about your neighbors? I know you weren't here the night of Cleo's disappearance, but it would help to understand the group dynamics outside of competition hours."

It took less than an hour to give him our impressions, during which Gustavia and Julie raided our fridge to put together a hodgepodge lunch.

"Your spook squad nailed the timeline for us," Zack said, "which I confirmed early this morning when the owners let me into Cleo's cabin. According to the text she sent at 10:26, she heard what she thought was a cat crying outside and went out to check."

I nodded. That tracked with what the ghosts had said.

"The other vendors claim not to have seen or heard anything at the time of the disappearance. Sophia Clark states she heard Tommy O'Malley tending his smoker, which he always did at that time. Then she spoke with her mother on the phone for at least half an hour."

"That plays. She told us she makes that call every night at around the same time," Drew said, nodding.

Zack tapped his fingertips on the table. "She also told us she heard a heated discussion earlier in the evening between Cleo and a man she assumed was Chase Williams."

"They were an item until a few weeks ago," I repeated what little I knew about their relationship. "It's funny he didn't mention they'd spoken when he was here yesterday, though."

"I'm looking into it," Zack confirmed. "Then, there's Jake Ryder, who says he was "kicking ass on Diablo IV" with a group of online gamers from eight until nearly midnight. According to several players, he was only away from his computer long enough for bathroom breaks and not at all from 10:15 to 11:00, which puts him out of the running. No compelling motive there, either. Same goes for Sophia. Both only met Cleo the first day of the competition, and if winning's behind it, they'd have had to take out more than just her."

Stopping in the middle of spreading butter on a chunk of bread, I waved my knife. "Ollie thought Cleo was the one who damaged his truck, so he might have wanted revenge."

"It's possible, and his alibi is weak. He says he was in bed by then."

Drew and I exchanged a look. "Makes sense," he said. "Ollie's an early riser who goes to bed before dark most nights. And he has a bad shoulder. I can't see him having the strength to overpower Cleo. She's not—if you'll forgive me, Amethyst-sized."

Amethyst did not seem offended.

"I still think we have to keep him on the list." I squinted, trying—and failing— to picture him in the role of kidnapper.

"They're all on the list until I've had time to double-check their alibis." Zack drained his glass of iced tea. "Plus, Cleo has ties to the community, which widens the scope, but so far, I've found nothing to indicate she had bad blood with anyone in town."

"Iris will be glad to hear that." As soon as it left my

lips, I realized I shouldn't have mentioned her name. She wasn't Beetlejuice or Bloody Mary, but saying any ghost's name was to be avoided if one didn't want a visit.

"Glad to hear what?" She popped in with her entourage not far behind. I sighed.

"Iris is here," I warned the living. "So are Edna and Howdy. Iris wants an update."

Kat glanced around the room like the others, not seeing anything since the ghosts hadn't tried to show themselves. "You really can't see them, can you?"

She shook her head.

"I had an idea about that." Not giving me any warning, Edna's hand landed on my shoulder. Or in it, to be specific. I shuddered at the sensation, then watched Kat do the same when Edna leaned across the table and completed the metaphysical connection between us by touching Kat's hand.

"Oh. Hello," Kat's gaze snapped to Edna's face. "You must be Iris."

"Edna." She made Iris and Howdy touch her, waiting until Kat's gaze fell on each one, then dropped her hands and stepped back. "Can you see us now?"

"I can. Sorry about the name mix-up." Kat turned to Iris. "You must be Iris, then."

"Right." A grin split Iris' face. "And this is Howdy."

Howdy bobbed his head. "Pleased to meetcha."

"What did you do?" I pinned Edna with a look. "Didn't we discuss my touching rules?"

She waved that away. "I used your energy and mine to

tune her in. We talked about this the other day. She just needed to change channels."

"Like a radio?" Kat's brow furrowed.

"Precisely." Edna bobbed her head. "She'll see us now. If she wants to, that is."

"You mean she'd have a choice?" I found the notion highly unfair since none of the ghosts who'd bugged me had given me a chance to say no.

Edna shrugged.

"Does it work with just you or with all ghosts?" I had questions.

"Just us, I expect. I can't say for sure, though. I'm not an expert on these things. It was just an idea I had. Looks like it worked, though."

Kat's gaze locked onto mine, her lips twisting into a wry smile that let me know I probably hadn't done her any favors. Too late now, I supposed.

"What's happening?" Gustavia's head swiveled between Kat and me. "I hate being left out."

I gave Iris a nod. When she showed herself, Gustavia's breath caught in her throat. "Oh, well then," she said. "Hi, I guess."

Julie sat mute while Amethyst mumbled something unintelligible.

"What's happening? What will I be glad to hear?" Iris prodded until I told her what we'd learned. By the time I got through it, her energy had already begun to flag, which told me Kat's retuning had taken a lot out of them, or worse, the three of them might have been up to something before they showed up here. I didn't get a chance to ask, though. Once she'd heard everything Zack had to say, she thanked me and said, "See you around. The three ghosts winked out as quickly as they'd come.

"That was..." words failed Zack.

"Yep," I said, knowing how he felt.

Later, once everyone had gone, my mom called to check in.

"We saw that missing woman from Oakville on the news. You're not tangled up in whatever's going on down there, are you? The news didn't mention anyone was dead." She didn't bother with the niceties, like asking if we were enjoying our honeymoon.

"We're fine, Mom. How are things there?" I didn't exactly lie, but I wanted to avoid the lecture I considered myself old enough to have outgrown. What she didn't know wouldn't hurt her.

"Oh," her voice went bright. Suspiciously so. "Everything's just fine here. Don't you worry about a thing, dear. I just want you to have fun and enjoy this special moment. Now, I really must be going. Have fun!"

She hung up without another word.

"Everything okay?" Drew asked.

"I think so." But I wasn't sure.

CHAPTER SIXTEEN

*T*he cool lake water enveloped me as I dove in, washing away the last traces of makeup and hairspray from the photo shoot. I surfaced with a splash, grinning at Drew as he swam toward me, his hair slicked back and glistening in the afternoon sun.

For a moment, all thoughts of missing persons and ghostly mysteries faded away, replaced by the simple joy of swimming with my husband on a perfect summer day.

Playing water fetch with Molly, the sight of the section of beach in front of the rental cabins caused a twinge of guilt. Here I was, enjoying myself while Cleo was still missing. The thought must have shown on my face because Drew squeezed my hand as we waded out of the water.

"Hey," he said softly. "It's okay to be happy right now. It doesn't mean you don't care what happens to Cleo."

I sighed, wringing out my hair. "I know, it's just—"

"It's just that you want to fix it. Whenever something goes wrong, that busy mind of yours automatically starts working on possible solutions."

"It's how I'm wired." That he noticed something about me that most people only understood when it benefited them was just one more reason I'd married him. "I'm not sure I can let it go. Cleo, I mean. I know solving mysteries was supposed to be off the table for our honeymoon, but I can't just turn my back on her."

"I'm not asking you to." He took hold of my arm, turned me into his embrace. "Not only because Iris wouldn't let you, but because I want to know what happened, too. Any ideas on what to do next?"

Since Molly still wanted to play, we settled side-by-side at the end of the dock and dangled our feet in the water.

"Chase would be the likeliest suspect given their current relationship status. Except, I can't see what he'd hope to gain by hurting or kidnapping her."

"A chance to plead his case, I suppose. I'll be honest, though, I don't see him as the type."

I threw the toy for Molly while I considered. "Besides, if he had her stashed away somewhere, wouldn't he be spending more time trying to convince her to take him back than moping around here and poking at Zack on her behalf? I just don't see it. Unless Kat's wrong, and Cleo's dead, which would change things."

"If she was, I assume she'd have shown up by now. Her ghost, I mean."

"Maybe. I mean, if he took her into the woods and killed her, she might not know how to get back to the cabins."

Drew called Molly out of the water. "It's a possibility. So's one of the other vendors getting her out of the way of the competition. Then, there's the local connection. Past issues, old enemies."

"Not according to Zack. Or Iris, for that matter. But we probably shouldn't discount her fans. If a group is willing to come here and deliberately trash the other vendor's reputations all over social media, one might have developed an unhealthy obsession."

Molly shook off, thankfully not all over us, and settled on the dock while we continued through the suspect list.

"That would turn the suspect pool into a suspect lake. You don't think that's the case, do you?" Drew asked.

Not according to my gut. "I don't. Not when you look at the timing and the whole picture. Two trucks were sabotaged before Cleo went missing. What if Tommy or Ollie caught Cleo in the act and made sure she couldn't do it again? Nothing else has happened since she disappeared."

Leaning back on his hands, Drew considered. "Sophia heard Tommy tending his smoker that night. Ollie's the only one without a solid alibi, but his shoulder? I don't see it."

I sighed. "I know. Jake would be physically capable, but according to Zack, his alibi holds. Plus, his salads are fantastic, but he hasn't placed above third in any of the categories. Cleo wouldn't be the only threat to his winning. With her gone, Tommy's in the lead. Especially when Ollie's pizza isn't as good since he's been using the temporary ovens. That leaves Sophia and Jake battling it out for the bottom of the pile. He'd have to take out Tommy and Ollie to stand a chance."

"Hence the sabotage?" Drew wondered.

"Possibly." I considered the implications for a moment. "If the competition figures into the motive, Jake has to be high on the suspect list. If it's love, as these things so often are, then we have to look at Chase. Money or power? That's where it gets really muddy since I don't have enough information to speculate."

Drawing his feet under him, Drew rose effortlessly and held out a hand to help me up.

"We'll figure it out. We always do." He drew me in for a hug, and I pressed my face to his chest.

"You know, I wasn't planning on getting married again. I'm glad I changed my mind."

"Me, too. In the interest of enjoying our honeymoon even amid mystery, how about a boat ride?"

I grinned, pushing sodden curls out of my face. "Now that sounds like a plan. Let me just do something about my hair first. 'Dried by boat wind' is not a good look on me."

"I disagree." He kissed me on the nose.

Minutes later, we were gliding across the glassy surface of the lake, Molly's ears flapping in the breeze and my hair tamed by the magic of the hair tie. All the tension from the past few days melted more with each passing ripple.

"You know," I mused, hanging my arm over the side and trailing my fingers through the cool water, "I could get used to this lake life. I see why Momma Wade practically lives up to camp during the summer."

Drew chuckled, his hand steady on the wheel. "I was just thinking the same thing. It'd be nice to have a little slice of paradise to escape to, wouldn't it?"

"Mmm," I hummed in agreement. "Just imagine: quiet mornings with coffee on the dock, afternoon swims, and evening bonfires under the stars."

"Don't forget the occasional ghost popping in for a chat," Drew teased, and I stuck my tongue out at him.

As we rounded a bend, Drew pointed to a weathered cabin nestled among the pines at the far end of the lake. "Now that's what I call remote. A bit too isolated for my tastes, though."

"Belongs to someone from out of state, now," Howdy said, making me jump since I hadn't felt his presence when he appeared in the boat. "But Patrick Boilard built that camp back in the sixties. My grandfather helped set the foundation."

"Good to know." Or entirely useless information, but I didn't want to hurt his feelings by pointing that out. I repeated his statement for Drew.

"You ain't fishing, are you?" Howdy scanned the boat for signs. "Wrong time of day."

"We're just out for a ride. But we should be heading back now. I'm getting hungry again."

Drew nodded, turning the boat around. "Your wish is my command, milady."

Howdy rode with us until he got distracted by two kids on jet skis and floated off to keep an eye on them.

Alone again, we spent the rest of the day thoroughly enjoying ourselves, so much so that later, when Tommy lit the nightly vendor campfire and the scent of mystery wafted over from the tiny cabin compound, I found myself tempted to join in.

"Want to take advantage of the open invitation and talk Tommy out of another glass of peach wine?" I posed the question to Drew, who shrugged affably.

"Might as well."

The crackling fire cast its heat over the little gathering as I settled next to Drew, his arm snaking around my waist. The scent of pine mixed with the aroma from Tommy's smoker created a quintessential summer evening atmosphere completely at odds with the strained tone of the group.

Barely talking, Ollie slumped in a camp chair, a beer cooler at his side, while Sophia sat as far from him as she could. Surprisingly, Jake chose to remain outside on this occasion rather than retreat to his cabin, but still sat well away from the fire.

Attempting to break the tension, I asked, "How'd the competition go today?"

Prescott whined from inside Chase's cabin at the sound of my voice. Glancing over, I noted both the shuttle and Chase's car were gone. I assumed Chase would be out looking for Cleo, but it wasn't like Tommy to be absent during fire time.

"I won," Sophia said, handing me a plate of something that looked like a cross between a cupcake and a pastry. "But it was dessert day. I made kouign-amann." She pronounced it queen uh-man.

I snagged one and bit into sticky, sugary heaven.

"I can see why you took the prize, Sophia. This might be the best thing I've eaten...today." I very nearly said ever, but realized that might not be the best comment to make in present company.

Ollie scoffed, taking a slow sip from his beer. "Don't let her fool you. That little pastry almost lost to my chocolate hazelnut calzone."

"Ollie gets cranky when it's past his bedtime," Sophia kept her tone mild, but the glitter in her eyes wasn't just from the firelight. "And when he doesn't win."

Ollie grunted but didn't respond. His mood had been unpredictable since Cleo's disappearance. Tonight, though, his discomfort was noticeable in how his knee bounced and his fingers twitched around his beer bottle.

Sophia shrugged. "People have a sweet tooth. What can I say?"

The splash of headlights put the conversation on pause. Tommy parked the shuttle in its customary spot and joined the group. Without asking, he nipped a bottle from Ollie's cooler.

"Find anything?" Ollie didn't seem bothered by the beer theft.

"Just a headache." He drained half the bottle in one gulp. "Not that I expected to. I don't think anyone will find Cleo sitting on a rock beside some old dirt road that isn't even on the map. Toss in a truckload of jabbering groupies and you've got yourself a recipe for disaster."

"Tommy offered to take some of Cleo's Collective out for a search," Sophia explained, though I'd figured that much out on my own.

"They should have postponed the competition when Cleo went missing." Jake finally found his voice, stringing together the longest sentence I'd heard him utter. "It doesn't feel right."

Two sentences in a row. Wow.

The comment sent a ripple through the group.

Ollie was the first to speak, and his voice was a little too even. "Maybe not. Or maybe she'd have been disqualified by now, anyway."

"What's that supposed to mean?" Tommy's bouncing knee stilled.

Ollie shrugged. "Just saying, some folks like to play fair, and some folks don't. This isn't the first time something has happened at a competition."

"You're talking about sabotage?" Drew turned toward Ollie, hoping for clarification.

Jake made a soft noise in the back of his throat that was barely audible from a distance, but didn't say anything.

"I've heard things, and you can't deny what happened here. Not just one instance of sabotage, but two."

"Which," Tommy pointed out, flicking the toothpick

he was chewing on from one side of his mouth to the other. "Stopped when she disappeared."

Sophia frowned. "Come on, Tommy. I know Ollie's convinced, but you don't think—"

"I don't think anything," Tommy interrupted, gesturing vaguely with his bottle. "But it does make you wonder, doesn't it? My truck was hit, then Ollie's. And the next thing you know, Cleo's gone, and that's the end of it. Awfully convenient, isn't it?"

Sophia stiffened. "Cleo didn't have to cheat to win. She got here the same way we all did, by rising to the top in the regional heats."

"No?" Ollie tilted his head. "Then where is she now? If she didn't run, if she didn't have a reason to disappear, why hasn't she come back?" His voice took on an almost reasonable tone. "And what if she wasn't done? What if what she did the first time didn't work, so she tried again? What if someone caught her in the act and made sure she wouldn't do it again?"

I exchanged a look with Drew. This wasn't the first time Ollie had voiced suspicion of Cleo, but this was more than that.

Tommy slammed his beer down on the cooler, the thud cutting through the crackling fire. "You got something to say, Ollie? Just spit it out."

Ollie took another long sip and shook his head. "Nothing I haven't said before."

Tommy let out a harsh breath, muttering something

under his breath before grabbing another beer. He fumbled with the cap, his movements jerky.

The tension was thick enough to cut, and the crackling of the fire was the only sound for a long moment. I almost wished Drew and I had stayed inside, but only almost.

Tommy, clearly at the end of his patience, stood abruptly. "It's late. I've had a filthy day, and I think I should go inside before Ollie paints a big red X on my back."

Ollie lifted an eyebrow. "I'm just being practical."

"No, you're stirring the pot like you have been since I edged you out." Sophia shook her head. "I hope to God Cleo comes back and shuts you up."

Ollie only smiled, slow and smug. "We'll see."

I let out a slow breath and reached for another kouign-amann, needing something to do with my hands.

Drew's arm tightened around my waist, and I could tell he'd picked up on the same thing I had.

Ollie was playing a game. He was shifting the suspicion, planting seeds. But why? Sophia had heard Tommy tending his smoker on the other side of the compound at the time of Cleo's disappearance, and unlike hers, his truck had also been sabotaged. I could see it if Ollie had tried to implicate Jake or Sophia, but he'd gone for victim shaming instead. Why?

The trill of a cell phone ringtone cut through the tense atmosphere like a knife. Sophia fumbled in her pocket, her face illuminated by the screen's glow. Once she answered, I watched the color drain from her cheeks.

"What? No, that can't be right," she stammered, rising to her feet. "I'm on my way."

"Sophia?" I asked, my heart racing. "What's wrong?"

She looked at me, eyes wide with shock. "My truck...there's a fire. At my truck."

The words hung in the air for a moment before chaos erupted. Everyone started talking at once, a cacophony of concern and confusion.

Drew's voice rose above the din. "We'll drive you," he said, already fishing his keys from his pocket and directing a look at Tommy. "We'll get there faster, and I haven't had anything to drink."

"I'm coming with." Jake rose, his face grim in the firelight, he skirted widely, and followed us toward the lake house.

"I can't believe this is happening," Sophia moaned. "Everything I've worked for..."

I squeezed her shoulder. "Hey, let's not jump to conclusions. It might not be as bad as you think."

But even as I said it, I couldn't shake the feeling that this was just another piece of a puzzle I couldn't see enough of to solve. My fingers drummed an anxious rhythm on my thigh as Drew navigated the winding lakeside road.

"What do you think, babe?" I asked, breaking the tense silence. "Coincidence or something more sinister?"

Drew's jaw tightened. "I don't know, Ev. But I've got a bad feeling about this whole situation."

"Join the club," I muttered, staring out at the dark

water of the lake as we sped past. Whatever was waiting for us in town, I had a sinking feeling it would change everything.

CHAPTER SEVENTEEN

*W*ith the moon hidden from view behind the looming pines, the drive down the camp road seemed to take ten minutes longer than forever. Drew's reassuring grip on the steering wheel steadied me as we headed toward the scene of Sophia's food truck disaster.

"What if it's completely ruined? All my recipes, my equipment..." Her voice trembled almost in rhythm with the fingers she continued to wring throughout the entire trip.

"Is your truck insured, at least?" I asked, hoping for some shred of silver lining amidst the cloud of worry swirling in her mind.

"It is," Sophia managed to squeak out, her brown eyes wide and glossy with unshed tears.

Next to her, Jake, looking every inch the stoic guardian angel in his worn baseball cap, spoke up, his voice low and laced with an undercurrent suggesting experience. "Fire is a merciless beast. It eats what it wants without distinction—wood, dreams, even lives."

"Cheery thought, Jake," I quipped, trying to lighten

the mood while secretly admiring his way with dramatic truths.

We pulled up behind the throng of emergency vehicles clustered around Sophia's truck, their lights still flashing. Emergency personnel moved through whatever mysterious errands the aftermath required, but without urgency. Sophia barely waited for the car to stop moving before she hopped out and made a beeline for the scene.

I followed in time to hear her say, "I'm Sophia Clark, and that's my truck."

From what I could see with lights still flashing in my eyes, the truck hadn't suffered catastrophic damage. My next breath came easier when Drew and Jake stepped up behind us.

The fire marshal, a burly man with a mustache that looked like it could smother a blaze, approached with a clipboard clutched in his beefy hand.

"Miss Clark? You got real lucky today," he said, a hint of relief in his tone. "One of our local guys was off duty nearby. Saw the flames licking up the awning and managed to pull it down before it could spread. Could've been much worse."

"Thank goodness," Sophia breathed, her shoulders sagging as she took in the sight of her beloved truck, the once cheerful awning a scorched, sad-looking pile on the ground. Although smoke stains marred the once vibrant exterior, the truck stood resolute, wounded but alive.

"Looks like you'll be back on your feet in no time," Jake said, placing a comforting hand on Sophia's shoulder. His touch seemed to bolster her, and I caught a flicker of gratitude between them. And maybe something else, but that could have been my imagination—and probably was, I decided.

"Back on my wheels, you mean," Sophia corrected with a weak smile, finding her sense of humor among the ashes. Jake's mouth twitched, a rare glimmer of amusement in his hazel eyes.

The crunch of tires behind us announced new arrivals, and I turned to watch Tommy O'Malley approach. I hadn't expected him to follow, but there he was, accompanied by Ollie, whose usual jovial expression seemed tempered by the gravity of the situation and the fact that he was up way past his bedtime.

"Looks better than I expected. Quite a stroke of luck you've had," Tommy bellowed across the parking lot, his voice ricocheting off the surrounding fire trucks like a misfired cue ball. His attempt to be supportive resembled the rallying cry before a football match.

"You got off easy," Ollie added, his tone subdued as he surveyed the damage, but I spotted the way his eyebrows pinched together when Tommy clapped him a little too heartily on the back. Was that irritation flickering in Ollie's eyes, or just a reflection of my emotions?

"You didn't have to come," Sophia replied, focusing on the firefighters as they packed their equipment.

"Little elbow grease will clean up that smoke damage. If you're lucky, the interior won't smell too bad. Might lose some of your stock if it does, but better than losing the whole kit and caboodle," Tommy continued, his laugh a notch too loud.

"Johnny's right," Iris's voice trilled beside me, her form as solid-looking as ever except for the blurry edges and the telltale chill that seeped into my bones. She peered at Tommy with a quizzical tilt of her head. "We had a minor fire when I ran the bakery. Bit worse than this, but you'd be surprised how quickly sugar picks up the scent of smoke."

"His name is Tommy, Iris," I corrected under my breath, amused by her mix-up.

"Is it?" she exclaimed. "I'd have sworn it was Johnny... Johnny—" She snapped her fingers as if trying to pull up a last name from memory, failed, then shook her head.

"More trouble?" Edna asked, materializing next to Iris, her outline slightly blurred as well. She clasped her hands in front of her, an expression of mild disapproval etching her spectral features. "I knew this food truck business was bad for the town. Didn't I tell you that when they showed up here, Iris?"

"More than once," Iris caught my eye and winked.

"It won't be for much longer," I murmured, feeling the familiar sensation akin to slimy bog water as Iris patted my arm. "Provided there's anyone left to compete by the end."

"You think this was intentional?" Edna sighed, shaking her head slowly. "What has the world come to?"

"Tell me about it," I replied, only half-joking as I watched the scene unfold. Tommy had launched into an anecdote about a grill fire he'd once tamed single-handedly, embellishing the details while the firefighters worked around him to return hoses to trucks.

"Back in my day," Iris began, her words ripe with nostalgia, "people respected others' things. If someone burned something down, it was their own building. You know, for the insurance money."

My snort, while an appropriate response to Iris' comment, was out of place given the circumstances. "Iris," I said when Drew quirked an eyebrow at me.

"I'm not saying that was the case here." Iris absently patted me on the arm again, ignoring my shudder. "But if it was, she did a lousy job of it."

"Have you been sniffing glue?" Edna drew herself up to her full height and pointed at Sophia. "Honestly, look at that poor girl. She can't decide whether to smile or cry, so she's doing both. That is not the face of an arsonist."

"Maybe not," Iris agreed, but I suspected she wasn't fully convinced.

Having stepped away from the bulk of the living crowd while I dealt with the not-living, I happened to be in the right place at the right time when Jake walked up to the Fire Chief.

"Mind if I take a look?" he asked, his voice low but carrying an undercurrent of authority I hadn't heard from him before.

"You got some experience with this kind of thing?"

Jake's jaw clenched for a moment before he answered, "Ten years on the job. Two off. Give or take."

"Whereabouts?"

"Port Harbor." Jake's tone was clipped.

"Fleet Hill fire?"

Given the pause before he spoke and the chief's tone, the fire in question must have been bad. Really bad.

"I was inside when the first tank went up. Barely made it out." Jake's words were matter-of-fact, but I caught a glimpse of something haunted flickering in his eyes—a memory that lingered like the smoke still clinging to the night air.

"Belly of the beast," the chief muttered.

"After my stint on the J's, I tried going back on the 40, but I—" Jake broke off, stuffed his hands in his pockets, and dropped his gaze to his feet.

"Nothing to be ashamed of, son. Fire eats whatever it can. Sometimes that includes the piece of you that's fool enough to keep fighting it. That's the price of the job."

"It was for me. That's what I told my chief when he came by last week to try and talk me into coming back. I haven't been able to deal with active fire since that day, so I spent my savings on a food truck and ended up here."

Jake's absence from the nightly campfire and cold food truck offerings made more sense now. I'd avoid fire, too, if I'd nearly died in one.

"I told her not to leave those lights on when she wasn't here." Jake moved toward the blackened remains of Sophia's awning, his squared shoulders showing renewed purpose as the fire chief handed him a pair of gloves. "Ten bucks says that's what started it."

"They're brand new, though," Sophia said, a tear leaking down her cheek. "The LED kind. They're supposed to be safer. It said so on the box."

With precise, methodical movements and hands that betrayed no tremors, Jake located what was left of the fairy lights.

"Here," he said when he'd found and untangled them from the rest of the awning. "This is your origin point right here. Something nicked the jacket hard enough to fray the wires. All it took was a little spark and something flammable like the awning."

The chief leaned in, scrutinizing the indicated section that was charred more than the rest. "Could be the wires rubbed against the awning frame. We get a steady breeze off the water. If she didn't have them lashed down well enough and there was a burr on the metal, they'd wear through fairly quickly."

"Or someone tampered with them," Jake added, the edge in his voice slicing through the air.

"Tampered?" Sophia gasped, her face paling. "But why would anyone—"

"Let's not jump to conclusions," the chief chided gently, though his brow furrowed in concern.

Jake shook his head. "Not much of a jump given two other vendors' trucks have been sabotaged."

"But not yours," Tommy pointed out.

"Since I'm running dead last, I'm probably not enough of a threat to warrant anyone messing with me." Jake faced Tommy more confidently than I'd seen him show since we'd met.

"Nothing wrong with your food that putting a little heart and soul into it wouldn't fix." Ollie offered a backhanded compliment.

To everyone's surprise, Jake laughed. "You nailed that in one. Food trucking is a good way to make ends meet, but it isn't my thing."

The laughter transformed more than just his face, lightening everything about him as if he'd shrugged off a great weight.

Standing, he handed the lights to the chief, pulled out his phone, turned on the camera app, and zoomed in on the frayed spot. "I need more light."

"Right here." Prepared as always, Drew pulled out the penlight he kept on his keychain and shined it on the wires while Jake took several photos.

The crunch of gravel underfoot announced Chase's arrival before I even saw him. He sauntered onto the scene, hands tucked into the pockets of his faded jeans, his scruffy beard doing nothing to hide the concern etching lines between his brows. His presence was like a pebble dropped into the still waters of our little gathering —ripples of tension spread out in every direction.

"What's going on here? Did something happen to Sophia's truck?"

"A fire of possibly suspicious origins," Tommy answered before anyone else could. "Where have you been all evening?"

"Not out setting fires, if that's what you're asking." Chase bristled and stepped aside to show he wasn't alone. "Ask Tawny."

"He was at the bar talking to Wes Delaney all evening," she said, lifting her chin as if expecting an argument. "And I'm not the only one who saw him there. You can't pin this on Chase. He's innocent."

"No one is trying to pin anything on Chase," Drew said sternly. "Or anyone else, for that matter. Not until the cause of the fire has been determined."

"Which is what we're trying to do right now," the fire chief warned. "Step back and let us work."

"I'm not a licensed investigator, but I've studied my fair share of origin points," Jake said as he showed the images to the chief. "Do you see what I see?"

"You've got a good eye, son. Looks like teeth marks to me."

Jake turned to Sophia. "There was tampering all right, but not of the human variety. I'd say a rodent chewed on these. Unless Chase has squirrel teeth, I think he's in the clear. For this, at least."

"But not for Cleo? You're way off base, there, Tex. I know for a fact he wasn't anywhere near those cabins when she went missing. Tell them, Chase."

His face a dull red, Chase said, "Shut up, Tawny. Or you'll have to find another ride home."

"You shut up," she retorted, slamming her hands on her hips and facing him down. "I'm only trying to help. Chase drives an electric car, and we only have one charging station in town, which just happens to be across from the walk-in clinic where I work. You're the only person in the area with one in that pretty blue color. I saw you when I went out on break at nine, and again at eleven when I got off work. I bet Wes saw you there, too. He goes on at ten."

Tawny worked at a medical facility? Remind me to never get sick in Oakville.

Still, the revelation distracted Sophia from the aftermath of the fire. "That must have been after he argued with Cleo that night."

"Chase argued with Cleo?" I frowned at Sophia. "Why didn't you say anything before?"

"I figured it wasn't important because I saw her after he stormed out of her cabin."

"It's not," Chase insisted.

Tawny, who had been defending him only moments before, turned on him with whiplash speed.

"You did this." She slapped him smartly across the face, then grabbed his shirt as if holding him in place. "Where is she? What did you do with her?"

"Nothing. I swear. I didn't do anything to hurt Cleo."

Every hair on my body lifted as Iris puffed up, her emotions sliding over my skin like a palpable wave as she asked me, "Is he the one?"

"Here we go," I muttered under my breath, glancing at Drew, whose eyebrows lifted in a silent question when his arms sprouted gooseflesh. At least I wasn't the only one who felt something this time.

"I don't trust him," Iris spat out, her tone laced with fury, "I saw him flirting with that pastry pushing Jezebel when he was supposed to be in love with my grand-niece. If he knows anything about Cleo, I'll haunt it out of him. Don't you think I won't. I'll haunt whoever I have to, make no mistake."

"I think Chase realized he was over Cleo on Karaoke night."

Chase responded to the statement he thought I'd directed at him. "That's right. Sophia helped me see my way clear. That's what we talked about at the bar. Ask her. She'll tell you."

Sophia nodded. "I did do that." When she caught my skeptical expression, she said, "What?"

"It looked like you were flirting with him."

"Maybe I was. A little. I have a thing for people who need saving," she admitted. "He wasn't interested."

I'd seen that for myself.

Chase looked like he wasn't sure if that was a compliment or a slam. "I did talk to Cleo, but it wasn't about us. I had money tied up in her business. Do you have any idea how much it costs to wrap a vehicle that size? I spent almost ten grand putting her face—her brand—on that food truck."

Whatever I'd expected him to say, that was not it.

"We were arguing over setting up a payment plan. Not about getting back together. If she's not selling tacos, I'll never see a dime of that money back. Doing anything to hurt her is not in my best interest, and I stand by what I said. Cleo would not have left her truck behind. It meant more to her than I ever did."

"Is he telling the truth?" Tawny let go of Chase's shirt.

Bitter much? Yeah. Telling the truth? Again, yeah. Chase was not the guy.

If the sudden absence of chill in the air meant anything, Iris had come to the same conclusion.

"Horse feathers," she swore, her nose wrinkling, her hands on her hips. "These trucks didn't sabotage themselves. Cleo didn't disappear into thin air, and you're not being nearly helpful enough."

I shrugged. I'd ruled out another suspect. What more did she want?

"You need to tell Zack what you've just told us," Drew suggested. "It might help the investigation."

"I already did. He hauled me in for questioning this afternoon. Now, if you're done accusing me, I need to get back to my dog. Prescott must be going out of his mind by now."

"So much for the love motive," I said.

"Obviously, someone wanted her out of the way," Edna offered her opinion. "I still don't see how sabotage fits into the picture. This mystery has more twists than a telephone cord."

"Except," I sighed, rubbing my temples. "Tawny just alibied Chase out. And this fire wasn't sabotage."

"What's next? You need to come up with a new plan. Or else." Iris meant me, of course.

"Can you just give me a day or two before you start haunting more of the townspeople?"

"One day." Iris held up a finger, her gaze lingering on mine as she slowly faded away. Her final, "One," wafted into the night on a whisper.

Great.

I rejoined the group just in time to hear Jake say, "I'll withdraw from the competition tomorrow."

"What did I miss?" I'd only been gone two minutes.

"Jake's leaving the competition to pursue a career as an arson investigator," Ollie explained. "And then, there were three."

With the excitement over for the night, Sophia and Jake opted to ride back to the cabins with Tommy, leaving Drew and me alone to discuss Iris and Edna's reaction to the state of events.

"And we have one day to figure out what happened to Cleo before Iris starts scaring the bejesus out of her prime suspect, whoever that might be."

"I can't imagine, now that Chase is out of the running. Who's next on the hot seat?"

"It's not about what I think. Iris has her own ideas. To tell the truth, I'm tempted to let her do her thing. Maybe she can flush something out because I'm at a loss."

CHAPTER EIGHTEEN

The dream hit me like a sucker punch, yanking me from the depths of sleep into a swirling maelstrom of weird lighting and raucous laughter. I blinked, trying to get my bearings, but the scene before me refused to settle, vibrating with an almost manic energy that set my teeth on edge.

Cleo's truck wasn't just bright; it was impossibly vibrant, as if someone had cranked up the saturation on reality. From its once-cheerful exterior, her face pulsed with an otherworldly glow, one eye winking at me. Not metaphorically, but actually winking—the painted lid opening and closing with an audible click.

A long line of customers stretched from the service window, curling around the truck like a python. The people waiting didn't just stand there; stuck in Selfie Mode, they preened and posed, shifting their weight from one foot to another in practiced stances that would photograph well. Someone tossed their hair or laughed a little too loudly every few seconds.

I pushed closer, weaving through the throng of bodies, trying to catch a glimpse of Cleo.

This filter is absolutely giving me life," said a woman

in front of me, though she wasn't holding a phone. Her cheekbones caught the light in a way that seemed to defy the laws of physics.

"Hashtag *taco goals*," replied her companion, making air quotes with his fingers. He wore a t-shirt that read 'I'd rather be scrolling' in a font that constantly changed before my eyes.

"I'd kill for a taco right now!" a man in a suit exclaimed, his eyes wide and manic. The knife in his hand suggested he meant that literally.

"Cleo is *everything*," a woman in a sequined dress giggled, her laughter high and brittle.

Underneath it all, Iris's voice repeated like a metronome. "Find Cleo."

The air thrummed with an undercurrent of menace, the laughter taking on a darker edge as I finally reached the front of the line. And there was Cleo in all her glory.

Except she looked different.

Her hair wasn't just styled; it was performing, ombré waves catching the neon lights and reflecting them back with interest. She wore a bright pink apron with the words "PAYBACK TACOS" splashed across the front in blood-soaked red letters. Around her neck was the silk scarf I'd seen her wear before—a swirl of emerald and cobalt that somehow complemented the pink of her apron despite the clash of colors.

"Everly! My fave customer!" she exclaimed, her voice oddly melodic, as if she were speaking through an audio enhancer. "What can I get for my bestie today?"

I hadn't decided. I hadn't even seen a menu. But my mouth moved anyway. "The usual," I heard myself say.

"One 'Truth Bomb' taco coming right up!" Cleo winked and turned to her grill with a flourish.

Her hands moved with hypnotic precision as she worked, chopping invisible ingredients and stirring pots that materialized only when needed. Every few seconds, she'd reach up and touch the scarf around her neck, fingers tracing the pattern as if checking that it was still there.

"Don't forget to like and subscribe," she whispered, leaning out the window. The scarf tightened around her neck as she moved, and for a moment, I saw panic flash across her face.

I looked more closely at Cleo. Beneath the carefully applied makeup, her skin had a grayish undertone, and the hand not touching the scarf trembled slightly as she handed food to the next customer.

The line of customers began to distort, their features blurring, bodies elongating until they were nothing more than smudges of movement against the night.

Cleo touched her scarf again, but the gesture was more frantic this time. She opened her mouth to speak, but no sound came out. Behind her, the shadows coalesced, taking vaguely human forms—figures with limbs that moved too fluidly, faces that weren't quite faces.

One shadow-hand reached out, wrapping around Cleo's wrist. Another tugged at her clothing. She struggled against their grip, her movements hesitant and jerky like a buffering video.

"Wait!" I called out, reaching for the window, but my hand passed right through it.

The shadowy figures pulled Cleo backward into the truck's darkened interior. I caught one last glimpse of her face—eyes wide, mouth open in a silent scream—before the shadow-hands clapped over her mouth.

The scarf came loose in their grasp, floating in the air like a bird pausing in flight before being swallowed by the darkness. I tried to move, to help her, but my feet were rooted to the spot, my limbs heavy and useless.

And then, as suddenly as it had begun, the dream shattered, leaving me gasping and alone in the lake house bed, my heart pounding a frantic rhythm against my ribs. Hands shaking, I sat up and pushed sweat-damp hair away from my face, then pressed my palms against my eyes until I saw stars. Anything to clear away the images clinging to my mind like cobwebs.

I told myself it was just a nightmare, but even as the words formed in my mind, I couldn't shake it off.

I glanced at the empty space beside me, feeling Drew's absence like a physical ache. I needed to talk to him, to share the worry that had settled into the pit of my stomach. But first, I needed to convince myself that the sunlight streaming through the windows was real, not just another trick of my subconscious.

With a sigh, I swung my legs over the side of the bed, bare feet landing on the solid hardwood floor, anchoring me back to reality, but the dream still lingered like the scent of smoke after Sophia's fire as I shuffled into the kitchen.

Drew stood at the stove, his back to me, shoulders working rhythmically as he manipulated something in a cast-iron skillet. Morning light slanted through the floor-to-ceiling windows, cutting sharp angles across the sleek countertop and turning his sandy hair gold. I paused in the doorway, taking a moment to appreciate the view—not just the lake stretching beyond the glass, but the man who'd chosen to share his life with mine. A picture of domestic bliss that couldn't quite chase away my lingering unease.

"Morning, sleepyhead," Drew said without turning around, somehow sensing my presence. "Thought you might sleep till noon."

"What time is it?" My voice sounded raspy, as if I'd been shouting in my sleep.

"Just past nine." He glanced over his shoulder, his smile fading as he got a good look at me. "Hey, you okay? You look like you've seen a ghost."

"Not yet today," I said, attempting levity. "But give me time. It's still early."

The kitchen light felt too bright, too harsh against my raw nerves.

Needing something to occupy my hands, I pulled condiments from the caddy Drew had set on the table, lining them up in front of me like chess pieces on a board. The flashy red ketchup bottle caught my eye, reminding me of Cleo's vibrant personality and equally bold fashion sense.

Picturing the layout of the cabins, I placed the bottle where Cleo's would be, selected the mustard bottle for Chase, and set it in the appropriate position. Why Drew thought mustard went with eggs was one mystery I'd decided never to solve. Best to ignore it altogether.

"What are you doing?"

"I don't know. I had a weird dream about Cleo. Unsettling."

Drew dropped a kiss on my head and slid two eggs onto my plate before pulling a stack of buttered toast from the oven where he'd been keeping it warm, and lowering into the chair opposite.

"Cleo's the ketchup." I dipped the edge of my toast in the runny egg yolk and took a bite. "Chase is the mustard."

As if this were normal breakfast conversation, Drew picked up the bottle of barbecue sauce and added some to his sausage—another cringeworthy breakfast choice in my opinion, but each to his own.

When he was done, he placed the bottle where Tommy's cabin would be. "Tommy's the barbecue sauce, obviously."

"Ollie's the pepper," I added him to the mix, gesturing with my fork. "Which leaves Sophia and Jake."

I picked up the sugar bowl, thinking of Sophia's sweet nature and how she always had a smile for everyone, even when things were tough. "Sophia's the sugar. And Jake..."

I trailed off, spotting the toppled salt shaker, a few stray grains scattered across the tabletop. "Jake's the salt, I guess. Off the table—pun intended— now that he's leaving the competition. Zack wouldn't let him go if he was under suspicion."

Drew grabbed Ollie and Jake, adding seasoning to his eggs before replacing them. "But what if the barbecue sauce was in the refrigerator when the ketchup went missing?" he asked, his eyes sparkling with mischief.

I couldn't help but laugh, the sound bursting out like a cork from a champagne bottle. It felt good to let some of the tension building in my chest escape. But even as the laughter broke the dream's hold over me, the unspoken knowledge that we were no closer to finding Cleo than we had been the day before put an edge on things.

"Based on what we learned last night, it was the mustard in the refrigerator, which is where it should remain at breakfast time. Just saying."

Drew snorted.

"You know," I continued, spearing a bite of egg with my fork, "if we don't figure this out soon, Iris plans to start haunting the suspects. Can you imagine her popping up in Tommy's smoker or Ollie's pizza oven?"

Drew's eyes lit up with mischief. "Or reciting her favorite recipes in Sophia's ear while she's trying to bake."

"She could follow Chase around, whispering food puns until he cracks," I added, warming to the theme.

"'Donut give up on finding the truth!'" Drew intoned in a wavering, ghostly voice.

"'I've got my pie on you!'" I countered, waving my fingers in what I hoped was a spooky manner.

Under the table, Drew's foot nudged mine, a silent gesture of comfort and support. I nudged him back, grateful for his presence and how he always seemed to know exactly what I needed, even when I didn't know myself.

"Did the condiment reenactment shake anything loose? Except for the salt on my eggs, anyway."

"Not really." Something Drew said earlier had triggered a thought, but it slid away as quickly as it tried to surface, which wasn't helpful. I put the condiments back in the caddy.

We finished our breakfast in companionable silence, only broken by one sharp bark from Molly when Effie and Carlton drove past and honked the horn on their ATV.

"The Paulsons are living it up," Drew observed with a grin.

"Effie would love to help with this investigation, you know," I said, imagining her pulling out endless supplies from her enormous purse. "She'd probably offer Cleo's kidnapper a breath mint and a Band-Aid."

"And a lecture about proper hostage-taking etiquette," Drew added.

We laughed again, the sound chasing away some of the morning's lingering darkness until we'd finished eating and Drew took his plate to the sink.

I rose from my chair, circled the table, and wrapped my arms around Drew from behind as he stood there. I pressed my cheek against his back, feeling the solid warmth of him through his T-shirt, listening to the steady beat of his heart.

"Thanks," I murmured.

"For cooking breakfast?" he asked, though I knew he understood what I meant.

"For not telling me I'm crazy for chasing after missing food truck owners on our honeymoon."

Drew turned in my embrace, suds clinging to his fingers as he cupped my face, careful not to get them in my hair. His eyes, blue as the lake outside our windows, held mine with unwavering certainty.

"Everly, I knew exactly who you were when I married you. Ghost-seeing, mystery-solving, trouble-finding you." He kissed me softly. "Besides, what's a honeymoon without a little amateur sleuthing?"

I smiled against his lips. "Most people would say 'romance.'"

"Most people don't know what they're missing." He kissed me tenderly.

While Drew headed upstairs to shower, I gathered up the dishes and carried them to the dishwasher, then picked up my phone from where it had been charging on the kitchen counter. Leaning there, I texted Jacy, who'd been unusually quiet the past few days.

What's up?

Long moments passed before I got a two-word reply.

Nothing much.

Everything okay?

Peachy!

Without news from home to distract me, I turned to social media. Cleo's, to be specific. She stared back at me from her profile picture—a perfectly lit selfie with a sunrise behind her. Her bio read: "Slaying the taco game one bite at a time. Food truck dreams. Living deliciously." The emoji parade that followed was a confetti of tacos, flames, and hearts.

Her lack of recent posts told the story of her absence with sobering clarity. Behind the artful shots of her signature creations, the comment sections shifted into something somber. Nestled between queries about her secret spices and gluten-free tortilla tips, messages expressing concern and prayers for a safe return turned her feed into a virtual altar where her followers laid their hearts bare.

I scrolled through the endless stream of well-wishes and worries, my eyes straining against the screen's glow, searching for anything to help me figure out who might have wanted to harm her. It was like panning for gold in a digital river, sifting through the silt of hashtags and emojis, waiting for a glimmer of truth to catch the light.

And then, I saw it.

Sandwiched between a teary-eyed selfie and a fan-made missing persons poster, a grainy video flickered to life. Posted by a fan who'd camped out near Cleo's truck overnight to be first in line the next morning, its time-stamp marked it as the day Ollie's truck had been sabotaged. The footage was shaky, but there was no mistaking the figure that darted across the frame. Even with his face obscured by shadow, his build and gait were quite familiar.

Tommy O'Malley had been skulking around Ollie's truck on the night someone sabotaged the electrical panel. Coincidence? Probably not.

My heart hammered against my ribs as I reversed the video and re-watched him slink behind Ollie's truck, his movements furtive and quick. The video ended abruptly, cutting to black before I could see what he did next, but the implications were clear. If Tommy had been near Ollie's truck that night, what else was he hiding?

CHAPTER NINETEEN

*P*ieces of the puzzle began to slot into a whole new configuration, forming a picture that made my stomach twist. Could Tommy be the saboteur?

And if Tommy was the saboteur, was he also a kidnapper? Could he also be lying about his alibi for the night Cleo disappeared? No, because Sophia had been the one to supply it. She'd clearly stated she'd heard him checking his smoker like he did every night. Had they both been lying? Were they working together, or was Sophia an unwitting pawn in Tommy's game?

Could the man who had spent hours driving searchers around in the shuttle after he'd worked all day also be the reason for the search? Talk about hiding in plain sight.

I closed the app and slipped my phone into my pocket, my mind racing with possibilities. I needed answers, and I needed them now. But confronting Tommy directly felt like a risk I couldn't afford to take, not without more evidence to back up my suspicions.

Sophia, on the other hand...

I pushed off from the counter to pace the kitchen while I brought up her contact info and waited for her to answer my call.

The phone rang three times before Sophia answered, her voice bursting through the speaker like a sugar rush.

"Everly. Is everything okay?"

"Sure. I just wanted to check in and see how things were going after last night."

"Oh," she sounded rushed. "Everything's fine. After what happened to Tommy and Ollie, I'd been extra careful about closing and locking my windows up tight. Not enough smoke got inside to cause any damage."

"I'm glad to hear that," I said, pacing the room. "I know you're probably busy, but could you just go over what you remember from the night Cleo went missing again?"

Sophia huffed, and I could almost see her blowing a stray curl from her forehead.

"Well, like I said, I called my mom a little after 10:00. We talk every night before bed—it's our thing."

"And you're sure about the timing?"

"Positive. I heard Tommy messing with his smoker, which he does at precisely 10 pm. That was my cue to pour a glass of wine and make the call."

"Sophia," I said carefully, "would you mind checking your phone's call log? Just to confirm the exact time?"

"My call log? Why?" Her voice took on a hint of wariness.

"Just being thorough. Sometimes our memories play tricks on us, especially during stressful times."

There was a pause, then the sound of her setting something down. "Hang on, let me check." I heard her murmuring to herself as she navigated her phone. "Okay. Outgoing calls...Mom...here it is."

The silence that followed stretched long enough that I wondered if we'd lost the connection.

"Sophia? You still there?"

Drew walked back downstairs, his hair damp from his shower. I put the call on speaker.

"Yeah, I'm here." Her voice had changed, confusion replacing certainty. "That's weird. According to my call log, I called Mom at 11:05, not 10:05. We talked for about forty minutes, so it would have been closer to midnight when we hung up."

An hour late. An hour when Tommy could have been doing something nefarious.

"Is something wrong?" Sophia's voice sounded confused.

"Not really. Wouldn't your mom have noticed if you were an hour late to call? Especially at that time of the night." My mother had a firm rule. Any call after ten had better be an emergency, or heads would roll. It didn't even matter that she never went to bed that early.

"She works the evening shift."

"Sophia," I said softly, "I need you to think carefully. Are you absolutely certain that what you heard was Tommy at his smoker? Did you actually see him, or just hear noises you associated with him?"

The line went quiet except for Sophia's breathing, which had grown slightly faster. I could almost see her fingers drumming nervously against the counter—a habit I'd noticed she employed when thinking.

"I didn't see him," she admitted finally. "But I know it was Tommy. He whistles when he turns his meat. Besides, who else would be messing with a smoker at that hour?"

"You're sure about the whistling?" Drew asked, speaking for the first time.

"Drew! Hi," Sophia said, startled by the new voice. "Um, yeah. It's the same tune every night." Her voice warbling, she imitated what she'd heard.

"Okay. Thanks, Sophia. I appreciate your time."

After we hung up, Drew let out a long, slow whistle. "Tommy's alibi just went up in smoke."

"Like overcooked brisket," I agreed, pocketing my phone.

"The question is, what do we do with this information? Go to the police?"

I shook my head. "Not yet. We still don't have definitive proof of anything, just circumstantial evidence. I think we need to confront Tommy directly, see how he reacts when backed into a corner."

Drew's expression tightened with concern. "That could be dangerous, Ev."

"That's why we'll do it together," I said, reaching for his hand. "And in a public place. But first, let's get all our facts straight. We need to be prepared for whatever he might say."

I jammed my phone into my pocket, mind racing with scenarios for confronting Tommy. The evidence against him had crystallized from vague suspicion to something solid and jagged—a timeline that didn't match, a video showing him where he claimed not to be, and a potential motive wrapped in competition. My fingers trembled slightly as I picked up the car keys, not from fear but from a crackling anticipation that made my skin feel too tight for my body.

"Ready?" Drew asked, pulling on a light jacket despite the warm day. His expression was grim, a stark contrast to the honeymoon relaxation that had softened his features just hours earlier.

"As I'll ever be," I replied, shoving my sunglasses onto my head. "Keys, phone, righteous indignation—I think I've got everything."

The car's engine roared to life, and we pulled away from the lake house, gravel crunching beneath our tires. We'd gone perhaps a quarter mile when Drew suddenly slammed on the brakes, the seatbelt jerking tight across my chest as we lurched to a stop.

"What the—" I started, then saw what had brought us to such an abrupt halt.

Sprawled across the dirt road like a beached whale was a battered, rust-tinged boat with a decrepit trailer that listed dangerously to one side. The contraption effectively blocked the entire road, its weathered hull suggesting it had been abandoned there rather than simply fallen from its moorings.

"Well," Drew said after a moment of stunned silence, "looks like old Captain Rusty here is blocking our drive."

Despite my frustration, I couldn't help the snort of laughter that escaped me. "Captain Rusty? Really?"

Drew grinned. "Would you prefer Admiral Tetanus?"

"Both excellent nautical villains," I conceded, unbuckling my seatbelt. I stepped out of the car to assess the situation more closely, and Drew joined me a moment later.

The boat was substantial—at least eighteen feet long —and though time had not been kind to its exterior, the hull appeared solid enough that simply trying to push it aside wasn't an option. The trailer's left wheel had utterly detached, explaining why the whole setup was canted awkwardly.

"We could wait for someone to move it," Drew suggested, though his tone made it clear he knew how long that might take out here.

I shook my head, already forming an alternative plan. "The lake is faster."

Drew caught my meaning immediately. "The boat. We can cut across the lake and dock in town."

"Exactly."

We hustled back to the lake house and ran to the dock. The delay was frustrating, but at least we had other options. Ones that made the caper feel like a proper adventure, the kind that would make for a good story afterward—assuming, of course, that the ending wasn't tragic.

My mind was so focused on Tommy and what we might discover that I barely noticed the beauty of the day around us—the perfect blue sky, the gentle breeze carrying the clean scent of the water, the distant call of a loon before it dove. We should be savoring these moments on our honeymoon, instead of racing against time to confront a potential kidnapper.

But then, when had anything in my life gone according to plan? Between my ability to see ghosts and my apparent magnetic attraction to mysteries, ordinary had never been in the cards for me—or, by extension, for Drew. Thankfully, he seemed to take it all in stride.

"We're low on fuel," Drew noted, tapping the gauge with a frown. "But we should have enough to get to town."

"*Should* being the operative word," I muttered, securing our supplies. "Can't anything go smoothly today?"

Drew shot me a quick grin. "We're chasing a missing food truck owner across a lake because a rusty boat is blocking our road. I think 'smooth' left the chat a while ago."

He reversed the throttle, and we eased away from the dock, the water churning white beneath us. Once we had enough clearance, he shifted gears, and the bow lifted as we surged forward, cutting a clean path across the lake's surface.

Without warning, a speedboat cut across our path, closer than was safe or courteous. Its wake hit us broadside, sending our boat rocking violently. I lurched forward, then back, my hand shooting out instinctively to grab something for stability.

"Sorry!" Drew called, wrestling with the wheel to steady us. "Guy came out of nowhere!"

I waved off his apology, more annoyed with the reckless speedboat driver than with Drew. As the boat settled back into a smoother rhythm, I realized I had wedged my hand between the seat cushions in my quest for stability. Something soft and silky brushed against my fingers.

Curious, I pushed my hand deeper into the crevice, my fist closing around what felt like fabric. I tugged, expecting to find a handkerchief or a cleaning cloth that had slipped between the cushions.

What emerged in my hand sent a jolt of adrenaline through my system.

A scarf, but not just any scarf. Emerald and cobalt silk swirled together in a pattern I recognized immediately, from my dream. The one that had been around Cleo's neck the day we'd arrived.

"Drew," I said, my voice barely audible over the engine. "This is Cleo's scarf. The one she wore the day we met her. I'd recognize it anywhere."

Drew cut the engine, letting us drift as he stared at the scarf. "How did it get in our boat?"

I shook my head, my mind racing through possibilities, each more unsettling than the last. "I don't know."

My mind, usually quick to connect dots and form theories, seemed to stall, catching on the impossible fact that Cleo Martin's signature accessory had somehow found its way into our rental boat. Drew's face mirrored my own bewilderment, his brows drawn together in a line as straight and hard as the horizon behind him.

"Let me see that," he said, reaching for the scarf. His fingers brushed mine as I handed it over, a small point of warmth in the sudden chill that had nothing to do with the lake breeze.

Drew examined the silk closely, turning it over in his hands. "It's definitely hers?"

I nodded.

"No blood or anything. It looks clean, almost like it was placed here deliberately rather than lost in a struggle."

That observation hung between us, its implications unfurling like the scarf itself.

"Someone put it here," I said slowly. "And that someone had to be Cleo."

"How do you figure?"

I didn't answer right away. My mind raced through possibilities until only one remained.

CHAPTER TWENTY

*I*ris McCann hovered near Sophia Clark's dessert truck, her ghostly form solid to anyone who could see the dead, which, unfortunately for her gossip quota, didn't include Sophia. Iris adjusted her apron—a habit from years of baking—and watched Tommy O'Malley unload a tray of smoked brisket from his shuttle, her eyes narrowing with the expertise of a woman who'd spent decades appraising pastries and men.

"That is one good-looking brisket," Iris murmured, her plump ghostly hand fanning her face as Tommy bent over to lift another tray. "And I do mean young Johnny."

Edna Mayfield materialized beside her, arms crossed over her cardigan. The former librarian's disapproving frown had once silenced rowdy teenagers with a single glance. Death hadn't diminished its power, but it had little effect on Iris.

"Really, Iris. Must you be so crude?" Edna's words were pressed flat, like petals tucked between the pages of a book. "And stop ogling the man. It's unseemly."

The two ghosts stood unnoticed by the living, though a young woman walking past Sophia's truck shivered and pulled her cardigan tighter. This happened often enough that neither ghost paid it any mind.

Iris snorted. "Honey, I've been dead for a lot of years. Ogling is about all I've got left."

The warm scent of cinnamon and sugar wafted from Sophia's truck as she leaned out the service window. Her curly chestnut hair was piled atop her head, secured with what appeared to be a pencil, and flour dusted her arms like the remnants of a snowfall.

"Tommy!" Sophia called, her voice bright as a copper penny. "Could you spare half a cup of honey? I'm completely out."

Tommy glanced up, his eyes catching the sun's glow. "Sure thing, Soph. I'll bring it over once I finish unloading."

Edna's head swiveled between Sophia and the man unloading meat. Her gray-blue eyes narrowed when they landed back on Iris. "If you must ogle the man, at least get his name right. It's Tommy."

Iris squinted, leaning forward like an extra few inches might make all the difference. "Have you gone barmy? That's Johnny Boilard."

Edna crossed her arms, her transparent form becoming increasingly rigid with annoyance. "I am in complete control of my faculties. The man's name is Tommy O'Malley. I can read his truck sign from here." She pointed to the large, bold lettering on the side of his food truck.

"Well, he's the spitting image! If that's not Johnny Boilard, it's his doppelganger."

"Or maybe a relative," Edna tilted her head and surveyed Tommy more closely. "Didn't Patrick Boilard have two kids? A boy and a girl."

Iris nodded. "John and little Susie. She married a fellow from Boston and moved down that way. Had a couple of kids, if I remember right. She came back when Patrick took sick, and left again once he'd gone. Took her mother with her, too. Johnny Boilard sold off whatever Patrick left him and moved away soon after."

"Did you say Boilard?" Howdy's ghost suddenly materialized beside them. "As in the Boilards who owned that cabin way out on the far side of the lake? The one past Miller's Point?"

"That's the one." Iris nodded vigorously, her earrings swinging through the chilly air surrounding her. "Patrick left it to the kids, and they sold it to someone from out of state, didn't they?"

"And you say that barbecue fellow looks like Johnny? Could they be related?"

Edna's posture, already rigid in life, seemed to calcify further in death. "I doubt there's any connection. You must be misremembering something."

"I might be dead, but my memory's sharp as a tack. The eyes are the same, and even under that beard, you can see he has the same chin." Iris tilted her head and looked Tommy up and down. "Same rangy form, and it certainly is a good one. Besides, how many Boilards do you think there are in the area? It's not the most common name."

Sophia drummed her fingers nervously on the counter of her truck, watching Tommy sort through his supplies. The rhythmic tapping seemed to follow some internal melody only she could hear.

Howdy scratched his chin, a habit from life that carried over into death. "That camp's been abandoned for years. I don't think it's been accessible by road since the big ice storm of '98. You can get there by boat, of course. Perfect place to..." He trailed off, the implication hanging in the air like the mist rising from the lake each morning.

The three ghosts exchanged glances, the same realization dawning on each of their faces.

"Cleo," Edna whispered, the name falling from her lips like a key turning in a lock.

"You don't think—" Howdy began.

"That Tommy, or whatever his name is, had something to do with Cleo's disappearance?" Iris finished, her ghostly eyes widening. "And that she might be at that remote cabin? I think someone should check it out."

Howdy pulled at his mustache, water droplets scattering in the air. "Competition can make folks do crazy things. I saw two men who'd been friends for decades come to blows over who caught the bigger trout at the Oakville Fishing Derby of '95."

"This is more serious than a fishing competition," Edna said, her voice dropping to a whisper even though no living person could hear her. "If Cleo is being held at that cabin, we must alert the authorities immediately."

"But how?" Howdy asked. "It's not like we can waltz into the police station and file a report."

"You know the lake better than we," Edna said. "Check the cabin. See if Cleo is there, and find Everly. The more living folk we can mobilize, the better."

Howdy straightened, seemingly pleased to have a purpose that played to his strengths. "I'm on it. I'll head there now." He tipped his hat and vanished, leaving only a few spectral water droplets that evaporated seconds later.

"Come along, Iris," Edna said, already moving with the purposeful stride that had her dead friend struggling to keep up. "We've much to do."

"Always so bossy," Iris muttered. "Even in death, some things never change."

Still, she stayed behind long enough to watch the man unload supplies and had just caught up with Edna when Tommy noticed something that sharpened his gaze.

*
**

Zack Roman watched the older woman's hands with the focused intensity of a hawk tracking a field mouse. Effie Paulson moved through the crowd near

Tommy's BBQ truck with the inherent slowness of age, but with the finesse of someone who'd perfected her craft over decades. Her flowered dress and grandmotherly smile provided the perfect cover as her fingers, artful and precise, slipped into an unsuspecting bystander's back pocket. Zack stepped forward, his movement casual but purposeful, catching her wrist just as she extracted a leather wallet.

"Mrs. Paulson," he said, his voice low enough not to cause a scene but firm enough to convey authority. "I think you have something that doesn't belong to you."

Effie blinked at him, her expression shifting from startlement to grandmotherly confusion in a heartbeat.

"Oh my! Officer Roman, you scared me." Her voice carried the sweet, tremulous quality that had likely helped her escape detection for years. She clutched her oversized purse to her chest with her free hand. "I was just returning this gentleman's wallet. It fell, you see, and it's hard to catch up to someone walking so briskly at my age."

The lie slid from her lips with practiced ease, but Zack had been a police officer long enough to recognize a load of BS when someone tossed it his way. He maintained his grip on her wrist, gentle but unyielding.

"That's very thoughtful of you," he said, not bothering to hide the skepticism in his tone. "Why don't we chat about your Good Samaritan work in my cruiser?"

Effie's smile dimmed a few watts, but she nodded amiably, as if he'd invited her to tea rather than to be questioned pending arrest. "Of course, dear. Let me just tell Carlton—"

"I'll make sure Mr. Paulson knows where you are," Zack interrupted. Not wanting to create a scene that would disrupt the food truck festival, he deftly retrieved the wallet from her hand and nodded to the oblivious victim, who was still engrossed in comparing menu options.

"Sir," he called, "you might want to keep this more secure."

The man turned, confusion washing over his face as he patted his empty pocket and then gratefully accepted the wallet from Zack. "Thanks, Officer! I had no idea—"

"Just doing my job," Zack replied, already turning his attention back to Effie, smoothly guiding her through the crowd with a hand on her elbow.

"Mrs. Paulson, you have the right to remain silent..." He continued reciting her rights as they walked, Effie's floral perfume mixing with the scent of barbecue smoke and funnel cakes.

From behind Tommy's BBQ truck, Carlton Paulson watched the scene unfold with mounting panic. His weathered truck driver's face paled beneath his cap, and he pressed himself against the side of the vehicle, hoping to blend into the shadows. When his wife of fifty years was escorted out of sight, he let out a shaky breath that sounded like a deflating tire at the end of a long haul.

Zack guided Effie to his running patrol car parked at the

side of the street. The reflective POLICE lettering caught the sun, spelling out Effie's misfortune in bright, unmistakable flashes. Attempting discretion, he shielded her with his body as the cuffs clicked into place with a soft metallic snap. Criminal or not, she reminded him of his grandmother, so he put them in the front for the sake of comfort.

"Are the handcuffs really necessary, dear?" Effie asked as Zack helped her into the back seat. "At my age, where would I run to?"

"Standard procedure, Mrs. Paulson," Zack replied, though his mouth twitched with the hint of a smile. "I'm sure you know the drill."

"I don't know what you're talking about. I've done nothing wrong."

"Oh, I think my body cam will beg to differ." He opened the handbag he'd taken from her before he'd cuffed her and counted four wallets. "The third lift wasn't as smooth as the first two I caught on record. Obviously, I missed one."

"You know, Officer Roman," Effie said as he opened the cruiser's back door, "that last wallet belongs to a young man who's been woefully undertipping all week. I like to think of what I do as price adjustment."

"His tipping habits are between him and his conscience, Mrs. Paulson, not your sticky fingers." Zack helped her into the backseat, impressed by her ability to maintain dignity even while being arrested.

He closed the door and was about to walk to the

240 | REGINA WELLING & ERIN LYNN

driver's side when his wife and her three best friends rushed across the street.

"Tommy O'Malley's possibly related to a family that once owned a cabin on the lake—we think he might be holding Cleo there!" The words tumbled out in a rush, at odds with Kat's usually measured speech.

Zack glanced at his watch, then at Effie sitting patiently in his cruiser. His duty as an officer pulled him in two directions.

"How solid is this information?" he asked, knowing the answer. Kat's psychic insights had proved reliable too many times to dismiss.

"Rock," she replied. "Iris and Edna just figured out the relationship. They've sent Howdy to check the cabin, but we need to get there now, Zack. Howdy said it's only accessible by boat."

Decision made, Zack radioed dispatch. "Roman here. Send one of the deputies to the corner of Main and Third to transport a suspect to the station. Elderly female, detained on a pickpocketing charge. She's in my ride, but I need to pursue a lead on the Martin case."

"Copy that, Officer Roman. Deputy Wilson is five minutes out," came the response.

"Thanks," Zack said, then returned to Effie, opening the door to explain the situation. "Mrs. Paulson, another officer will be taking you to the station. I have an emergency to attend to."

"Oh, sweetie," she cooed, undeterred by her circumstances, "you seem stressed. I have some homemade cookies in my purse if you'd like one. Made them fresh this morning."

Zack shook his head, unable to suppress a brief smile at her persistence. "I'll pass, thanks."

After ensuring Effie was secure and comfortable, he closed the door and, with quick strides, headed toward the marina and the police-issue boat bobbing gently at the dock.

"We're coming with you."

"Don't even try to stop us," Gustavia declared, her eyes resolute in a way that Zack knew better than to argue with. His sister took after their mother—stubborn to the bone and ornery with it when need be.

"All of you?" He looked at the small boat, mentally calculating its capacity.

"Yes," Amethyst said, her purple hair catching the light that bounced off the water. "All of us. Howdy's been sent to warn Everly as well."

"They're closer to the camp than we are," Julie added, already stepping into the boat without waiting for permission. Her athletic build made the maneuver look effortless.

Gustavia nodded vigorously, her necklaces clinking together like wind chimes. "Besides, strength in numbers. If Tommy has done something to Cleo, you might need backup."

"Fine," Zack conceded, "but follow my lead, stay back if there's any sign of danger, and no heroics. Clear?"

"Crystal," Amethyst replied with a smile that suggested compliance was a flexible concept in her mind.

They boarded quickly, the small craft rocking under their combined weight. Zack took the helm, starting the motor with a twist of his wrist. The sound echoed across the water, swallowed quickly by the lake's vastness.

"Damn it!" Only a couple of lengths from the dock, he noticed the lack of fuel, spun the boat in a tight arc, and swore again when he noted two other boaters waited to fill up at the pump.

Time stretched infuriatingly slowly, the fifteen minutes passed weighing on Zack's patience. When they finally pulled away from the dock once more, Kat's hand found his knee in a comforting gesture.

"Howdy said the cabin is past Miller's Point, tucked into a small cove that's hard to spot unless you know what you're looking for," she said, raising her voice above the motor's drone.

"I know the one." Zack steered the boat past the channel marker.

"Naked male insecurity," Gustavia shook her head and rolled her eyes at the same time. "That's what's at the heart of it. He couldn't beat her by fair means, so he resorted to foul."

"Fouler than foul," Amethyst spat out her opinion with a side of vitriol. "And for the record, I bet Kat twenty dollars that Tommy was involved somehow. I never win these bets, but I think I'm about to break my losing streak."

CHAPTER TWENTY-ONE

*D*rew pushed the throttle forward, sending the boat across the waves while he steered with a steady hand. The engine hummed along, and the gentle splash of water against the hull might have soothed if my nerves weren't wound so tight. We were close to finding Cleo, I could feel it in my bones. Still, I hadn't expected Tommy to be the culprit.

"I should have picked up on the clues," I raised my voice to be heard over the wind. "Like how Tommy pointed Ollie toward Cleo when his truck location got switched. And again with the sabotage."

"He damaged his truck to throw off suspicion," Drew reminded me. "That's why it was so easy to fix, and it worked. No one expects a victim to be the bad guy."

"Do you think he's cruel enough to kill Cleo? Kat said she was still alive, but who knows what he might have done to her since then."

"We'll get there, Everly," Drew said, reading my mind.

I nodded, but my eyes stayed glued to the shore, willing it to move faster. The wind whipped my hair, and I tried not to think about what would happen if we were too late.

When the engine sputtered to a stop, I nearly jumped out of skin that had taken on an otherworldly chill.

"There you are." A voice as familiar as it was unwelcome came from next to me as I turned to catch Howdy in the act of pulling the choke.

"What did you do that for? This isn't the time, Howdy," my voice rose to match my inner turmoil. "We're kind of busy. We think we've figured out who's behind Cleo's disappearance, and we're trying to get to town to do something about it."

More agitated than I'd ever seen him, Howdy said, "You're not the only one with big news."

Drew was already working on restarting the engine, his focus split between the boat and my one-sided conversation.

"Remember how Iris kept calling that barbecue fella the wrong name?" Howdy said, his voice picking up speed. "Turns out it wasn't a mistake. Well, it was a mistake, but a good one, I think."

"Talk faster," I snapped my fingers to indicate he should talk faster.

"Turns out she was mixing Tommy up with Johnny Boilard because of how they look alike. Anyway," he finally got to the point, his excitement palpable. "We figured out that young Tommy might be a relative of Johnny's. Johnny's father was Patrick Boilard."

"So?" I couldn't see what that had to do with anything, but then the name triggered something. "Wait. I've heard the name Patrick Boilard before."

"The cabin at the far end of the lake," Drew supplied.

Howdy practically danced with excitement. "That's the one. If Tommy's a relative, he might have known about the cabin."

It made a terrible kind of sense.

Drew was still fiddling with the engine, but I caught his curious glance and repeated a shortened version of Howdy's story.

"You think Cleo's at the cabin?" Drew finished up whatever repairs he'd been making, his face grimly satisfied.

"I do, now. We should go check it out," I decided. "If we can get this thing moving again."

As if on cue, the engine roared back to life.

"Nice work," I called to Drew, relief flooding through me.

He gave me a quick grin and turned the boat toward the far end of the lake.

I sent Howdy off to let Kat know we were heading to the cabin and clutched the side of the boat, my mind whirling. If Tommy had been connected to this Boilard, and Cleo was being held at that cabin, she must have been there when Howdy pointed it out the first time. My imagination supplied a far too vivid image of Cleo hearing the boat and thinking she was saved, only for us to turn around and leave. My stomach clenched. I should have put this together sooner, but there was no point in dwelling on it now.

"Hurry," I urged.

"Hang on." Drew pushed the boat to its limits, sending it cutting through the water with enough chop to make for a bumpy ride. I watched him steer us toward the cabin, my heart pounding with the engine's rhythm and hoping we'd find Cleo alive.

Drew docked the boat with precision, but the eerie quiet of the place sent a chill over my skin. The weathered camp appeared unchanged since we'd seen it before—its cedar shake siding weathered to a silvery gray, most of the paint peeled off the trim. Boards covered every window, and the front steps listed slightly to one side. After he tested them, I followed Drew up, every creak and groan echoing in the stillness.

Overhead, the pines stood tall and silent, as if holding their breath, and the air was thick with anticipation. I wasn't sure what we were walking into, but we had to get to her if Cleo was inside.

Drew pushed me behind him as we reached the door, his protective instincts kicking in. "Stay close," he said, his voice low and urgent.

I didn't argue.

The door opened with a groan of rusted hinges, and the sight that met us stopped me cold. Cleo was slumped on a ratty old sofa, her hair hanging in limp strings around her face, her wrists bound with rough rope, and her ankle shackled to the wall by a heavy chain.

"Oh my God," I breathed, rushing forward.

Drew was right behind me, his pocketknife already

out. "Cleo," he said, kneeling beside her. "We're going to get you out of here."

"About damn time," her voice came out muffled and tired.

CHAPTER TWENTY-TWO

*N*o wonder Kat had seen Cleo in a dark place. With the windows tightly boarded over, barely any light filtered into the cabin. Despite the panic that clawed at me, I forced myself to stay calm, pulled out my phone, and flicked on the flashlight.

Guided by its meager glow, I found an old wrench and attempted to undo the shackle bolts. "Sorry it took so long, but we've got you," I said, my voice firm. "Just hold on."

"How long?" Cleo's voice rasped.

One hand for the phone and one for the wrench wasn't working well. "Four days." About as long as it would take me to get these shackles off her without better tools.

"Who?" Was her next question.

Didn't she know who'd taken her? "Tommy," I said as Drew pulled out his pocket knife. "He was behind the sabotage, too."

"Trade." He handed it to me, hilt first, and took the wrench. Shrugging, I applied the sharp blade to the ropes and began to cut her free.

"Stay still," I urged gently. "I don't want to nick your

skin." Her wrists had to be sore, given the vicious welts she'd raised in her attempts to struggle free.

"Come on," Drew muttered, working at the nuts that didn't want to loosen.

"No." She shook her head, the motion nearly causing the knife to slip. "Who's winning?"

"It's not important now. Besides, I'm not sure." I'd only managed to saw through the first coil of rope when a distant sound caught my ear. The low rumble of an engine, getting closer by the second.

My heart skipped a beat. "Do you hear that?"

Drew's head snapped up. He went to the door, opened it a crack, and looked out. "ATV," he said, his expression tightening. "It's Tommy."

The name sent a jolt through me. "What do we do?"

Already on his feet, he pulled me up with him. "I want you behind the door. It will take his vision a few seconds to adjust. That should give me plenty of time to take him down."

"What if he has a knife? He's a chef, remember?"

"Won't be my first knife fight," Drew said grimly. "Just stay out of sight. But if he gets past me, remember your training. He won't be expecting you to fight."

I looked at Cleo. She looked at me, and my resolve hardened. "Got it. We'll get you out, Cleo. Trust us."

"Kick his ass," she said, her eyes glittering in the dim light.

It wasn't much of a plan, but it was all we had time for.

"Okay," I said, trying to sound more confident than I felt. "Let's do it."

With the rumble of the ATV's engine growing louder, filling the cabin with its menacing roar, we moved into position. My heart pounded in my ears, and I hoped we weren't making a huge mistake.

Drew's hand gripped mine. "Ready?"

"Ready." I nodded, squeezing back, then letting go to take my place behind the door. We braced ourselves, every muscle tense, as Tommy closed in.

My life's pattern had become distressingly predictable: find dead body, solve murder, enjoy a brief period of normalcy, then stumble into another life-threatening situation. Standing pressed against the rough-hewn cabin wall, hardly daring to breathe, I realized I'd skipped a few steps this time and jumped straight to the life-threatening part. The cabin smelled of mildew and something worse—the distinct scent of unwashed human desperation. Poor Cleo.

Across from me, Drew mirrored my position, his jaw set in that way that meant he was preparing for trouble. Between us, the door we expected Tommy O'Malley to walk through remained stubbornly closed while Cleo struggled against the half-cut bindings just a few feet away.

Hearing him coming, Cleo made small whimpering sounds that tugged at my heart. She wasn't gagged—Tommy hadn't gone that far—but being so close to freedom and seeing it snatched away had to be doing a number on her. I couldn't blame her. The thin walls of the decrepit cabin barely kept out the elements, and she'd been trapped inside for what, four days now? The thought made my stomach twist.

"Stay calm," Drew mouthed at me from across the doorway, his blue eyes intense, focused. Right. Calm. Because that was so easy when my heart was doing its best impression of a jackhammer against my ribs.

A floorboard creaked somewhere to our left, and Drew's attention snapped toward the sound. The cabin was small, just one main room with a kitchenette in the corner, and a single bedroom at the back. Waiting near the front door, it never occurred to us that Tommy might come in another way.

Stupid. So stupid.

The bedroom door burst open with enough force to bang against the wall, and there he stood—beard even more grizzled than usual, hand gripping a revolver that he pointed directly at me. Well, wasn't that just my luck?

"Don't do anything foolish," Tommy growled, his eyes darting between Drew and me like a cornered animal's.

I froze, my back pressed so hard against the wall I could feel every uneven ridge of the wood through my shirt. Across the room, Drew, his hands raised and ready, had gone entirely still. The only sound was Cleo's breathing, which had quickened to short, panicked gasps.

"Tommy," I said, keeping my voice deliberately soft, even as my mind screamed at me to duck, run, do something. "You don't want to hurt anyone. I know you're not that kind of person."

His hand trembled slightly, making the gun waver. "You don't know what I want. You shouldn't be here. Nobody was supposed to find this place. I was supposed to win the competition, take my money, and disappear forever. Get a new start. Then, I'd let someone know where Cleo was. I didn't plan to hurt her. You weren't supposed to find her yet."

"But we did find her," I said, attempting to sound more reasonable than terrified. "And now we need to figure this out together. You haven't hurt anyone, Tommy. Not yet. Let's keep it that way."

Something flickered in his eyes—uncertainty or maybe even relief. I didn't care which, only that the gun lowered a fraction of an inch. "You don't understand," he said, but the edge in his voice had already dulled.

"Help me understand," I said. "This isn't you, Tommy. Everybody's favorite uncle who makes great food—that's you. Not this." I gestured at the gun with my chin, not daring to move my hands.

Tommy's shoulders sagged, but the barrel remained pointed vaguely in my direction. "I needed the money. You have no idea how much I needed it. I've made some stupid decisions."

"Gambling debts?" I ventured, remembering the chip Effie had found.

He looked at me sharply, then gave a bitter laugh. "Everyone knows, don't they? 'Poor Tommy O'Malley, can't stop throwing good money after bad.' It wasn't always like this. I built my business from nothing, you know. Had a good reputation and a little extra cash, so I put some on a horse named Smoke. Seemed appropriate"

Drew shifted his weight slightly, and Tommy's attention snapped to him, the gun following. "Don't," Tommy warned.

"I'm not moving," Drew assured him, voice calm as still water. "We're just listening, Tommy. What happened with Smoke?"

"He won, so I bet on another one. And then another. It got away from me after that."

"I'm sorry," I said, hoping a little sympathy would help.

Tommy's focus returned to me, but he didn't relent. "Fifteen grand," he said with a hollow laugh. "That's what I owe. Might as well be fifteen million for all the chance I have of paying it back. The truck's been struggling. Everyone wants fancy fusion food now, not good old-fashioned BBQ."

He paced a few steps, gun still trained in our general direction, his free hand compulsively flexing. "I thought maybe I could win it back. Isn't that what they all say? Just one more game, one more bet. And then suddenly you're in so deep you can't breathe."

I glanced at Cleo, who had gone still on the sofa, clearly listening. "So you sabotaged Ollie's truck and took Cleo," I said softly. "To ensure your victory?"

Tommy gave a jerky nod. "The prize money from the

competition. Twenty-five thousand dollars. It would have cleared my debt and given me enough to start over somewhere else." His laugh was sharp, brittle. "But my bookie called and said I needed the money sooner. I didn't have it."

"Of course not," Drew said, his voice filled with sympathy. "What happened next?"

"You lost your boat key, so I made a copy. I figured I'd sell it and use the money to buy myself some time. I had a buyer all lined up. Even a couple of grand would've been enough to keep me from losing a pound of flesh." Tommy's voice cracked. "But then, I went out to turn my brisket, and Cleo was there."

"And you couldn't resist taking out your biggest competition," Drew said, his tone neutral but firm.

Tommy's face twisted. "I guess. It just happened. I didn't think about it. I grabbed her from behind so she wouldn't know it was me."

"Like I couldn't tell by the smell." Cleo's voice came out scratchy and muffled.

"She struggled, so I choked her until she passed out. I wasn't trying to kill you, Cleo. I swear, I wasn't."

"Asshole." She glared at him.

Ignoring that, Tommy swiped at his face with his free hand.

"I couldn't take a chance on getting her into the shuttle, so I used the boat key and brought her here. But then people started looking for her, and I didn't dare to sell the boat because it was the only way to keep an eye on her. I knew it was a stupid idea almost as soon as I did it, because it cost me what I needed to buy some time. I had to offer an extra five grand to keep from getting kneecapped."

The gun sagged lower in his grip. I could see the realization that his options were narrowing written in every line of his body. This was a man on the edge, and I wasn't sure which way he'd fall.

As if the situation weren't precarious enough, a familiar chill washed over the room. Great. Just what we needed—an audience from the afterlife. Two figures materialized near the cabin's small kitchenette: Edna, looking prim as ever, and Iris, clutching her hands to her chest. Wonderful. The dead were dropping in for the show.

"I just kept thinking if I could keep all the balls in the air until I won the competition, everything would be okay. But then I heard that cop say he was heading out here." He gestured with the gun, which was now pointed more at the floor than at either of us. "So I figured I'd better grab Cleo and clear out, but now you're here, mucking up the works. How did you figure out she was here, anyway?"

Half the truth was all he was getting. "Someone posted a selfie with a fuzzy image of you in the background, skulking around Ollie's truck on the night you sabotaged it. That got us looking at you, then someone mentioned you might have a connection to the owner of this place, so we came to check things out."

"It was me, you two-bit Johnny lookalike," Iris

shouted from across the room. "You aren't worth a hair on his backside."

I had to clench my jaw to keep from snorting.

"You know the rest," Drew said. "What matters is what happens next, Tommy."

His fingers tightened on the gun, then loosened. "I don't know what happens next," he admitted, voice barely audible. "I never meant it to go this far. But I can't go to jail. I just can't."

"You kidnapped someone, Tommy," Drew said quietly. "There's no walking away from that."

Tommy's face crumpled. "The guys I owe money to, they don't care if I'm in jail or not. They'll find me. They'll make me pay one way or another." His breathing grew more ragged. "I'm trapped. Don't you get it? I'm completely trapped."

In that moment, I saw him clearly—not as a villain, but as a desperate man who'd made one terrible choice after another until he couldn't see a way out. It didn't excuse what he'd done to Cleo, but I understood the fear that had driven him.

"It doesn't have to end with someone getting hurt," I said softly. "Put the gun down, Tommy. Let's figure this out together."

For one hopeful moment, I thought he might do it. His arm lowered another inch, the fight seeming to drain out of him. Then something hardened in his eyes.

"In the Steinman case of 1978," Edna announced to no one in particular, completely ignoring Tommy's confession, "the kidnapper was thwarted when the victim's sister noticed a peculiar detail in the ransom note. People always leave clues, you see."

"Oh, that was a scandalous affair," Iris agreed. "Though not half as scandalous as when Mayor Plimpton's wife ran off with the butcher in '62. Left nothing but a lipstick message on the bathroom mirror!"

The surreal juxtaposition of Tommy's grim confession and the ghosts' commentary was enough to make my head spin. Drew, meanwhile, inched forward almost imperceptibly, his eyes never leaving Tommy's gun hand.

"No," Tommy said, raising the gun again, this time with more resolve. "No, I've come too far to give up now. I need to get out of here—away from Maine, away from everything, and I need money to do that."

"And how exactly do you plan to get it?" Drew asked, his voice still steady despite the escalating tension.

Tommy's gaze darted around the cabin, then settled on me. "That cop is on his way, so we're going for a little walk in the woods. I'll do what I have to do, then I'll figure something out."

My stomach dropped. He was spiraling, desperation pushing him toward even more dangerous thinking. I'd hoped we were making progress, but now I saw the truth: the more trapped Tommy felt, the more dangerous he became.

Behind him, Iris slipped into full tizzy mode, her ghostly hands fluttering around her face. "Oh my stars and garters," she stage-whispered, loud enough that I had to fight not to wince. "That poor girl on the couch! And Whatshisname with a gun! Everly, you've got to do something. He looks dangerous."

Like I wasn't already aware of that, thanks very much.

Edna, bless her staunch heart, held on to her composure. She adjusted her glasses and assessed the situation with the same critical eye I could imagine her having on students researching a paper due the next day.

"I don't think I can walk," Cleo announced, her voice a thready rasp.

Tommy didn't care. He fixed his gaze on Drew, nodding toward Cleo. "Help her up. There's no time to waste."

"Do something," Iris shouted at me. "Before he hurts her."

"What about me?" I responded to Iris without thinking.

"You, too." Tommy gestured with the hand holding the gun. "One on each—"

His words trailed off in shock when the moldy roll of toilet paper Cleo had been forced to use flew across the room and hit him in the side of the head.

Go Edna. She'd remembered her emotion-fueled ability to affect the living world. I'm not sure who was more surprised about the fact, her or Tommy.

"Well, I'll be," she said, her face going grim with humor. "I guess I still have my throwing arm. Been a long time since I played shortstop on the softball team. Let's see if I can do it again." A citronella candle in a pink glass holder whizzed past Tommy's nose.

"How'd you do that?" Iris grabbed for a rusty tin can, but her hand went right through it.

"Get mad, and let her rip." Edna did just that, with everything in reaching distance.

"What the hell?" Tommy dodged the old tin pan Iris ripped off the nail it had been hanging on. Then a can opener, and an empty squeeze bottle with an inch of what looked like petrified ketchup in the bottom. "How are you doing that?"

Drew looked at me. I shrugged, but it didn't take much for him to figure out what was happening.

"Score one for the home team," Iris declared with unexpected glee, grabbing a fishing hat from a hook and launching it at Tommy's face.

"Foul ball!" Edna cried, somehow managing to sound both proper and utterly unhinged as she sent a stack of weathered playing cards flying like confetti.

"Two-point penalty for threatening innocent people!" Iris shouted.

"There are no penalties in softball, Iris. Don't you know anything?" Edna corrected while Howdy popped into the room, then right back out again.

The cabin erupted into supernatural chaos. A dusty lantern rocked on its hook. A box of matches rattled across the table. The ancient curtains billowed despite the windows being closed. And through it all, the ghosts provided running commentary that would have had me in stitches if my life hadn't been in danger.

"Take that," Iris announced, hurling a decades-old Farmer's Almanac with surprising accuracy, "You ungrateful cur."

The Almanac scored a direct hit on Tommy's gun hand. He spun in the direction it had come from just as Edna decided to show herself. Tommy's eyes went wide, his finger squeezing the trigger as if by reflex. Iris dropped to the floor before she remembered she was already dead, then struggled to regain her footing.

The gun went off with a deafening boom.

Gustavia leaned over the boat's bow like a figurehead, pointing the way. "There's Miller's Point. If we go around it, the cove should be right there."

Miller's point, a crooked finger of land with a few scrubby pine trees jutting into the sky, obscured their approach. Zack reduced the motor's speed as much for stealth as for navigating carefully around the minefield of submerged rocks that had previously claimed less cautious boats.

Past the point, the shoreline transformed from rocky outcroppings to a dense wall of pines that marched right to the water's edge, broken only occasionally by small gaps and clearings.

"There," Kat suddenly said, pointing to the weathered shack. "That's it."

Zack cut the motor, allowing the boat to glide silently toward the hidden cove. The only sounds were the gentle lapping of water against the hull and the distant call of a loon.

"Everyone stay back," he whispered, reaching under his jacket to ensure his service weapon was accessible. "This is police business, so you'll let me handle it. Understood?"

The women nodded, their earlier chatter muted by tension.

"Everly and Drew are already here," Gustavia noted the obvious when she saw their boat tied to the dock.

As Zack let the boat coast to a stop, a figure materialized at the water's edge—not stepping from the trees or emerging from the cabin, but simply appearing. Howdy's ghostly form was visible only to Kat, but she gasped loudly enough to make everyone freeze.

"What is it?" Zack asked, his hand moving to his gun.

"Howdy's here," Kat whispered. "He says Cleo's inside. Tommy's got the upper hand on Drew and Everly. He slipped in the back and caught them off guard."

"Okay." Zack's eyes narrowed as he secured the line and calculated his next move.

"There's more." Kat listened, then relayed what she'd heard. "Iris and Edna are in there, too. They're trying to help."

Inside the cabin, a gun went off.

"Stay here," Zack ordered, drawing his weapon fully. "This isn't a game or an adventure. It's my job. Let me do it."

With silent determination, he disembarked, the dock

creaking beneath his weight. As he moved toward the cabin, Gustavia stepped onto the pier.

"Hell with that," she said. "You coming?"

The others followed suit.

"Oh, I don't think so." Edna drew back a hand intending to slap Tommy silly, but it was a swing and a miss because her hand went right through his face.

"In all my seventy-three years," Iris announced, grabbing the cast iron grate from the dingy range, "I never met a man who couldn't be improved by a good whack upside the head at least once in his life!"

The grate spun through the air like a Frisbee and clocked Tommy in the chest at roughly the same time Drew gave me the nod, and we sprang into action. I went for Cleo. Grabbing the sofa with both hands, I heaved it up, tipping both it and her over so the base provided us both some protection as I covered her body with mine.

Tommy sensed the movement and tried to swing the gun around, but Drew was already on him. They collided with enough force to send them both staggering backward. Tommy's back hit the wall with a thud that shook dust from the ceiling. Drew reached for Tommy's gun hand, his face a mask of fierce concentration. Tommy fought back desperately, bringing his knee up toward Drew's midsection.

Pivoting, Drew avoided the worst of the blow. The two

men grappled, their shadows stretching grotesquely across the cabin walls in the dim light. Tommy's free hand clawed at Drew's face, but Drew ducked his head, using his shoulder to pin Tommy more firmly against the wall. His other hand camped around Tommy's wrist, forcing the weapon upward.

The gun went off again. I thought Cleo screamed, and I know I did while Drew and Tommy wrestled for control, but my ears were ringing from the gunshots, so it was hard to tell. Things happened fast after that. Edna picked up the tin pan Iris had thrown earlier and brought it down on Tommy's head just as Drew finally knocked the gun out of his hand. It landed on the floor with a thud.

Mostly stunned but unwilling to concede, Tommy made a half-hearted lunge for the weapon, but Drew got there first, kicked it away, and landed a solid punch to Tommy's jaw. When the gun slid past me, I abandoned Cleo, scrambling off her with less grace than I care to admit. My hand closed over solid metal as I rose off the floor and pointed the gun at Tommy.

"I've got it," I shouted in the loud tones of someone experiencing temporary hearing loss. Tommy froze as the cabin door burst open with enough force to rattle the hinges, revealing Zack Roman in full police officer mode, his stance wide and authoritative.

Behind him, four determined women crowded the doorway—Julie, Kat, Gustavia, and Amethyst—each with an expression that suggested they were fully prepared to handle whatever disaster lay inside. The cavalry had arrived, and not a moment too soon.

As relief washed through me, I sagged against the wall, my knees suddenly feeling as substantial as warm butter. Nothing says, "Your ordeal is almost over," quite like the arrival of an actual police officer and the posse of take-no-prisoners friends.

"Hands where I can see them!" Zack shouted, though the command had been rendered unnecessary. Tommy slumped against the wall, still dazed from Drew's punch, and Drew raised his hands to show he wasn't a threat.

"He's down," Drew said calmly, nodding toward Tommy. "Everly's got the gun."

"We heard shots. Is anyone hurt?" Kat and Julie rushed to my side while Gustavia and Amethyst hoisted Cleo off the floor.

"Mostly Tommy's pride," I said. "But Cleo needs medical attention. He shackled her to the wall."

Zack crossed the room in three quick strides, hand on his holster. He swiftly patted Tommy down for additional weapons, then pulled the handcuffs from his belt.

"Thomas O'Malley," Zack said, his voice taking on that official tone police officers must practice in the mirror, "you are under arrest for kidnapping and assault." He efficiently secured Tommy's wrists behind his back, continuing to recite Miranda rights as if he'd been waiting all day to use them.

Tommy barely struggled, the bravado and desperation that had animated him earlier collapsed into something closer to resignation.. He kept his eyes downcast, avoiding looking at any of us.

I'd barely registered our friends' presence beyond their timely arrival, but now I noticed Julie had a first aid kit in hand, and Kat carried a bottle of water and what looked like two energy bars.

"Let's get her free," Amethyst said, but Drew was already there, applying the wrench to the shackle bolts.

"It's okay," he told Cleo, his voice gentle. "You're safe now. We're getting you out of here. For real, this time."

I moved to help, taking Drew's knife and sawing through the bindings around her wrists. Days of struggling against them had tightened them until they cut cruelly into her flesh.

Once the ropes fell away, Drew put his hand under her chin and lifted Cleo's head. "You're safe."

"Water," she croaked, her voice rough from disuse or perhaps from crying.

Kat was there instantly, unscrewing the cap. "Small sips," she instructed, helping Cleo hold it to her chapped lips.

Cleo drank gratefully, but as the initial shock of freedom began to wear off, her gaze darted around the cabin, finally landing on Tommy. Something sparked in those tired eyes—a slow burn that quickly flared into rage.

"Loser," she said, the single word loaded with days of fear and humiliation.

Tommy couldn't meet her gaze and tried to melt into the wall and become invisible under Cleo's accusing stare.

"You kept me here," Cleo continued, her voice gaining strength with each word. "Tied up, in the dark, not knowing if you were planning to kill me."

"I wouldn't have hurt you," Tommy mumbled, still looking at the floor.

"Liar!" The force of her exclamation seemed to surprise even Cleo. She pushed herself to her feet, wobbling slightly. Drew moved to steady her, but she shrugged him off, determination etched into every line of her exhausted face.

"You don't think you hurt me?" She gave a brittle laugh that contained no humor whatsoever. "You knocked me out. Kidnapped me. Left me tied up for days, not knowing if I'd ever see my family again. What do you call that?"

Tommy had no answer, just a slight flinch at each accusation.

"Do you know what that's like?" she demanded, taking another unsteady step. "To sit in darkness, to feel your muscles cramping, to wonder if anyone is even looking for you? To hear a boat on the water and know it's too far away for the people to hear you because you've already screamed yourself hoarse?"

She stood directly in front of Tommy now. Zack moved as if to step between them, but something in Cleo's face must have stopped him. This was a confrontation she needed to have.

"Look at me," she ordered.

Tommy reluctantly raised his eyes to meet hers.

The slap came so fast I barely saw it happen—just a blur of movement and then the sharp crack of palm against cheek. Tommy's head snapped to the side, his eyes wide with shock.

"That's for taking days of my life," Cleo said, her voice trembling but strong.

Then, as quickly as her burst of energy had come, it drained away. Her knees buckled, and when Drew and I moved to catch her this time, she didn't resist. We guided her to the chair Julie had pulled out, easing her down gently.

"He deserved worse," Cleo said with a weak attempt at humor as Julie pressed a bottle of water into her hands.

"You were amazing," I told her. "Just amazing."

"She needs medical attention." Julie applied antibiotic cream to the raw abrasions on Cleo's wrists before wrapping them in soft bandages from the first aid kit. "Dehydration, malnutrition, and who knows what psychological trauma."

"I'll come back and process the scene later," Zack said. "For now, let's get these two back to town. I'll call ahead and have an ambulance waiting, but I think Cleo should ride with you. She'll be more comfortable on those padded seats."

Drew nodded. "Sure thing."

"I'll ride with you," Kat informed her husband. "You need a second set of eyes."

"Me too," Gustavia added, throwing Tommy a withering look. "If this creep tries anything funny, we'll toss him overboard."

"Ammie and I can ride with Everly and Zack." Julie unwrapped a protein bar, broke off a piece, and handed it to Cleo. "Small bites."

When Cleo attempted to stand, Drew shook his head. "Let me." He scooped her up in his arms as if she weighed nothing.

"My hero," she said, her gaze moving from his face to mine. "Both of you."

While we made our way slowly toward the door, I glanced back at the ghosts. Edna gave me a prim nod of approval. Iris beamed and waved enthusiastically. Howdy, it seemed, had found someplace better to be. A small smile tugged at my lips despite everything. The living might not always appreciate my connection to the dead, but it made all the difference today.

Once Cleo was settled, Drew started the engine, its steady rumble breaking the evening quiet. Zack did the same in the police boat. As both vessels pulled away from the dock, I watched the decrepit cabin recede into the distance.

Beside me, Cleo took another small bite of the protein bar, her eyes fixed on the horizon where Oakville waited. Her ordeal wasn't over—there would be statements to give, trauma to process, perhaps a trial to endure. But she was free, and no one had been killed. For now, that would have to be enough.

CHAPTER TWENTY-THREE

*C*oming back from a harrowing rescue mission shouldn't involve so much fanfare, but when your victim is a social media darling with thousands of followers, all bets are off. Word must have traveled fast because the docks buzzed with activity. Paramedics waited to assess Cleo's condition while onlookers used their cell phones to capture her dramatic return for posterity.

"You okay?" Drew asked, his eyes meeting mine briefly.

"Define okay," I muttered. Fans of Cleo's social media presence who'd been in town for the food truck competition crowded the paramedics trying to roll a gurney onto the dock. Their eager faces reminded me of vultures circling wounded prey, cell phones raised high to capture every moment of drama.

After handing Tommy off to one of his deputies, Zack ordered the crowd back to let the paramedics assess Cleo's condition. She waved them off when they would have lifted her from the seat, and stood under her own power to face her fans.

While the breeze from the boat ride had whipped my

hair into a tangled mess, it had somehow restored some of Cleo's curl and body. Remnants of bold makeup smudged beneath her eyes, highlighting them subtly. Instead of looking like the disheveled survivor of a harrowing experience, she gave off a subtle warrior vibe.

A lesser woman might hate her a little.

"I wish I had my phone," she said in a low voice. "Make sure they get my good side."

I blinked at her, momentarily stunned. "You've just been rescued from a kidnapping, and you're worried about angles?"

A weak smile played at her lips. "Brand management never stops, honey."

I couldn't decide if she was the most resilient person I'd ever met or simply the most singularly focused. Maybe both.

The crowd pressed closer, a sea of unfamiliar faces punctuated by the occasional recognizable one. Ollie stood to one side, his usual jovial expression replaced by something more complicated—concern, indeed, but something else lingered in his eyes as he watched Cleo be tended to. His thick fingers fidgeted with the edge of his apron, smudged with what looked like pizza sauce.

Beside him, Sophia tapped nervous fingers against her leg. She caught my eye and smiled encouragingly, but her attention focused mainly on Cleo.

Drew helped Julie and Amethyst from the boat, but Cleo grabbed hold of my hand when he got to me and wouldn't let me go. "Stay with me," she begged, so I did, but only after one of the paramedics said it was okay and convinced Cleo to let them help her onto the gurney.

"You need fluids." The other paramedic, a capable, no-nonsense woman whose calm demeanor reminded me of my mother, prepared an IV. "Just a little poke, and you'll be feeling better in no time."

Cleo winced when the needle slid into her vein.

"Oh, Cleo! Thank God, you're okay!" Tawny pushed forward with such force that several onlookers stumbled backward. "I'll go in the ambulance with her. I'm her oldest friend. That makes me practically family, after all."

Cleo's hand shot up like a barrier. "No, you're not, Tawny. We were never friends. You couldn't be bothered to speak to me when we were kids. Now that I have a little fame, you're just someone trying to get a taste of it." The words cracked through the air with unexpected venom, causing Tawny to freeze mid-stride.

"That's just mean," Tawny pouted. "All I ever wanted was to be like you."

"You'd be better off," Cleo nodded in my direction. "If you were more like Everly. She's the real deal."

The paramedics exchanged glances and continued their work, securing Cleo to the gurney. She gave my hand a final squeeze before letting go. "Thanks for everything. I'll never forget it," she murmured, her voice softer now, vulnerable in a way I hadn't heard before.

While the gurney bumped over uneven dock boards, Chase, hands shoved deep in his pockets, uncertainty written across his face, stood next to the waiting ambulance.

"Cleo," was all he said.

"It's okay," she responded.

The sun flashing off a phone screen nearly blinded me when Tawny, recovered from her rebuff, raced forward to film the moment, her lips moving in what appeared to be running commentary for her followers.

"Is she for real?" I muttered to no one in particular.

Cleo shot me a look. "Is anyone?" She asked as if that explained everything about Tawny's behavior. Maybe it did.

I stepped back, watching as they closed the doors. The ambulance pulled away, its siren wailing into the late afternoon air, leaving a strange emptiness in its wake. Though many lingered, the crowd began to disperse, typing furiously on their phones—no doubt updating their social media accounts with first-hand reports of Cleo's return.

"She good?" Drew asked when I returned to where he stood with Zack and the rest of our friends.

"She'll do. There's steel under that socially polished exterior. She asked me to call her mom."

"Already done," Zack caught my eye and nodded. "She's on her way to the hospital as we speak. I need to deal with Tommy now. You folks can go on back to the lake house. I'll come by later to take your formal statements."

"We'll all come by the lake house later, if that's okay,"

Gustavia spoke for the group. "With celebration pizza. I want to hear everything that happened before we got there. I'll text you the details."

"Sounds good." Drew slipped an arm around my waist and winked at me with the eye that wasn't turning black. "You ready?"

"More than." I let him lead me back to the boat, but didn't say much while he slowly backed away from the pier and steered toward the gas pump for a much-needed fill-up.

"Quite the honeymoon we're having," Drew remarked once we were underway again, his eyes fixed on the water ahead.

I laughed, the sound surprising me with its genuine mirth. "Never a dull moment, huh?"

His hand found mine. "Wouldn't have it any other way."

The house came into view, its modern lines and floor-to-ceiling windows reflecting the lake at us. After the crowded dock and the rescue drama, the sight of our temporary home filled me with unexpected comfort.

Molly barked a warning when she heard our steps on the deck, and her face popped up in the window. Seeing us, she barked again, this time in greeting.

I noticed a plastic container sitting on the step. "Looks like we had visitors," I said, bending to pick it up.

Someone had left us cookies—perfect golden-brown circles studded with chocolate chips. The note taped to the lid read: "A little sweetness for a lovely couple. Sorry to have missed you! – Effie and Carlton."

"That was thoughtful of them," Drew said, unlocking the door. "I wonder where they went."

Inside, Drew ruffled Molly's fur while I set the container on the kitchen counter. The lake house welcomed us back with silent comfort—no crowds, cameras, or drama. Just the two of us and the gentle sound of the water lapping at the shore outside.

The sofa called my name, but so did the container of cookies. After today's excitement, they felt like a reward.

"Want one?"

"They smell amazing," Drew murmured, taking a bite, his eyes closing in appreciation.

"And taste even better," I agreed.

"I think they're even better than Patrea's," he said, a playful glint in his eye as he referenced our friend's famous—and famously guarded—cookie recipe.

I laughed and waved my cookie at him. "Don't you dare say that to her. We'll never hear the end of it."

The evening air carried the tang of pine and lake water as it swept across the deck of Bailey's Lakeside Getaway. Citronella-fueled torches kept bugs at bay and, along with patio lights, created a glowing oasis in the otherwise velvety darkness. I sat with my feet propped up on an empty chair, nursing a glass of wine and trying to process the day's events, when the crunch of tires on gravel announced the arrival of our friends. My stomach growled in anticipation of the pizza I knew they'd bring—nothing builds an appetite quite like saving someone from a kidnapper.

"They're here," Drew called from inside, his footsteps crossing the hardwood floor toward the front door.

I smiled into my wine glass, oddly relieved. After the day we'd had, the normalcy of friends gathering for pizza felt like a lifeline to sanity.

The sliding door to the deck opened, and out poured several of my favorite people in the world, arms laden with pizza boxes. The rich aroma of melted cheese, tomato sauce, and freshly baked dough wafted ahead of them, making my mouth water.

"There she is—our very own Nancy Drew," Gustavia announced, her looping braids adorned with what appeared to be tiny silver fishing lures that caught the light as she moved. She set down a stack of pizza boxes on the outdoor table and enveloped me in a vanilla and spice-scented hug.

"Pretty sure Nancy Drew never had to deal with kidnapped food truck competitors," I said, returning her embrace.

"Or ghosts," Kat added quietly, her blue eyes meeting mine with understanding. As a fellow medium, she was one of the few who truly understood what it was like to see the dead as clearly as the living.

Zack followed behind her, carrying a cooler, his police uniform exchanged for jeans and a casual button-down.

"Brought beer," he said simply, setting it down with a solid thunk. "For after the statements."

Amethyst breezed past, her purple hair a vibrant streak in the soft deck lighting. "And wine," she added, lifting a bottle in each hand. "Because some situations require options."

Reid trailed behind her, giving me a warm smile. "Thought you might need reinforcements after today."

Julie and Tyler were the last to emerge onto the deck, arms linked, carrying paper plates and napkins. "We come bearing the essentials," Julie announced.

"And gossip," Tyler added with a grin. "So much gossip."

"Food first," Finn declared, opening the top pizza box and releasing a fresh wave of mouthwatering scent. "Statements and gossip second."

Drew followed with the tray of glasses we'd prepared earlier. For a few minutes, chaos reigned as everyone helped themselves to slices of Ollie's pizza—the irony of eating food made by one of the food truck competitors after rescuing another wasn't lost on me—and poured drinks.

Finally, we settled into a loose circle of chairs, the glow of the deck lights illuminating faces that had become so dear to me. For a moment, no one spoke, just the sounds of contentment as hunger was satisfied after a long, stressful day.

"So," Amethyst broke the silence, leaning forward with her elbows on her knees, "are we going to talk about how you two managed to find trouble on your honeymoon, or are we pretending this is normal?"

"In their defense," Gustavia said, waving a slice of pizza for emphasis, "trouble does seem to find Everly rather than the other way around."

"It's a gift," I deadpanned, sipping wine.

Zack cleared his throat, his expression shifting subtly from friend to police officer. "I'd like to get your official statements about today. The sooner we document everything, the better."

Drew nodded, setting aside his empty plate. "Where do you want us to start?"

"How did you figure out where Cleo was?" Zack said, pulling out a small tablet and stylus from his pocket.

I exchanged glances with Drew, knowing some of our story might not make it into the official reports.

"Well," I described seeing Tommy somewhere he shouldn't have been on one of Cleo's followers' posts. "We were heading to town to talk to him when Howdy showed up with the news that Tommy had ties to Oakville, specifically, to a remote cabin."

Drew picked up the thread seamlessly. "We'd seen it from the water before. To think we were that close and had no idea Cleo was there...well, it's hard to swallow."

We ran through the chain of events. It didn't take long.

"I didn't expect him to have a gun," Drew admitted.

"It belonged to a man going by the name of Carlton Paulson. Tommy 'borrowed' his ATV."

"That's right," Drew nodded. "Carlton told us he carried one in case he and Effie ran into a bear or something."

"It took at least a year off my life when we heard it go off," Gustavia said, a shudder going through her body.

"If not for some unconventional help, he'd have taken more than a year off our lives," I explained.

"We saved your butts, is what we did." Making the extra effort to show herself to all, Iris shimmered into visibility almost as soon as I'd felt the unmistakable chill of her presence.

"Unconventional! Is that what we are now?" Edna Mayfield materialized beside the railing, her tall, thin frame as precise and proper as ever, even after confronting a criminal. "I prefer to think of it as 'specialized assistance.'"

Howdy appeared next. "Oh, don't be so touchy, Edna. The girl's trying to give a statement without sounding crazy."

I suppressed a sigh. "I'm pretty sure that ship has sailed."

Zack didn't flinch, to his credit, though his pen paused over his notebook. "Ladies," he acknowledged with a respectful nod. "Howdy."

"We're here to make our statements, too," Iris said, her eyes twinkling. "For as long as I'm dead, I'll never forget the look on Johnny's face when that roll of toilet paper hit him."

"His name is Tommy," Edna corrected. With the ghost's help, we filled in the rest of the blanks.

"Drew tackled him," I said, unable to keep the pride from my voice. "And then you showed up."

A moment of silence fell over the deck as Zack finished writing. Then he looked up, his gaze shrewd. "I'll keep the flying toilet paper out of the report and just say you were able to subdue the suspect."

"So we don't even get a mention?" Edna sounded annoyed. "Howdy wasn't any help, but Iris and I did our part."

"Sorry," Howdy said, his tone sounding anything but apologetic. "I got distracted. Young Jeb Peterson caught Biggie Smallie. Can you believe it? After all these years!"

"Biggie Smallie?" Amethyst frowned. "Is that a rap artist? Or some small-time mob boss?"

"No," I snorted out a laugh. "It's a fish."

"Not just any fish!" Howdy protested, pacing the deck and passing straight through Julie, who gasped at the sudden cold. "Biggie Smallie! The legendary smallmouth bass that's been eluding fishermen on this lake for decades! I lost my life trying to land that monster!"

"I've heard of that one," Reid nodded. "I thought it was an urban myth...or what passes for urban around here, anyway."

Howdy pushed his fishing hat farther back on his head, his ghostly face alight with awe and envy. "Twenty-seven pounds! Can you believe it? That's the catch of a lifetime. Too bad it wasn't mine."

Still, as Howdy spoke, something strange began to happen. A subtle glow emanated from nearby space, growing steadily brighter until it illuminated his entire form.

"Howdy?" I asked, suddenly understanding what was happening. "Is Biggie Smallie your unfinished business?"

The ghost fisherman paused in his excited pacing, looking down at his hands in wonder as they began to shimmer with golden light. "Well, I'll be," he murmured. "I guess it was. I always said I wouldn't rest until that fish was caught."

Edna sniffed. "Rather mundane, if you ask me. My unfinished business involves the proper return of seventy-three overdue library books."

"Nobody asked you, Edna," Iris chided softly, her eyes fixed on Howdy as the light grew more intense.

"I think Howdy's crossing over," Kat explained quietly, her eyes fixed on the glowing figure. "I usually only talk to spirits after they've crossed, so this is something I've never seen before."

Howdy's face split into a wide grin as the light enveloped him completely. "Well, it's been real, folks! Guess it's finally my time. Tell Jeb I said 'nice work'!"

And with that, he expanded into pure light before collapsing into a single bright point and disappearing altogether. A sense of peace washed over the deck, replacing the chill that had accompanied the ghosts. While they hadn't crossed, Iris and Edna went to wherever ghosts go when they're recharging.

I blinked, my eyes readjusting to the regular deck lighting. "He's gone," I said softly. "Rest in peace, Howdy."

Zack cleared his throat, drawing our attention back to his notebook. "So, to summarize: social media intel led you to the cabin where you found Cleo and apprehended Tommy. Is that correct?"

"That's about the size of it," Drew confirmed, squeezing my hand.

Zack made a final note, then closed his notebook with a decisive snap. "Well, that's all I needed. Tommy confessed to everything. The gambling debts, the tampering with Ollie's truck, and the kidnapping. He didn't mention anything about ghosts, but the rest is enough to put him away for a long time."

"How did he get hold of Carlton's gun?" Drew wanted to know. "You said he borrowed the ATV?"

A small smile played at the corners of Zack's mouth. "Interesting you should mention that. Your next-door neighbors were picking pockets at the food truck festival."

I nearly choked on my wine. "What? Effie and Carlton? The sweet little old couple celebrating their fiftieth?"

Zack nodded, looking amused. "Not their real names, as it turns out. We've been tracking a pair of con artists who target crowded events—they pose as friendly tourists while lifting wallets and jewelry. I caught 'Effie' in the act. 'Carlton' managed to swoop in and rescue her before backup arrived to take her into custody. According to bystander accounts, Tommy stole and took off with the ATV while the pickpocketing seniors got away."

"But they left us cookies," Drew said, sounding almost offended on their behalf.

"Genuine fondness for you, maybe," Finn suggested with a chuckle. "Con artists are people, too, I guess."

Conversation flowed more freely after that, the tension of the day's events gradually easing as we listened to the water lap against the dock. The deck lights cast shifting patterns across our faces, and laughter punctuated the night air.

I leaned back in my chair, letting the voices of my friends wash over me. Drew's arm draped casually across my shoulders, a comfortable weight that anchored me to the present moment. Despite our honeymoon's bizarre twists, I found myself relaxing for the first time in days.

Sometimes the strangest circumstances led to the most perfect moments. And sitting there under the stars, surrounded by friends who accepted every weird facet of my life without question, I decided this was exactly the kind of honeymoon I was meant to have.

EPILOGUE

*T*wo days passed in relative peace before we packed up the car and bid farewell to Oakville. The remainder of our honeymoon had been gloriously uneventful—no more kidnappings, no new ghosts, and not a single picked pocket in sight. Still, as we pulled into the driveway of our home in Mooselick River, a piece of me was glad it was over, and we could get back to our usual routines.

Molly let out a welcoming bark when she saw our familiar front porch. Drew killed the engine and turned to me with a smile that still made my heart skip. "Home sweet home, Mrs. Parker."

"Home sweet home, Mr. Dupree." After everything we'd been through—murder accusations, ghostly interventions, and a honeymoon that veered wildly off-script—the simple fact that we'd made it to this moment felt like a minor miracle.

We sat for a moment, soaking in the familiar sights. I noted the hanging ferns I'd worried would die in our absence, looking suspiciously healthy. I made a mental note to thank my mom for remembering to water them.

I noticed a package by the front door as Drew hauled our suitcases toward the porch. It was wrapped in brown paper and tied with simple twine, with only our address on the shipping label.

"What's that?" Drew asked, setting down the bags.

"No idea." I approached cautiously, my habit of ending up adjacent to murder having taught me a healthy suspicion of unexpected deliveries. "No return address."

"Secret admirer?" Drew suggested, the corner of his mouth quirking up.

I rolled my eyes. "More likely someone trying to kill us with a mail bomb."

"Always the optimist."

"Hey, my life is weird. You never know."

Molly sniffed at the package, her tail still wagging, which I took as a positive sign. Dogs could sense evil, right? Or was that just ghosts? I couldn't remember.

Curiosity overcoming caution, I picked up the package. It was lighter than it looked. Probably not a bomb. I carried it inside and set it on the kitchen table while I hunted down a pair of scissors to cut the twine. Inside lay a folded blanket, its hand-crocheted texture and color instantly familiar.

"Recognize this?" I called to Drew, running my fingers over the impossibly even stitches.

He emerged from the bedroom, my blue bikini top dangling from his fingers. "Effie?"

"That's right," I said, running my hand over the softly blended colors.

"Huh." Drew sat beside me, reaching out to touch the blanket. "So our criminal neighbors sent us a handmade gift. That's... oddly thoughtful."

"Even on the run from the law, Effie thought of me," I mused, unable to suppress a smile. "I'm torn between being touched and concerned about my ability to attract the weirdest people."

"You attract all kinds," Drew said, dropping a kiss on the top of my head. "Including perfectly normal fitness center owners who have a fondness for these." He waved the bikini top.

"You're the exception that proves the rule," I teased, snatching the scrap of blue from his hand and setting it aside. "Come on, help me unpack. I want to get settled before I let everyone know we're back."

For the next hour, we fell into the comfortable routine of returning to real life—unpacking suitcases, sorting laundry, and checking the mail accumulated in our absence. Molly thoroughly sniffed all her favorite pee spots and made new deposits.

Eventually, with the worst of the unpacking done and laundry humming in the washing machine, I collapsed onto the couch and pulled out my phone.

"I'm sending out a blanket text," I announced to Drew, who was in the kitchen investigating the state of our refrigerator. "Just letting everyone know we're home and alive."

"Good idea," he called back. "Also, we need groceries.

Unless you want condiments and one suspicious apple for dinner."

"We'll order from Berties." I quickly composed a text to our central circle of friends and family: "Home safe and sound. Honeymoon was eventful—ask us about the food truck kidnapping and our criminal neighbors sometime. Hugs to all!"

A notification from one of my social media apps popped up as I hit send. For the past two days, I had studiously ignored these, but the preview caught my eye —a photo tagged with names I recognized. Curiosity piqued, I tapped to open it.

The image filled my screen: Tawny Ray and Chase Williams, their heads tilted together in what was unmistakably a couple's selfie. His arm wrapped around her shoulders, and he gazed at her with an expression I can only describe as besotted. The caption read: "Found someone who appreciates authenticity over likes! #NotJustCleosLeftovers #NewBeginnings."

I burst out laughing, the sound carrying through the house.

"What's so funny?" Drew asked, wandering back from the kitchen with a glass of water.

I held up my phone, still chuckling. "Tawny and Chase are a thing now. Apparently, he's moved on from Cleo to her biggest fan. Or maybe not so much anymore."

Drew peered at the screen, his lips twitching. "She's changed her hair. It's almost the same color as yours. Did you notice?"

I hadn't.

My phone rang, cutting off further commentary. I glanced at the screen to see Jacy's name.

"Hey, Jace," I answered, settling back against the couch cushions. "We just got home."

"I know, I saw your text," she replied, her voice carrying that particular lilt it got when she was bursting with news. "I'm glad you're back. You won't believe what happened while you were off having your drama-free honeymoon—someone was murdered."

We know you're wondering what's next for Everly now that her life has settled down—well, as much as it can when ghosts are involved. Get ready for something a little different.

Keep reading to learn a little bit about the next book, Soul Proprietor. Also, if you're wondering what happened with Carlton, Effie, and Tommy right before the big showdown, check out our bonus content for that deleted scene!

~Also Available in Audiobook & Paperback Versions~

Quick Author's Note

One thing we're sure you've noticed about this book was the lack of murder. There were two solid reasons for that.

The first is that this book took place in Oakville as a crossover with the Psychic Seasons crew. If you've read the four main books in that series, you will already know that it wasn't a murder mystery series. In fact, Oakville is entirely murder-free and Everly wasn't about to be the one to change that.

The second reason is that we've tossed an awful lot at Everly leading up to, and on her wedding day. We just didn't have the heart to add one more death to the toll. She deserved a honeymoon sans dead body, so we gave her one. She didn't come away completely unscathed in the mystery department, but for once, she didn't rack up a body count.

The same, however, cannot be said for what went on back in good old Mooselick River in her absence. The next book in the Everly series will give you the inside scoop on what happened there while she was gone. Jacy and the rest of the gang—which includes Kitty and Leandra—solve a murder. Uh oh.

While Everly's away, the sleuths will play... and naturally stumble over a body.

With Everly and Drew off honeymooning, Mooselick River enjoys a rare moment of calm—until Jacy, Neena, and Patrea sign up for a girls' night at the town's newest

attraction and find themselves locked in an escape room...
with a dead man.

The victim? A charming travel vlogger whose visit was supposed to bring positive buzz to *The Strand Escape*, a handmade experience crafted by newcomer Kari Palmiscno in the back room of the old Strand Cinema. What was meant to be good publicity turns into a nightmare when Kari becomes the prime suspect. But something doesn't add up.

As the mystery deepens, the sleuth squad recruits Kitty and Leandra to help unravel a case filled with hidden motives, small-town rivalries, and the kind of ghostly interference Mooselick River is famous for.

Anyway, if you've come this far with us and not decided we're complete and total whackadoodles...and especially if you have, we're offering a chance to sign up for our newsletters— the best place to get new release updates, sales notifications, and other fun content.

You can sign up for ReGina's newsletter and/or Erin's newsletter and as a thank-you gift for hanging out with us, you'll also get a FREE novella that isn't available anywhere else. And of course, we promise not to SPAM your inbox!

Love, hugs, and happy reading,

ReGina & Erin

P. S. If you enjoyed this book, it would be great if you could leave a review or recommendation on Amazon, GoodReads or BookBub.

Your reviews help indie authors sell more books!

*T*he honeymoon was over, and given the way it had turned out, I was okay with that. I mean, the lake house was terrific, and having access to the boat had made it all the better. But considering my life trajectory, I probably shouldn't have expected the peace of a ghost-free vacation, anyway. But no one had died for once, and that was a plus I could live with.

Besides, we'd needed the chance to decompress after the chaos surrounding the wedding and then the aftermath. Fifty cents said Drew would be looking through real estate sites for lakefront property within twenty-four hours. Fingers crossed, there would be something. I hadn't realized how much I enjoyed time on the water. But that was a problem for another day.

By the time we'd unpacked and sorted through the mail my mother had left on the hall table, I was more than ready to collapse on the couch with a glass of wine, a hot slice of Bertino's finest, and—since one of those pieces of mail contained the DVD—a front-row seat to the wedding I'd barely had time to enjoy the first time around.

"Ready?" Drew asked, remote in hand, the box containing a loaded pizza resting on the coffee table between us like an offering to the gods of greasy comfort food. He'd already cued up the menu screen.

"Hit it," I said, tucking my legs under me and stealing a pepperoni slice off the top before the video even started.

The opening chords of something vaguely classical swelled as the screen lit up with an intro showing our names and the date before panning to an exterior shot of Wentworth House, the porch dressed in floral finery. Just as the camera landed on my arrival, in the classic car I'd gifted to my father, the doorbell rang.

"Wonder who that is," Drew said, grinning as he punched the pause button.

Two fast knocks followed the bell, telling me exactly who stood outside my front door, which swung open before I could reply.

Jacy.

She burst into the house like she was trying to outrun her personal demons. Winded, red-cheeked, and carrying the energy of someone who'd mainlined espresso, she made a beeline for me. Honey-colored hair swung free around her shoulders, a clear sign she'd been in a hurry to leave the house without pulling it back into its usual tail.

"Are you—" Was all I managed to get out after I got my breath back when she hugged me so hard almost dropped the slice I'd just pulled from the box.

"I'm sorry, I know, we were planning to come over tomorrow and hear all about the honeymoon, but I couldn't wait that long." She hugged Drew next. "I want to hear everything, and I mean everything, but first—"

She went quiet when she caught sight of the TV screen, which had frozen on an image of me walking ahead of my father as he ushered me into the house.

"Ohhh," she breathed, seeing the paused wedding footage. "Look at him. He's beaming and trying not to cry." Her eyes went glossy. "Gets me right in the feels. It was such a beautiful day. You know...mostly."

She flopped onto the couch, grabbed a slice of pizza like it was her emotional support snack—which I happened to know it wasn't—and took a bite.

"I have to tell you what happened while you were gone. Unless your mom already did." Jacy sounded as if she might be disappointed if that were the case.

"Unless it has to do with the snafu at the annual book sale at the library, I think you're safe."

"Good." Jacy took her first full breath. "Then do I ever have a story for you."

"The adult version of 'what I did on my summer vacation'? I can't wait to hear it. Let me get you a drink first." Drew went to the kitchen and came back with a glass of iced tea, which Jacy gratefully accepted and sipped to wash down another bite of pizza.

"It all started the day after you left."

And just like that, I wasn't the main character in my own story anymore. Jacy was.

***Okay. So. You know how sometimes you just know something's going to go sideways, but you do it anyway because you think maybe this time will be different?

That's how we ended up at the escape room.

Well, sort of. Let me back up.

It actually started with those local business owner meetings—you know, the ones you never come to because you "don't technically own a business," which is just a fancy way of saying you're too smart to get roped into three-hour discussions about sandwich board placement and bulk discounts if we all chip together and buy from the big box store in Bangor.

Anyway, that's where I met Kari. Kari Palmiscno. You remember her? New in town, married to this super chill guy named Michael. Michael will be taking over as manager at the bank next month, and Kari's working there, too. But the best thing is they're both heavy into amateur theater in their spare time, and absolutely determined to bring The Strand back from the dead. Which, if you ask me, is both a noble and slightly cursed pursuit. Everyone knows the place is haunted.

Still, they're planning to restore the building—get the projector running again, eventually host live productions, add a gaming annex in the back, and maybe even put together a summer program for kids who want to act. The whole nine yards. But of course, restoring the seats would cost a fortune, and their finances were already stretched thin just buying the building.

Then they got hit with the news they'd have to update the projection equipment because everything's digital these days. And so, they came up with the idea to turn the backstage area into a temporary escape room to raise extra money. I thought it was genius.

Theater people know drama, right? And they're gamers besides, so they figured they could blend everything they love into building a good story. And who knows props and puzzles better than someone who's had to rig a trapdoor with fishing line and duct tape between the first and second act of a play?

They named the escape room The Final Curtain, which felt appropriately dramatic. When Kari asked if we'd beta-test it before it opened to the public, I practically jumped in her pocket and dragged Neena and Patrea along for the fun.

I mean, it was supposed to be a girls' night. A little bonding. A little puzzle-solving. Maybe a fake ghost or two if we were lucky. With you off in honeymoonland, the real kind wasn't in the cards, but you know how it is.

What we didn't expect was to find a real, live dead guy. But I'll get to that.

We were just about to head into the third room when it happened. Kari and Michael had set the whole thing up like a haunted theater mystery—think doomed production, cursed scripts, moody lighting. Honestly, it was kind of brilliant. She said the next version might even have a fog machine if Michael could figure out how to run one without tripping the fire alarm or making anyone sick.

We were having a blast. Patrea was taking notes as if she were preparing to audit the room, while Neena was muttering about lighting choices and the proper paint technique to give the props more flair, and I was mainly just giggling and dancing around like a gremlin in a glitter closet.

Then we heard it.

This dragging sound, and then a thump. Followed by silence.

Neena froze. Patrea's eyes narrowed. And me? I immediately assumed it was part of the game.

I mean, c'mon. It's called The Final Curtain. Of course, someone's going to fake their death dramatically. I figured it had to be a requirement or something. We got through that room and then had to navigate a spooky passage before we reached the next one. And then...

The door clicked open, and we stepped into what was supposed to be the old dressing room scene. That's when we saw him.

At first, I thought he was a prop. Some kind of incredibly lifelike mannequin sprawled on the floor behind a dressing table.

It wasn't.

It was Brett Haskins.

And he was very, very dead.

"Jacy, stop."

Everly's voice cut through my word sprint like a brake screeching right before the worst happens.

I blinked. She was still holding her wine glass—untouched since I started talking.

"Start over," she said. "From the beginning. With breathing this time."

"Who's Brett Haskins?" Drew interrupted

I opened my mouth to protest because I was right there, about to describe the blood and the footlight and the letter opener, but the look Everly gave me channeled her mother. You didn't mess with that look. You just didn't.

So I nodded, took a breath, and started again.

Soul Proprietor is available now. Keep reading for a preview of the free novella you'll get for joining our newsletters.

A FREE STORY FOR YOU

*E*njoyed meeting Everly? Not ready for her story to end?

Sign up for either or both of our newsletters and you'll receive *A Snowball's Chance in Spell*, a prequel novella featuring characters from the *Mag & Clara Balefire Mysteries*, the *Haunted Everly After Mysteries*, and the *Psychic Seasons* series.

Christmas is canceled! Lexi Balefire's faerie godmothers didn't mean to knock Santa Claus and his sleigh out of the sky, but now his reindeer are missing, and it's up to Lexi to find them all before time runs out and Christmas is ruined!

Excerpt from A Snowball's Chance in Spell

～

*L*ightning flirted in shadows of the dark clouds hovering over my house when I came home from work the afternoon before my twenty-second Christmas Eve. Nothing unusual there. With three elemental faeries living in the house, weird weather happened all the time. Or rather, every time my temperamental godmothers mounted some sort of snit.

The godmothers idled at snit.

Going back to work wasn't an option. I'd cleared the last match of the year—a lovely couple with a shared affection for online gaming—and I was no coward. When it came to diffusing faerie fights, I consider myself an expert, and this one didn't look like it rated more than a two on the volcano scale.

Yes, you heard right. I measure faerie fights on the scale of whether or not a volcano might erupt in my backyard. Living with faeries is never boring. Occasionally dangerous—especially because I have yet to come into the magic that is my birthright, but never boring.

A quick check proved they'd contained the madness to the inside and/or the backyard. The two feet of snow on the front lawn was still there and still white—you try explaining black snow to your neighbors sometime. I didn't see any winged denizens—fae or otherwise— dotting the roof ridge, or hear any ominous sounds. If not for the fact that lightning is rare in Maine during the winter, and rarer still when confined to a single area, I'd have thought it was a quiet day in the household.

In my head, I downgraded the threat to a level one, and went inside.

For the most part, my place looks like an ordinary, New England style home. Built by my great grandparents, it's the oldest house in a neighborhood that grew up around it when the suburbs expanded into what was once a rural area. Because, I think, the faeries wanted to give me a normal upbringing, they left the house in mostly the same condition it was in when they came to take care of me and only added on a wing for their own use.

I stepped into the front hall expecting...well, just about anything. Did I mention the faeries love holidays? Maybe they don't have them in the faelands, or maybe they do and go overboard there, too. I can't say since I've never been, but I could tell at a glance there were more decorations than there had been when I left.

"Terra!" I yelled, but got no answer. Terra, faerie of earth, held sway over all the flora and fauna found on dry land. She would be the one responsible for the pine boughs twining over anything that held still long enough. Fire faerie, Soleil, contributed by setting sparks of faerie light to twinkle inside the delicate ice bubbles crafted by her sister, Evian, mistress of water. The effect was lovely, but not as lovely as the three women could be when their faces weren't twisted, as they were now, with rage.

I came upon them in their favorite fighting grounds: the kitchen. It looked like I'd caught this one early since there was relatively little damage done so far. Steam rose from a puddle of water at Soleil's feet which I assumed had come from Evian. Vines snaked from between the kitchen tiles to twine around Evian's ankles, and there were a few smoking embers dotting Terra's hair. Nothing more than a minor spat.

Keeping it casual, I asked, "What's going on?" There's no rhyme or reason to what will settle a fight or send one into the red zone.

Terra turned one granite pink eye in my direction. "This doesn't concern you." The fingers of her left hand twitched and the vines slithered from Evian's ankles to her knees.

Retaliating, Evian conjured a gush of water from thin air, and doused the smoking embers. The scent of pine boughs couldn't compete with the stench of burnt hair, or the pungent funk erupting from the flowers that burst into bloom near her feet.

"Now look," I pointed out to Terra before she conjured something worse. "Evian is trying to help."

"Was not." Evian snapped her fingers and turned Terra's wet hair white with frost, except because the vines were now questing higher, she overshot the mark and doused a few of Soleil's decorative sparkles.

That was the moment I lost control.

Oh, who am I kidding? I never had control.

Soleil let out a screech and lobbed a fireball at Evian, who encased it in a ball of water and batted it toward Terra. I felt scoured clean when Terra called all the dirt and dust in the house to form a layer over the bobbing ball of doom which now resembled a small planet whizzing back toward Soleil.

It might have ended better if I'd have kept my mouth shut, but I didn't.

"You're going to put an eye out with that thing."

The ire of three faeries is a potent thing, but not as potent as a flaming mudball. I ducked, rolled, and hit the latch on the patio door in what I'd like to think was a graceful move. Probably looked like a seal rolling off a rock.

The flaming fireball arced over my head, its warm breeze tossing my hair, and rocketed off into the sky.

Crisis averted. Except, it wasn't. I should have known.

A Snowball's Chance in Spell is only available by signing up for one of our newsletters here:
https://reginawelling.com
https://erinlynnwrites.com

OTHER BOOKS

*I*f you'd like to meet more people who live rent-free in our heads, here's a list of other series we've written. Our books are all set in fictional towns in Maine, and some characters like to flit back and forth between series. The cast of Psychic Seasons hangs out with Everly and also with Lexi Balefire from the Fate Weaver series. Mag and Clara Balefire are Lexi's grandmother and aunt!

Psychic Seasons
Four women, four love stories, and a whole lot of supernatural surprises. In the quaint town of Oakville, Maine, psychic visions, ghostly whispers, and fate itself conspire to change lives—and hearts—forever

Haunted Everly After
Everly Dupree came home for a fresh start—not a full-time gig solving ghostly murders. But when the dearly departed start demanding justice, what's a reluctant medium to do?

Ponderosa Pines Mysteries

Nothing bad ever happens in the weird little town of Ponderosa Pines...until someone dies. Now it's up to best friends Chloe and EV to solve the mystery—before the town's secrets bury them too.

Fate Weaver
Lexi Balefire—matchmaker, witch, and accidental fate-weaver—must balance love, magic, and a family legacy of chaos before destiny decides for her!

Mag and Clara Balefire Mysteries
Sister witches Mag and Clara Balefire move to a sleepy Maine town for a fresh start—only to find themselves conjuring up trouble, solving murders, and keeping their magic under wraps in this charmingly witchy cozy mystery series

Laurel Haven Witches
Four witches, destined by blood and magic, must embrace their power, battle a dark legacy, and surrender to the love that could break the curse—or bind them to it forever.

Nell Page: Accidental Investigator
Nell Page owns a bookstore, drinks too much coffee, and has a habit of noticing things she probably shouldn't. With warmth, wit, and an accidental talent for investigating, Nell tackles mysteries that don't always involve murder—but always matter.